White Death

White Death

Philip Baridon

Winchester, UK
Washington, USA

First published by Roundfire Books, 2013
Roundfire Books is an imprint of John Hunt Publishing Ltd., Laurel House, Station Approach,
Alresford, Hants, SO24 9JH, UK
office1@jhpbooks.net
www.johnhuntpublishing.com
www.roundfire-books.com

For distributor details and how to order please visit the 'Ordering' section on our website.

ISBN: 978 1 78279 080 8

A CIP catalogue record for this book is available from the British Library.

Design: Stuart Davies

Printed and bound by CPI Group (UK) Ltd, Croydon, CR0 4YY

CONTENTS

Chapter 1

Rise of the Triumvirate

Barranquilla, Colombia, November 1968

El Patron turned to one of his lieutenants, "Get rid of the body." His voice sounded flat, emotionless. *El Patron* had just shot a drug mule twice in the head at point-blank range. Perhaps a little too close, as he casually flicked a piece of brain matter from his shoulder. "Cut off both hands, leave the wedding band on, return the truck to the factory with the right hand, and tell them to find drivers who won't short me a brick. The left hand is for the widow. Make the message clear: Cheat me, and you die."

As a wisp of smoke curled up from the barrel tip, he held the gun flat in his hand and eyed it for a moment. This C-96 Broomhandle Mauser, a top-loading 9 mm, was a trophy that always brought him good luck. He believed the story Marcus Sterling, his Cuban partner, told him when Marcus gave him the gun: An old soldier, down on his luck, had taken it from a dead German officer in 1944. The Cuban had picked it up for a fraction of its value, one more piece for *El Patron*'s extensive gun collection.

The gun brought back the scene about six months earlier. He had met Sterling in a Miami hotel and a new partner. Tyrone (the Professor) Jones was a respected and self-educated heroin dealer in Washington D.C. The Professor had been well-recommended by associates trusted by Gonzalez and Sterling for years.

With the amphetamine market in tatters, cocaine they agreed could fill that void. People would be willing to pay for stimulants. In addition, a new middle-class market was emerging, one that did not attach a stigma to cocaine use. Jones had a well-established distribution network in place, which already controlled most of the city's heroin, adding cocaine would not be difficult. Of course, the plan required hiring some white dealers who could fit into the go-go bars and suburbs.

Sterling was enthusiastic, but Gonzalez less sanguine and clearer about potential problems. The production of cocaine paste was scattered from the Upper Huauaga Valley of Peru to the San Jorge Valley of Colombia. "Who is going to oversee the three distinct steps? Specifically – leaf to paste; paste to base; and base to the final product, cocaine hydrochloride. The paste also has a short shelf-life and must be converted rapidly to base. This last step requires a yet-to-be-constructed laboratory near Barranquilla."

Gonzalez's questions were pertinent and to the point. He then offered, to nobody in particular, that he had established a friendship with a Paez Indian chieftain, who had left his tribe to join the Colombian military to fight the FARC – a five-year-old communist insurgency, which had already clashed with the Paez. "They may be interested in money or arms to help protect their lands, and they cultivate significant amounts of leaf and convert it to paste."

Sterling said he would be willing to fly to Peru to investigate possibilities for establishing reliable connections there.

Jones asked about the lab. "What will it cost? What does it need? How much space is required?"

Gonzalez had replied, "A good lab consists of several buildings including dormitories, eating facilities, generators, and filtering and drying equipment. The cost is considerable."

After further discussion, the three men agreed to divide lab costs evenly, but profits as follows: Gonzalez 35 percent; Sterling 30 percent; and Jones 35 percent. Jones argued that his risk exposure was greater, and the primary function of Sterling was logistics. The plan included construction of the lab in an industrial zone in Barranquilla, a convenient location close to the

Ernesto Cortissoz International Airport.

These men had just formed the Barranquilla Cartel, which would control cocaine from Richmond to Philadelphia.

Yes, thought Gonzalez, as his gazing at the gun ended. It had seemed so much easier then, when risks could be assessed and shares divided.

Chapter 2

Ambience

Washington, D.C., May 1969

I worked in the Fifteenth Precinct in the northwest part of the city, a short block from Georgia Avenue, a principal urban corridor. After a year of cajoling, my friend Mike had signed up with the Metropolitan Police Department (MPDC), completed "Rookie School," and was assigned to my precinct. A converted old brick colonial, the station house's gray slate roof had seen a half-century of winters. On the main floor, cheap partitions replaced walls, and government furniture made in federal prisons was dropped everywhere. Painters, apparently, had been told to use light green or brown on every non-moving thing. The building stank of fast food, cigarette smoke and, during hot spells, sweat. Telephones rang from everywhere, and both emergency and non-emergency calls came into the desk sergeant's area. Across from there was a space for paperwork and informal interviews, full of metal desks facing each other and never enough wooden chairs.

Walking toward the back of the station, a right turn led you to a cellblock for short-term detentions. A standard prank was to lure a rookie into one of the cells and lock him in for at least an hour. A left turn in the precinct brought you to a circular staircase, perhaps reminiscent of a grander time, which led upstairs to the roll-call room.

The basement—cluttered with desks, mechanical typewriters, and government-issue ballpoint pens—featured one table with stacks of forms for all necessary reports. Officers interviewed and processed prisoners here, including, for example, a standard Form 252 for each misdemeanor or felony arrest. The most coveted desk sat by a rusting cold-water pipe that ran vertically near the corner of the room's entry. One cuff fit around the pipe and the other around a wrist, while the officer completed the paperwork.

Officers with dangerous or agitated prisoners got priority. Out the back center door was an overhang where police brought in prisoners, and cruisers rolled in to be "hot-seated" during shift changes. The motor kept idling; the radio turned up loud; and the relieving officers were often handed a clipboard with new radio runs that the prior crew was unable or unwilling to take. Squabbles about fast-food trash in the back, or shoved under the seat, were common.

An eight-foot cyclone fence enclosed the area around the building, including a parking lot and a gas pump.

The workload was intense during late afternoons and night. The "power shift" ran from 6:00 p.m. to 2:00 a.m. Roll call for each shift started one-half before. Therefore, day work began at 5:30 a.m.; the evening at 3:30 p.m.; and midnights at 11:30 p.m. (As a paramilitary organization, they use the 24-hour time system.)

Coming late was never an option, and tonight we worked 3:30 p.m. to midnight. Outside the room hung a grease board with the "uniform of the day" written on it. The official uniform could be short sleeves, long sleeves, blouses, or heavy jackets. Beefs about short sleeves in fifty-degree weather or blouses in ninety-degree heat were common. Nevertheless, changing was not negotiable. In fact, nothing was changeable. Uttering the word union would cause lightning to strike your cruiser. The brothers shuffled into roll call alone, in pairs, or small groups, at least fifteen minutes early.

The banter and bravado often boiled down to, "I got more testosterone than you do." The room was self-segregated, with black officers on the right and white on the left.

"Hey, Brinson," came the taunt from the left, "you are one seriously ugly motherfucker." Brinson's voice on the radio was one of several that you wanted to hear when you needed serious backup, fast. Brinson swaggered up to the podium and addressed the room. "I'm the biggest, blackest, and meanest, nigger in this room. Anybody got a problem with that?" Hearing no objections, he returned to his seat, only for the usual buzz to resume. Footsteps pounding up the stairs signaled the beginning of work.

Sergeant Townsen and Lieutenant Dominik scanned the room for missing faces in the platoon. As usual, the next thirty minutes followed an orderly sequence of assignments (partners, special details); teletype (who has been robbed, shot, or flimflammed in the last sixteen hours); and the distribution of auto "hot sheets."

Today, he circulated an artist's sketch of a man wanted for the murder of a Maryland state trooper. The look-out-for was a red Ford model 110 with Maryland tags. Everybody memorized the information not only to avoid being the next victim of a shotgun clamped to the inside of a driver's door, but also to acknowledge how often the fraternity of police crossed jurisdictional and racial boundaries. It could happen to anyone. In this case, as the trooper approached, the killer opened the door to the correct angle and shot him. All listened to assignments with anticipation, because the chemistry between you and your partner (if you had one) would color the next eight hours.

"Rip and Country in 64; O'Day, you're alone in 65; Preacher, you're also 10-99 in 66; 67 is out for brakes. If you assholes don't stop riding the brakes with your left foot, I'm going to put you on permanent midnights, on foot beats eight and nine, and you can eat that biker-bar food. Grabowski and Crash in the wagon. Grab, you drive; Flyboy, you got Jansen the rookie, three and four beats, pull on the half; PT, take one and two beats on the hour."

"Shit, Sarge," said PT with a huge smile radiating across the room. "Let's make it interesting," he pulled five new twenties from his pocket and spread them apart, like a poker hand. "I got a hundred dollars here that says, with a half-hour head start, I can pull every box, and you'll never find me."

Grabowski farted his approval of the proposed wager as laughter replaced the momentary silence.

This was a familiar jibe by PT, but Townsen was in no mood for it.

"Let's make it more interesting. You *will* pull every box, and I *will* see you on the street working your beat. If I don't, I keep the money, and you don't need directions to the Trial Board because you've been there before."

"Sure, Sarge," now with wild laughter. "You can blindfold me on the front steps of headquarters, and I'll still find the right room."

The litany of assignments continued. Roll call ended with an inspection of uniforms and revolvers.

Lieutenant Dominik looked at Grab's filthy pants. "When is the last time you changed the oil in your pants?"

"Huh?"

"For Christ's sake, Grab, take your uniforms to the cleaners before I see you again."

The lieutenant concluded with, "Take your beats, men."

Chapter 3

The Beat

Washington, D.C., May 1969

The next day, Jansen and I took PT's normal one and two beats. We had barely started strolling when I noticed a familiar-looking figure ambling down the sidewalk.

"Mike, I know that guy with the dark sweater stepping toward us. I arrested him a couple of years ago for selling stolen property out of the trunk of his car. As a second conviction, he pulled a little time."

"Leroy, you remember me?"

"Yeah."

"You must have built up your good time to be out so early."

"Yeah."

"Seems like you got a good job. Did I see you mowing fields in the park here?"

"Yeah."

"Pays good?"

"Yeah."

"Your parole officer happy?"

"Yeah."

"Nice talking to you, Leroy."

"Yeah."

"I can tell he's a close friend, Jake," said Mike, laughing.

"Yeah."

I reminded Mike about the blue call boxes every five or six blocks, with a phone going directly to the station. You pulled a box on the hour or half past it. Because the promised radios for footmen had not yet arrived, any arrests were taken to a box to call for transport – old-style police work. With a thin shift, we walked many beats alone at night. Citizens sometimes helped out officers with phone calls, but this unseen help gradually disappeared as the beats moved south into all-black neighborhoods. Here, many viewed the police as an unwelcome, even occupying army. One and two beats were on Georgia Avenue, about sixteen blocks in total. Beginning at Missouri Avenue, one and two moved south through a busy commercial corridor of clubs, cleaners, liquor stores, and bars.

Everyone knew one bar near the beginning of the beat: the Zombies. I passed through the rusting iron security bars welded to the back door and into the kitchen with Jansen in tow. Maude, the cook, was a somewhat heavy black woman in her late thirties, with astonishing mammary development. Even when adding a little extra grease to her recipe, she greeted all cops coming through the back with a special treat.

"Jake, honey, your hands look cold." She put each hand inside her stained blouse and used both hands to rub them in a circular motion around her breasts. Looking at Mike, she said, "I don't know you, baby, but you got that uniform on, so what's your name?"

I grinned at Jansen and said, "Close your mouth and use it to answer her."

"Mike," he replied weakly. As she was giving Mike "the treatment," she apologized that her boobs were "not as hot" because of my cold hands.

As we walked into the bar, I leaned over into Jansen's ear and said, "There are two ironclad rules here: First, don't eat Maude's food; and second, look but don't touch any of the women. We come here after a shift to buy half-price drinks. Every woman in here is a lesbian. It's a straight bar during the day. You can see that most of the barflies are beginning to leave. At 6:00 p.m., one of the dykes puts a ten-dollar cover charge for men in the window, in case they're new to town and think they just found paradise."

Some had begun to dance, a few were making out in the booths which lined the long wall, and others sat at the bar drinking and chatting. The Zombies was rectangular with a relatively small area facing the sidewalk and entrance, and Maude's kitchen was out of direct sight in the back. The bar faced out onto a nice wooden dance floor.

A bear dyke with a light brown crew cut walked slowly up to me with a half-smile on her face, her hobnailed boots clicking on the wooden dance floor as she approached. Large dykes, sometimes called "bear dykes," are lesbians who present themselves in a masculine manner. Big Carol and I had a symbiotic relationship, meaning I accepted her without overt, or even implied, criticism. Of course, I took heat for this from some of the brothers. Because no man had accepted her before, Carol felt "special" toward me. Sometimes, we sat and got drunk together, talking like two men. She would occasionally ask for advice on behalf of one of her "femmes," who constituted the majority of the bar's denizens. I, in turn, used Carol's apparently inexhaustible knowledge of the street scene. It was a delicate dance. I had to be hyper-alert not to push too hard or too often. Her information was almost always more credible than that of my other informants – two hookers and an ex-stickup man on parole looking at five years' backup time if he tripped up.

At six-foot-four-inches and about two-hundred-twenty pounds, Carol was larger than both of us. She wore motorcycle boots, jeans, a denim top, and a black leather vest with leather dangles.

"How you been, Flyboy? Looks like they gave you a newbie to break in." Jansen, who appeared recovered from Maude's treatment, was staring up at the toughest-looking woman he had ever seen. Big Carol continued, "I hope you've already told this boy to keep his hands off my girls."

Looking around distractedly, I replied, "Yeah, we covered the rules. I don't see Tina and Nina."

Tina was one of several dykes who, like most, kept her distance from me and the other cops. Nina, a gregarious femme, was Tina's favorite girl. They were an item in the Zombies. Carol froze a little at my implied question, then recovered.

"They got popped buying a little action."

I pushed, "Buck action caps, black beauties, greenies, or what?"

Carol hesitated, looked at the wall behind me as though it would help her avoid the question.

"Cocaine."

"Shit," I replied. "This is a smack and speed town. Where did they score coke?"

"I don't know, Jake; you got the badge and gun. I hear talk that it's starting to make the scene."

Although I was curious, I knew that Carol would not elaborate. After a few more minutes of socializing, Jansen and I took our beat.

We settled into a "footman's stride" – a little faster than a slow walk, but slower than a normal gait. The idea was to see and be seen. Storeowners loved cops on the beat and complained if they came too infrequently. Commanders had to balance this with the demand on resources and the volume of calls that cars could handle, in contrast to mostly uneventful foot patrols. We pulled the boxes, chatted with storeowners, and ate some greasy chicken along the way.

"Mike, turn slowly to the left and look across the street. See the big, light-skinned black man with the reddish-orange hair?"

"Yeah."

"He's Big Red, a notorious police fighter. They're rare, not really discussed much anywhere, not even among cops, but we need to know who they are. Until a few months ago, we had a woman police fighter with a well-known address. She was skinny as a rail, but fought like a wild animal each time we arrested her. When she overdosed, we breathed more easily. Big Red is meaner and much stronger. He has an uncontrolled, fanatical hatred for the police that respects no boundaries. Take a close look and stay away, if possible."

I asked Mike if he was up for a little fun. Mike had endured some of my fun in the Zombies and eyed his partner with suspicion.

"What do you have in mind?"

"There's a really tough bar called McCombos Lounge at the edge of our beat. It's a place with an attitude. The patrons are holdup men, thugs, a black motorcycle gang, Black Panthers, and other seedy characters. I like to walk in as a white cop and feel fifty eyes on me as all the conversation stops. I always order a Sprite and turn around for the stare down."

"Jake, you're as crazy as me. Let's do it."

At 6:00 p.m., as Mike and I entered, McCombos was filling up with the usual suspects. The bar was a male enclave, although a few brought their girlfriends. The smell of beer and cigarette smoke filled the air. Common interests dictated who clustered together. Bikers sat with bikers, Panthers with Panthers, and other characters seemed grouped by geography or criminal specialty. The bartender came over and asked the usual double-edged question: "What do you want?"

We ordered two Sprites and turned around for the stare down. Soon, we heard a taunt from one Black Panther to another.

"I guess the white pigs are here to show us how tough they are. Maybe we should treat them with the respect they deserve. You know, help them find the door."

A few chuckles and curses seemed to foreshadow a consensus for action. I turned to Mike and whispered in his ear, "See the biker covered with tattoos near the left corner?" Mike's head nodded gently. "He's wanted for a robbery homicide."

Meanwhile the Panther table seemed more agitated. We were running out of time. I turned to the bartender and said, "I need your phone for about a one-minute call."

"Fuck you," he replied.

"Listen, asshole, I can get the Alcoholic Beverage Control Board to shut this place down because I know you don't serve food. Now hand me the phone."

I called dispatch, telling them we needed at least two backup units at McCombos for an arrest in a hostile crowd. We would wait outside for help. I silently wondered how many guns were in the room.

"Finish your drink, Mike. The welcome mat has been pulled out."

As we headed for the door, several Panthers stood up and moved to cut us off. One was now directly in front of us with the door to his back. We probably could not fight our way out so I decided on one of Preacher's tricks, namely, kindness.

I smiled at him and said, "We appreciate you fellows offering to help us find the door, but I can see it now, and we are leaving."

The cordial tone caught him off guard and bought us enough time to slip past him to the exit.

Several cars pulled up within a few minutes, including Lieutenant Dominik. I explained the situation to him, but he took more time than I expected to respond.

"Are you pretty sure this is the guy who's been knocking off restaurants, the one who later killed the owner of the dry cleaners after he resisted?"

"Yeah," I replied. "The description is dead on, especially the red and blue tats on his arms."

Dominik called for additional units from the adjoining precinct and laid out the plan after they arrived.

"We are going to make the arrest with such a show of force that resistance will be unlikely. Although we will move rapidly and try to avoid trouble, we know what kind of people hang out here. If someone pulls a gun, defend yourself. I want Stone to go in front directly to the suspect. All of us will follow with drawn revolvers at our sides and sticks in the other hand. Questions?"

No one asked anything. The only sounds were sticks being pulled out of their carry rings and weapons from holsters.

"Okay," said Dominik. "It's show time."

The sight of ten or eleven officers walking in with drawn weapons had the desired effect. Nobody moved or talked. I cuffed the suspect, and all of us were outside in less than two minutes. The lieutenant thanked everybody. Meanwhile, a wagon had arrived to transport the prisoner to the precinct. Fortunately, the cold-water pipe was not in use. I gave the collar to Mike and coached him on the paperwork.

An Ugly Rite of Passage

Mike came to court the next morning with me to watch the process. The arresting officer sits down with an Assistant U.S. Attorney who reviews the arrest report and criminal history of the defendant. After a few questions for the officer, the AUSA decides whether to press charges or release the defendant for lack of evidence or improper police procedure during or after the arrest. Outstanding warrants for robbery and murder made the decision simple in this case. Later, we caught a few hours of sleep and arrived for the 3:30 p.m. roll call the same afternoon.

The room was full, like nobody was on leave or sick. Excess manpower translates into two-man cars and foot beats.

Townsen began bellowing out assignments. "Stone and Jansen, one and two, pull on the hour, and stay the fuck away from McCombos." A few ripples of laughter followed the admonition.

An occasional foot beat gave patrol officers the opportunity to meet merchants and common citizens alike, listen to their crime problems and complaints while trying to repair some of the mistrust and racial tension, hanging thick in the air after the riots of 1968. Fast-moving cruisers on the streets cannot take in details such as hidden alleys, fire escapes, apartments above stores, and other information that might be helpful later during a disturbance or pursuit.

Footmen also have the luxury of pulling a box, then ducking into a restaurant to eat real food. The greasy pork fried rice and Kung Pao chicken we finished off was fair.

Resuming our trek north on Georgia Avenue, I turned to Mike and said, "See those two hard cores in long coats who just entered the liquor store? Their fronts were open, and the one nearest to us was using his arm to hold something against his body."

"Like what?"

"Like a sawed-off, twelve-gauge suspended by a leather sling from the shoulder. Easy to conceal, ready for action. Holdup artists here use a lot of sawed-offs."

"Jake, what's the plan?"

"We walk in together with pistols drawn but down at our sides. If everything is cool, we quietly holster our weapons. If not, we make the collars."

As we approached the door, the shouting to hurry with the money gave me a shiver. This would not end well.

Rushing into the store, I screamed, "Police! Drop the weapons or die!" The clerk dropped straight down behind the counter as the shotgun swung directly at Mike. The ex-Green Beret fired a deadly two-round burst to the center of the chest, or as the instructors like to call it, the "center of mass." Standing behind and slightly to the left of Mike, I ducked instinctively as the other robber fired a wild shot into the wall near me. His eyes told me I was the target. I hopped to the left away from Mike and got two clear shots at the gunman's right shoulder. He twisted right as he was hit, and dropped to his knees; a .32 caliber semi-auto skidded harmlessly across the floor. In a few seconds, the action ended. The young man with the shotgun had locked eyes with Mike. Even heart shots can allow the brain a minute of oxygen before unconsciousness and death. For Mike, in those few moments, there was no right or wrong, no lawful killing, just humanity and death hanging in the air. Later, the grim setting would permeate the armor of most who came and went.

"This had to be wrong," Mike thought. "I am a Christian." The eyes pleaded and accused at the same time. *I'm going to die now because of you*, they said. Seeing the exchange, I tried to break it off by moving in front of Mike and yelling at the clerk to dial 911 and hand me the phone.

"I've got a robbery holdup with two bad guys down from gunfire. Georgia and Allison Streets. No officers or civilians injured. Stone and Jansen."

In a few minutes, officials from the precinct, Homicide Division, and one of the night inspectors converged on the crime scene. Order belied the apparent chaos. Ambulances carried both men to the Washington Hospital Center. Homicide officials separated Jansen and me for preliminary statements. A Homicide detective also interviewed the clerk, who was recovering from staring down both barrels of a shotgun. Lieutenant Dominik walked slowly up to us after listening to the statements.

"No widows to notify, two bad guys off the street, no civilians hurt, a righteous killing, it doesn't get any better. Great work." Dominik was sincere in his praise, but melancholy eyes belied his smile. "Both of you will be on administrative leave for about three days while Internal Affairs finalizes its investigation. Jansen, it is just a formality in these cases. Scout 66 will take you back to the station where you can turn in your badges and weapons to the desk sergeant."

Mike and I rode in silence, and we gave a perfunctory thank you to Preacher for the lift.

Desk Sergeant Joe Allen had done the paperwork. Two badges, two guns, and two signatures. For Mike the process was surreal – like this happens all the time.

"Mike, let's go to my place and talk. Karen is out of town."

No response. "Mike?" I tried again.

"Yeah. Fine."

"Karen's house," as I called her place, could be featured on the cover of *Southern Living*. Both of us, however, skipped the pleasantries, headed straight for the bar, and poured two stiff ones. The bar was located amidst beige leather chairs and sofas situated on thick, chocolate brown wall-to-wall carpet in a spacious, sunken living room. At the other end a huge picture window looked out over a manicured lawn and a Japanese-style garden.

"I have some idea where your head is," I offered.

"You don't have a clue," snapped Mike.

I kicked off shoes, leaned way back in my favorite chair, and said, "Tell me."

"I spent a year in 'Nam and didn't kill anybody. Some VC probed our positions once, but the South Vietnamese did all the dirty work. We counted the dead guys in black pajamas and gave them advice on perimeter defense. Tonight, I killed a man, up close and personal. As the two rounds jerked him back, I knew I made a heart shot. I couldn't break away from those eyes staring at me as he died."

I took a long drink. "Where is your head now?"

"Saying I should puke and resign."

"I had a similar reaction once; couldn't work for two days. My mistake put me on the wrong end of a gun. Would you care to hear the story?"

"Yeah."

"My partner, a rookie, and I responded to a domestic shooting call. The wife had shot her husband, who had managed to make it out of the front door with five wounds before collapsing on the steps. I asked the small crowd of neighbors who shot him. Several said, 'Mrs. Wilson, and she's inside.'

"I asked where the weapon was and someone said, 'Next door with her aunt.'

"I told the rookie to make sure an ambulance and Homicide had been called, do what he could to stop the bleeding, and get names and addresses of witnesses before they drifted away.

"This happened in 1968, and I wore a heavy reefer, which covers the service weapon. With the new Sam Browns, everything you need – gun, cuffs, nightstick are outside. That cold day, the reefer was buttoned. After all, the gun was next door, and she had finished off her target. Another routine, violent domestic dispute. As I walked in, I saw a middle-aged black woman rocking gently in her chair. She had a shawl over her lap.

"'Are you Mrs. Wilson?' I asked.

"'Yeah.'

"'Mrs. Wilson, I have several witnesses who saw you shoot your husband. You're under arrest and will have to come with me.'

"'Ain't no white motherfucker taking me nowhere cause I'm going to do you just like I done to the other sack of shit.'

"She casually pulled back the shawl with her left hand, revealing a loaded .38 caliber pointed directly at my chest. Less than ten feet separated us. I went speechless. Did you know, when staring at a cocked, six-shot revolver, you can see two live rounds on each side of the cylinder, which means one is at the bottom and one is under the hammer—waiting for the firing pin. I also noticed the six spent shells on the floor in plain view. I had really fucked up, and was now awaiting execution. I couldn't get to my gun, I couldn't run, I couldn't do anything except wait for the blast."

Mike sat forward, "You're still here. What did you do?"

"I pleaded for my life. It wasn't pretty. I started talking. Trying to buy time and wear her down. I gambled that her husband was abusive and asked how often he hurt her.

"'Often enough,' was the hard reply. 'You motherfuckers didn't do nothing except lock him up once for disorderly conduct.'

"I appealed to her self-interest saying the court might go easy on her because of the history of abuse. Her actions may even be self-defense. In contrast, for the first-degree murder of a policeman, she would die behind prison bars. I watched her shift in her chair for the first time. Some progress. I could hear sirens coming, and she looked up.

"'Your house will be flooded with police in a few moments. Don't add another body. I'm not your enemy. He's dead on the front steps. Just hand me the gun, and we'll walk out together.' She took a deep sigh and tossed the gun at my feet. I picked it up, de-cocked it, stuffed it in my reefer, and held out my hand to her. We walked out together just as a Johnny Yates, a Homicide detective I knew, was stepping around the body.

"'Any problems?' he asked.

"'No,' I lied. 'Here's the murder weapon. Based on her statements to me, her husband abused her for a long time. It may have been self-defense.' I kept quiet about her threat to kill me."

"Why?" said Mike.

"I wanted to put the incident behind me. She wasn't a danger to society. For a few minutes her rage, which had been building over the years, was displaced onto me. I almost paid the full price for being careless. I knew the Assistant U.S. Attorney would have charged her, resulting in some jail time. She was already a broken woman; I didn't want to pile on."

By then, we had poured a second, or maybe a third, round of drinks.

"I finished the paperwork, went home, and got drunk. The next morning my hands started to shake as I reached for the uniform. I couldn't put it on. I called in sick and reported to the police clinic, as we're required to do. The intake physician sent me to the shrink. He listened to the story, told me I did a great job, and should be ready for work after another day of rest. And I was. I still remember the date as sort of a second, secret birthday. I thank God for each day since."

"Wow, and I thought you were a hard ass."

"I am a hard ass," I said, perhaps a little defensively. "I try to maintain some perspective as the radio sends us from one calamity to another. Many of the brothers lost that ability long ago. For them, dealing with their emotions is not an option. Too complicated, too much pain. It's easier to lump people and situations into categories and drink away the pain with other cops who feel it too. I'm not immune from that. Few cops share their emotions with their wives; it's not macho. An unspoken bond says that only cops understand other cops, especially those who work in the city."

"You know," said Mike. "I might have to drop the hammer on someone the day after I go back to work. I don't know if I can do that."

"The odds are really small. Most cops retire without using deadly force. However, you have to know that it could be necessary again. Another thing, just to cheer you up. This incident will stay with you unless you accept that it was necessary; accept that it is part of the job; and accept that the people have a right to expect justice and safety. Hey, the store owner is alive and in business because of your actions."

"Man, did you practice that speech?"

"No, but remember how I said that most cops have trouble dealing with their emotions. Having strong emotions are inconsistent with the swaggering, tough-guy image of ourselves. And fear is a forbidden topic. You will find, as you rotate through partners, everyone who has killed someone in the line of duty has the need to tell you about it sometime during that eight-hour tour. You are expected to reassure him—it was a righteous killing, you did the right thing, had no choice—*especially,* if the killing was a little gray, unlike tonight. They have not accepted it and made peace with their actions. That must be your priority."

"Jake, you never seemed this smart before."

"Fuck you."

"Well, fuck you, too, and the horse you rode in on."

We laughed, and the tension broke. "I think Karen has an extra three or four bedrooms. Neither of us should be driving. Since we're unemployed for a few days, we can screw off tomorrow."

Chapter 4

Rain and Snow

Washington, D.C., May 1969

Sergeant Townsen put Jansen on one and two beats his first day back, no coincidence. He was partnered with "Crash" Dudley, a big man, about six-foot-three-inches, stocky, never said much. "Crash" was an ex-gravedigger, no social skills, and was such a bad driver that precinct officials always put him on a beat. Jansen would have a long tour, especially since the rain had begun to fall in earnest.

I drew Brady in 67, an imposing black man with an imposing reputation. Officers who worked with him believed he was the smartest cop in the section, with a nearly photographic recall. He memorized hot sheets before the end of roll call. Brady would usually nail one or two stolen cars a week, more than anyone else in the precinct.

Brady was senior and wanted to drive the first four hours. Normally, the eight-hour shift is divided, not only for driving, but also for discretionary matters. Some guys like to sit out of sight at light-controlled intersections and hand out "movers." Others just write enough tickets to keep out of trouble and prefer to keep driving. Do you lock up the drunk who just described your mother's sexual preferences, or do you let him go? The driver usually makes these low-level policy decisions.

After notifying Desk Sergeant Allen that the fifty-round box of ammo was missing from the trunk, I climbed into the right seat, stuffed my nightstick between the seat and backrest, and put more accident forms in the box between us. It is a rough-cut wooden box with one coat of gray paint and loaded with forms and flares. Rain means more accidents than usual.

As the cruiser mingled with the lighter-than-average traffic heading south on Fourteenth Street, Brady shouted, "That motherfucker is driving a stolen car – check it out."

"Nice work," I said with obvious admiration. "I'll verify it through WALES.[1]

"A '66 Olds, black over cream, DC 384-194 is definitely hot. Brady, look at the driver, he fits the general description of the High's store robbery yesterday."

"Flyboy, I think we got a two-for-one here."

Meanwhile, other units began to flank the car moving in parallel on Sixteenth Street and Georgia Avenue. More set up a roadblock about ten blocks south.

I grabbed the mike, "Scout 67 emergency, we're made, and the stolen vehicle is running south."

"All units in vicinity of Fourteenth and Upshur Street, black over cream Olds DC 384-194 reported running south."

I had flipped on the light bar and selected "yelp" as the primary unit. The next car should select "wail," but the system always failed when all hell broke loose. Riding shotgun, I managed communications. It was going to be a high-speed chase in the rain. Brady drove fast and continually cursed. The moaning sound of the Holly four-barrels cut in and out on the 383 Interceptor package as Brady fought to stay on the edge between maximum speed and controllability.

"Scout 67, he's turning right on Spring Road. Now right again on Sixteenth Street."

"All responding units, vehicle now fleeing north on Sixteenth Street."

"Scout 67. Ask the Park Police to cut off Military Road if that's his plan."

"Scout 67, say present position."

"67 just passed Decatur Street." Sixteenth Street was a straightaway here. Brady was fifty yards behind him doing one-hundred-ten in the rain. My adrenalin was off the scale as the yelp of the siren pounded in my head.

Both of us had graduated from Pursuit-High Speed Driving School and understood very well that, at this speed and in the rain, the tires had long since left the pavement. Water built up under the tires too quickly for the rain grooves to dissipate. Only tiny corrections to a straight course were possible. I was like a sponge, absorbing the joy of the chase and adrenalin, along with the fear that my life might end in a matter of moments. Most cops confess to each other the love of adrenalin. It's not socially acceptable, however, for a man who carries a gun for a living to admit it.

"Scout 67," barked the dispatcher. "Be advised that Park has set up a roadblock at Beach Drive."

"67 copies."

I had guessed right, the Olds slowed and turned left onto Military Road, perhaps thinking D.C. had no jurisdiction, or that the Park Police had not been notified.

"We got him," Brady said stonily.

As we approached the roadblock, Brady backed off to a safer distance. The Olds driver saw it too late, locked up his brakes, and began an almost leisurely spin down the road, through the barricade, over the curb and up on a grassy mound. He was lucky. Brady couldn't wait to cuff him.

"Let's go, hot stuff, out of the car, hands on the roof."

"Well," he replied. "I see nothing has changed; the niggers do all the work and your white boy rides along."

"Shut up, alley nigger; that's my partner."

While Brady cuffed him, I began to pat down the prisoner. "Get your hands off me, white trash." I ignored him and continued the search.

"Well, we have a .25 caliber revolver, and what's this?" I pulled out three bags of white powder.

"Brady, I've never seen heroin sold like this." I carefully opened a bag and put some on the tip of my tongue; it was bitter, had little odor, and for a few minutes I lost sensation on my tongue. The powder did not have the characteristic foul smell that comes from adulterants, and most street heroin was averaging less than ten percent pure. It didn't add up. How did this low life, stick-up man come up with these three bags – probably cocaine?

"Brady, let's ask Narcotics to bring their kit to the station."

"Good idea. This kid knocked off a High's store yesterday and he's carrying this much powder?"

I began to intone, "You have the right to remain silent..." In a quick movement, the kid stepped back and stomped on the top of my foot. I slammed his head into the car, breaking his nose and causing various cuts.

"Brady, did you see that? He tripped in the rain and fell on a rock."

"I saw the whole thing."

"If you want some more accidents, asshole, just keep fucking with me," I growled. "The accidents are going to get worse, and every cop here will swear to them. Do you understand, asshole? Well?" A bloodstained head nodded up and down slightly.

Meanwhile, the arriving MPDC officials made nice with the Park Police brass for their cooperation, and Lieutenant Dominik came by to look at the powder. He told me that another officer had found more in a sandwich bag under the seat. We put the prisoner in a cage car,[2] and a procession of police vehicles returned to the station in the pouring rain.

At the precinct, Brady cuffed the prisoner to the rusted pipe. We greeted the team from Narcotics.

"So, you found something interesting," said Detective Lieutenant John Roberts. "Let's have a look." Roberts was an intense fellow, barely meeting the five-foot-eight-inch height requirement, had a receding hairline, looked to be in his thirties, and was wearing the cheap, standard-issue polyester brown suit. Brady and I exchanged looks as to why the captain of Narcotics sent his second-in-command out to a precinct drug-bust.

Roberts poured some of the powder onto a clean sheet of paper and appeared to toy with it using a wooden coffee stirrer. To nobody in particular he said, "Cocaine is very hygroscopic—it absorbs moisture easily from any source, including the air. See how it looks and feels a little pasty. Let's see how pure it is."

Out of his bag came a device with a heating coil around the bottom of a Pyrex tube with a thermometer affixed to it. With a tiny spoon, he put in a couple of grams, mixed in a few drops of water, and plugged it in.

"What's your name, son?" he asked the prisoner.

"Slim."

"Do you know what you have here, Slim?"

"I don't even know how it got there. Somebody musta put it in my pants while I was sleeping."

Roberts silently eyed the rising temperature and the white paste, which began to melt at one-hundred-sixty degrees. Roberts made some notes and pulled the plug at one-hundred-seventy.

"Pure cocaine melts at one-hundred-ninety-five degrees. However, there is no such thing as imported 'pure.' Personally, this is as high as I have ever seen. I need to discuss these results with the higher-ups in the chain of command. Would you ask your lieutenant, the one at the crash site, if I could have a word with him?"

I went upstairs to find Dominik; he was busy, and asked what Roberts wanted.

"I don't know," I told him. "He said he wants a word with you."

Roberts walked over to the stairs and motioned for Dominik to join him near a largely abandoned indoor shooting range. Brady, "Slim," and I watched the sometimes-animated conversation. After a few minutes, the two men shook hands; Dominik left, and Roberts came back for his tester and bag.

"This is a standard chain-of-custody transfer log," began

Roberts. "I'm going to take the cocaine with me to headquarters. If you gentlemen will each sign here with me, I'll be on my way. For now, you have Slim on assorted felony charges including the High's store robbery, auto theft, and traffic charges. When you fill out the SF 252, put 'an unknown white powder' was taken from the subject and turned over to Narcotics for further processing."

"Why can't we have the coke bust," complained Brady.

"Oh, it won't disappear. But, I really must get back now. Please talk to your lieutenant, and thanks for the good work."

"I need my nose fixed," whined Slim.

"Shut up," I said. "First, you're going to answer some questions so we can do all this paperwork, then you're going to get printed upstairs, then you're going to central cell block, then maybe somebody will take you to D.C. General Hospital."

"Stone, let's walk over to the range and talk for a minute," said Brady.

"Sure. My goddam foot still hurts like hell."

The old range had five firing points, probably put in when they converted the building. No ventilation system existed to suck the toxic lead out of the air. Occasionally, one or two of the brothers would use it until the air in the range got too bad, which was for maybe a half hour.

"I've been here five years and you more than three," began Brady. "That's eight years of police experience without ever seeing cocaine. Now, they send a detective lieutenant here with his toy bag. You know something I don't?"

"Big Carol told me that Tina and Nina recently got pinched for possession. And coke was beginning to make the scene."

"She say anything else?"

"No, and her body language said the topic was closed."

"Well," said Brady. "I guess the big shots can sort it out. We fight crime; they make policy."

I smiled at the sarcasm. "Let's get Slim Jim upstairs for prints and hope that Sergeant Allen doesn't break all his fingers 'just to make printing easier.'" This was one of Allen's standard threats to any uncooperative prisoner. Allen had a dark side. In fact, many desk sergeants do. They could not make it on the street, so they manage paper and supplies, which mostly keeps them away from the public.

As we began to climb the stairs with Slim Jim, the Wagon crew with O'Day and Grab had arrived ahead of us with a prisoner. O'Day, it seems, had been tasting a little Jim Beam and seemed to be in rare form that night. Jansen and Crash had returned from their beat and were preparing to check off.

"Jansen," bellowed O'Day. "Do you know how to spot a holdup man?"

"No."

"Well, you're gonna learn." Allen stood behind the huge book that records all arrests with a smirk on his face.

"What's your name, asshole?" said O'Day.

"Reggie Jones."

"Are you married, single, widowed, or divorced?"

"Divorced, I guess. We don't have no official paper."

"What's your address?"

"I move a little from place to place."

"So, no fixed address."

Talking to himself, O'Day said, "Armed Robbery – gun," and continued writing on the Arrest Book.

"Jansen! Back to the cell block," bellowed O'Day again. Anticipation grew as Allen, a card-carrying redneck, had now joined the odd procession.

"I don't want to see this," said Brady. "You make certain your rookie friend understands these assholes are the exceptions and make our work with the public harder."

"I'll take care of it," I replied.

"OK, drop 'em!" screamed O' Day as he slammed the holdup man against the cellblock wall. The two old timers smirked as he screamed the order again; his face flushed, working himself into a cold rage. Allen had taken out his blackjack and was knocking paint chips off the wall, closer and closer to the lock-up's face.

In a single movement, O' Day ripped off the snap and tore the zipper as the pants dropped to the dirty floor.

"I told you so!" roared O' Day. "You show me a motherfucker with red silk shorts, and I'll show you a goddam holdup man. Jansen, you see that! Justice is putting holdup men in jail; you got the right man if he's sporting silk shorts."

Jansen remained stoic but appalled as he absorbed this lesson on the rules of evidence. O' Day and Allen giggled and walked away.

Chapter 5

Bail

Washington, D.C., May 1969

The next day Mike and I arrived early at court for the initial appearance and bail setting for "Slim Jim." Normally, this hearing was quite predictable. The Assistant U.S. Attorney pressed charges on the High's store robbery, the stolen car, and the other felonies – except the cocaine. She argued in court that he was a flight risk, had no fixed address, a long record, and required a high bond. The judge concurred, and set it at seventy-five thousand dollars. We smiled at ourselves for putting one more bum in jail until trial. He couldn't possibly post that much money. Having no other business, we walked outside in time to see Slim Jim talk to the driver of a blacked-out Lincoln, and get into the rear seat. We stared.

The rear window cracked a little. It was Slim Jim's voice.

"Yo! White cops. You can never win. We gonna out-slick you at every turn. Bye, assholes."

"Mike, I've never seen a big-shot criminal post bond for minor charges, and have a new limo waiting in front of the court. This is about the cocaine. Spot me a dime for a call to Detective Roberts."

We walked over to a phone booth, and I called the main number at headquarters. I had left his card in my bag and had to find him the hard way; every secretary is trained as a guard dog for the senior staff.

Finally, "Good morning, Lieutenant, it's Jake Stone."

"Good morning, Jake, what's up?"

I explained what had happened and gave him the tag number of the limo, which began with an "R" for rented. He said that he would send someone to the rental agency, but the owners always have faulty memories. They know most of their clients are not wealthy executives.

"Jake, how does it feel to have met your enemy."

"*My* enemy?"

"In addition to heroin, we now have cocaine on the streets. Both are white death. It was bad enough just dealing with heroin. Whoever rented that Lincoln is a vendor of death. You don't invent a well-oiled distribution system, better to use one that's in place. We know that, but so far, we don't know much else. I thought you might want to know that hospitals are reporting more overdoses, especially from speedballing.[3] This is a new problem, and the Baltimore and Richmond police are beginning to report it. We're starting a log of these reports to look for patterns."

"I didn't know."

"Don't feel bad. Most people don't, and it's not in the papers."

We exchanged a few pleasantries and hung up. His reference to "my enemy" still bothered me. What was he thinking?

Chapter 6

Return of the Titles

Washington, D.C., June 1969

Unfortunately for Washington D.C, it had wrested the per capita homicide title from Detroit and the bank robbery title from Los Angeles in 1969. Both the FBI and D.C. Police had established task forces to handle the enormous rash of bank jobs. With J. Edgar Hoover still at the helm of the FBI, there was little or no coordination between their efforts and ours.

About a week before, a deadly incident almost occurred in a Georgia Avenue Bank. The FBI had planted one agent inside as a customer doing paperwork at a table. Someone pushed the alarm by mistake, which went to the communication centers of both the FBI and MPDC. Sergeant Townsen was driving by the bank when the radio call went out for a robbery in progress. Townsen stopped his cruiser, grabbed the 12-gauge shotgun off its rack, and hit the front door running. Inside, the agent saw nothing amiss, but had pulled out his service weapon when Townsen burst into the lobby. Townsen fired a rifled slug into the ceiling over the agent's head and yelled, "Drop it or I'll cut you in half with the next one." The agent dropped his weapon and repeatedly screamed, "FBI, FBI, FBI..." Townsen decided he looked like a fed and told him to reach slowly into his pocket and show his "creds" (credentials). Although a tragedy was avoided, the agent needed to take his pants to the cleaners.

It was the end of day work, and Sergeant Townsen was about to start reading out the assignments.

"Hey, Sarge," shouted a voice from the back. "Can I get four hours of leave midway through the shift?"

"No fucking way. I'm shorthanded today, and I need every swinging dick out on the street. We're doing bank plants again."

"Brinson, you're 10-99[4] in 63; Preacher is 10-99 in 64; 65 is out for maintenance; Rip, you're in 66; Wilson you're in 67; PT take 1 and 2 beats on the hour; Crash, you take 3 and 4 on the half; O' Day and Grab are in the Wagon; Flyboy, Jansen, and Brady, see me for details on a plant."

D.C. used a three-man plant system, with one officer in a suit behind a "closed" teller position located on the non-entrance side. He wore an ear mike facing away from the door. Outside two guys sat in a private car wearing old clothes, talking, drinking coffee, and looking casual. On the back seat were two twelve-gauge shotguns covered by papers and clothing. They talked to the inside man and dispatch. In place of the regular service revolver, each carried a .45 caliber Colt, model 1911, semiautomatic for extra stopping power.

"Brady, you're the teller." Townsen handed Brady a brightly colored necktie to replace the usual, black clip-on tie we normally wore. "Stone and Jansen, pick up a radio and tell me which car you're using, including plates. All of you have done these plants. Any questions? The bank at Connecticut and Woodley has been hit before. Tellers told management they believe they're being cased again. Be careful."

After about three hours of nothing, Brady came on the air with, "I need ones and fives"—meaning armed robbery: two bad guys. Brady got down on the floor with the other tellers on "orders" from the robbers.

Jansen and I looked for a getaway car and didn't see one: bad news. Maybe it was out of sight with a shooter we couldn't see. We walked back to front to the side of the door, waiting for information from Brady. Sirens were approaching rapidly.

Gunfire! Multiple gunshots from inside, two different weapons. Brady was not supposed to identify himself in any way except in self-defense. Two bad guys burst out of the bank's front doors, weapons drawn. I swung my shotgun like a baseball bat catching one in the throat. His knees buckled, and he fell backward. Jansen pivoted right and put the twelve-gauge in the other's stomach with "Surrender or die." We quickly disarmed the two and cuffed their ankles together, as other units began pulling up.

Brady was not talking as we raced inside to find him and a teller wounded. The teller's ear was hanging from the side of his face, a penalty for not moving fast enough. Brady opened his side door and exchanged fire with the gunman who shot the teller. Brady took one in the stomach, but the round went through the door first, expending most of its energy. As I ripped open his shirt, I could see the tip of the lead lodged in his abdomen.

"Stay still," I said. "The paramedics will give you a Band-Aid so you'll be ready for work tomorrow." A weak smile rewarded the humor.

Lieutenant Dominik waited outside as the paramedics attended to Brady.

"Nice job, Flyboy, except you may have killed one of them."

"Say what?"

"According to the doc here, when you swung that barrel it would have been a triple at least. His larynx was crushed so they had to do a tracheotomy to save his sorry ass. Furthermore, he may have been without air for up to four minutes. We may have to deal with a moron defendant. 'Incapable of understanding the nature of the charges against him or assisting counsel in his defense.' Remember Criminal Law 101? Now, I gotta do a mountain of paperwork, and the city has to pay to heal this asshole to bring him to trial. By the way, I missed the advanced weapons course where they teach you to use a twelve-gauge like a baseball bat."

"I improvised."

"Well, don't do any more improvisations. You should have shot and killed the bastard. Less paperwork, and less expense for the city. I want a detailed SF 252 on my desk before you go home. You're off the next two days, right?"

"Yes, sir."

"Unwind."

I planned to unwind, but silently wondered if cocaine was partially responsible for the upsurge in violence this year.

Down Time

Karen had invited Mike and a lady friend over for dinner and drinks. Karen was a beauty with light skin and sandy red hair. The latter item had been the source of recent discussion among us. Her girlfriends said that with her fair skin, she should "go blonde." My father once gave me some advice about women's hairstyle and color: "Stay out! First, they won't pay much attention to you. Second, if they don't like it later, it's your fault."

"Mike, do you think I should color my hair blonde?"

Poor Mike had not even finished one drink. He looked at me, but Karen was sharp, watching both of us. I just stared ahead as if I hadn't heard the question. Lily, Mike's friend, came to the rescue.

"Karen, you are so lovely that it would be perfect either way."

"Lily, you're such a diplomat, but thank you."

"Karen, how did you and Jake meet?"

Mike began to analyze the design of his fork, and I looked straight ahead. Karen enjoyed fielding this one.

"Actually," she began. "I had never seen Jake before, and he chased me out of a U.S. Post Office while proposing to me."

"It's a little more complicated than that," I said lamely.

"No, it's not," replied Karen. "Later you confessed if you couldn't get to me before I got to my car, you were going to jot down the tag number and find out who I was – all illegal for non-law enforcement purposes. Right?"

"Your Honor, I invoke my Fifth Amendment rights in

declining to answer."

Lily sat with a smirk on her face, but said nothing.

"Now that we've had fun skewering me," I said, "Karen omitted a few things. First, she looked back at me, with interest, twice before leaving."

"If you were in fear for your life, wouldn't you want to give the police a good description?"

"After she left, Karen walked with a slow, deliberate pace toward her car, like she wanted to be caught."

"Excuse me. It was a gravel surface, and I was in high heels. I calculated the fastest possible speed to my car without a substantial risk of falling down."

"Time!" said Lily. "I'm so glad I asked this question. At whatever speed she was traveling, you obviously caught up with her. Then what?"

"I told her I had never seen such a beautiful woman with such a sexy voice. How can you sound that sexy telling a clerk to send a package?"

"Your turn, Karen."

"Well, he was handsome in sort of a rugged way, wearing jeans and cowboy boots, which nobody wears around here. He didn't sound like a serial killer. I told him I'd meet him for lunch in a restaurant with outside seating and lots of taxis nearby. We kept seeing each other and married a year later."

"Wow!" said Lily. "If there were a contest for unusual romantic encounters, you would win by acclamation.

"And now you do mostly philanthropic work?"

"I'm raising money to rehabilitate inner-city gyms, basketball courts, and other athletic facilities," replied Karen. "Also, I have agreements from some current and former professional athletes to work with the kids, or at least make occasional appearances at their gyms or events. These athletes are often the only male role models for these children. In addition, I'm working with Social Services to help find and fund alternatives to juvenile detention for first or non-violent offenders. If you tell a boy often enough that he is bad or delinquent, it becomes his self-image. I am a big believer in labeling theory. They need positive goals and aspirations while they are still malleable, not a label limiting their future to a life of crime. Some can't be helped. They graduate to become problems for Jake and Mike. If they're shooting hoops, they're not shooting drugs. What do you think?"

"I think it's a great idea," said Mike. "Too many of these kids come from families with no fathers. The police can't be male role models for them. The city still looks burned out after the race riots last year, and too many kids are taught that police are their enemies."

After telling the story of how we met yet another time, with a few more embellishments, the banter was light over drinks and dinner. Both ladies gently admonished Mike and me about our morbid interest in visiting the scores of civil-war battlefields from Gettysburg south into central Virginia.

Karen and Lily drifted toward the kitchen, and we headed into the living room. The picture window was stunning and kept so clean that birds routinely flew into it and broke their necks. The gardener disposed of them quickly to minimize Karen's knowledge of the problem. Although Karen lived in a world with little pain, she understood life outside the bubble. She had a tough streak alongside her humanity, which helped me stay grounded in a daily routine where the radio ensured we stayed focused on human cruelty.

Chapter 7

Steelworkers in Paradise

Washington, D.C., June 1969

Sergeant Townsen put Brinson and me on the power shift from 6:00 p.m. to 2:00 a.m., walking beats three and four. Beat two ends at the Zombies where beat three begins, heading north on Georgia Avenue. We stopped briefly in the Zombies, said a few "hellos," and headed north. We passed one of the few Chinese restaurants in the area. Cops in uniform who wanted a free meal could enter on the side and be served whatever food they brought out – no menu. Those wanting to choose their meal entered the front door, received a menu, and paid like any other patron.

It seemed unusually quiet. Brinson remarked, "Welfare checks don't arrive for another few days. So, they're short on liquor and don't feel much like fighting yet." I smiled at his cynical analysis, but there was some truth in it.

We had pulled the top box and turned to walk south when Brinson announced, "I'm bored. This is supposed to be the power shift."

"Well," I countered, "it proves we've done our job. Stopped crime along our beat."

Brinson smiled.

"Brinson, did you notice that table of rough-looking guys who were still in the Zombies when we made our social call at the beginning of the shift?"

We exchanged glances.

"Yeah I did. Are we thinking the same thing?"

"Uh huh. Let's pick up the pace a little to see if they have left quietly. If not, we may need back up."

We heard raised voices as we walked in the door. The manager, Susan, and Big Carol were in a heated discussion. Susan, a bear dyke with a jagged scar down one cheek and two missing front teeth, chain-smoked and served liquor, always trying to stay out of the bar's internal politics. She was civil, but brusque with the cops who came in after hours to drink. The argument centered on how to handle the roughnecks, the steelworkers from Pittsburgh. All of the dykes and a few femmes had gathered around the back table to make their views clear. One femme seethed that the, "Motherfucker pulled me into his chair, ripped open my blouse, and fondled my breasts."

Susan wanted to call the cops. Carol countered that they needed to settle these troubles themselves. "If we call the cops, it sends the message that we depend on them to take care of our problems. We've never called the cops for big things, much less to throw out a table of drunken bums."

Brinson and I stood inside the doorway, unsure about the politics of open intervention. I had a new footman radio and called for backup, but I told the dispatcher to have the cars come *code two* – no lights or sirens.

Tired of the argument, Big Carol abruptly stood up, ordered one of the girls to unplug the jukebox, and walked directly over to the biggest steelworker. The time for diplomacy had ended. When Carol tapped that guy on the shoulder, there wasn't a sound in the bar.

Carol began, "You listen real careful, motherfucker. If you don't want your balls on my watch chain, you take your friends and leave – *now*." He must have had too much whisky, didn't realize that major muscle was talking. He stood up and took a wild swing with his left hand. Carol stepped right to avoid it and knocked him to the floor with a hook to his temple.

"Oh, shit," said Brinson, "let's get into it." We waded into the fight, which deteriorated quickly into a brawl. The eight steelworkers did not go down easily. I watched one dyke and a steelworker crash through a plywood partition into the men's room. Soon water was spewing out of the bathroom as the exposed copper pipes were ripped out of the wall. Water mixed with the blood and beer on the slippery floor. Femmes joined in using chairs as weapons. Both sides were using broken beer bottles, as the fighting grew uglier and bloodier. I pushed the transmit button on the radio and just yelled, "10-33 at Zombies." Soon cops came pouring in and quickly subdued the remaining steel-workers.

I sat down exhausted on the floor near the bar, with a new uniform slashed by a broken beer bottle. The back of my head bled from a nasty cut.

Brinson looked at me and just said, "Flyboy?"

"Yeah, I'm okay. How about you?"

"I'm okay. I think they put Country into an ambulance. I'm going to call the Washington Hospital Center when we get back to check on him."

Lieutenant Dominik stood by the door looking at the carnage. "Listen up, everybody," he bellowed. "Stone and Brinson are going to do the paperwork. Anybody that wants to add important information should meet them at the station." Pointing at Susan and Carol, Dominik added, "You two are coming with me for statements."

"I don't want to," said Susan sourly.

Dominik thundered back, "I don't give a shit what you want. You come voluntarily or I'll arrest you right now as a material witness to multiple felonies.

"Stone, get one of the paramedics to examine your head. If it's as hard as I think, he can put a bandage on it, and you'll be fine. Work with Brinson. Not only do we have multiple criminal charges to sort out, I guarantee this melee will result in civil litigation. Be careful with checking and corroborating facts."

Turning to other officers, he ordered that no ambulance leave without a name, address, and phone of the injured party. Looking at the pipe still spewing water and the detritus around him, the lieutenant muttered, "What a cluster fuck," to nobody in particular. Then, as an afterthought, he added, "I want the list of injured turned over to Stone and Brinson." Turning to two officers, he said, "Get the names and addresses of everybody who was in this room when the fighting began. Some have already slipped out. Find out from the girls who they are. Preacher, compile a master list based on those names and give it to Stone or Brinson."

"Yes, Lieutenant," replied Preacher, clearly mindful of his uncharacteristically foul mood.

After I returned with a bandaged head and two aspirins, Brinson said, "I'm so fucking glad you cleaned up all the crime on this beat."

Chapter 8

Midnights

Washington, D.C., June 1969

Some officers asked for midnights; most of us hated them. When the bars close at 2:00 a.m., and the drunks are home by 3:00 a.m., either nothing or everything happens. No calls are routine until the city begins to awaken about 5:30 a.m. It was 3:30 a.m., and I slumped against the window trying hard to stay awake.

"Scouts 65 and 66, a shooting at 4921 Georgia Avenue, complainant refused; respond code one, 0332."

Sitting only a block away, I acknowledged, turned the corner and looked at one of the most infamous slum buildings in the city. As I hurried around to the trunk for the first-aid kit, past images of visits here darted across my mind. There was no elevator; just an empty shaft filled with rotting garbage overrun by well-fed rats. Many rooms had no doors to the hallways, where junkies dozed and men gambled. I raced past the debris and stench, carrying a gun in one hand and a kit to save lives in the other.

Screaming from two women told me where to go. My appearance in the hallway intensified their hysteria. The victim lay on his back in front of me. He had been shot in the chest, head, left shoulder, and arm. I could get no information from the women. Working feverishly, I ripped open his shirt to close off the air gurgling through a large caliber entry wound in his chest. A request to apply pressure to slow the arterial bleeding in his left arm produced more hysteria and no help. The wailing of Scout 66 was still in the distance. I had to control that bleeding. Sweat poured down my face as I improvised a tourniquet from his torn shirt and a broken curtain rod. His pupils were of unequal size; blood flowed from one ear.

I was losing him, and I knew it.

"Who wasted you, man?"

His breathing changed along with a slight body movement; he heard the question.

"Come on; you got to tell me who wasted you."

Down on my knees just off his right side, I bent forward to hear any sound or word he might utter. Nothing, but another slight change in his breathing. He couldn't talk. It was all over.

As I rocked back on my heels, the fingers of his right hand tugged at my right hand. Instinctively, I held his hand for about a minute and watched him die. His last friend was a cop who hated midnights.

The sounds of sirens and footsteps began to fill the air as I wiped a tear from my eyes. Cops don't cry about bums wasted on a contract. I vowed to check his criminal history, just to verify he was a menace to society. Then I thought better of it and accepted the humanity of his dying. The record didn't matter.

Johnny Yates arrived from Homicide, a friend from other such encounters and a good country boy. We sometimes frequented the same watering holes after work.

"Johnny," I said. "You must love fresh stiffs. Good to see you, I guess. I don't have any witness information or anything other than what you're looking at. He pissed off somebody. Do you know him?"

"No," he replied. "Did you notice the track marks on his arms? You could run Amtrak service on them."

I smiled at the well-worn joke.

"Hey, you seem a little down," said Johnny. "I've got just the right medicine to cheer you up. After you get some rest in the morning, can you meet me at the morgue at 6:00 p.m. sharp? Go into the side entrance on Eighteenth Street, off Massachusetts Avenue. I'll wait for you there."

"And how is the morgue going to cheer me up?"

"Let's just say we're having a special event for a new Homicide detective."

I looked at my friend who was wearing a smug grin.

"Okay, Johnny. I'll meet you at 6:00 p.m. for your event."

The next afternoon I arrived a little early, parked, and saw Johnny smoking a cigarette by the entrance.

"Here's the deal," he began. "A few other Homicide dicks will be inside pretending to review cases, looking for something, and so on. We just walk in and do the same, ask the Medical Examiner something about this case. He'll be lecturing the new detective on how the morgue functions, as well as some pointers about on-scene observations. Our real job is to watch."

A large rat scurried past us as we entered. The paint on the walls appeared to be old, and the dirty institutional green clashed with the bright, stainless-steel tables. Four detectives sat at a cheap table surrounded by folding chairs, with case folders strewn in front of them. Numerous file cabinets sat with open drawers. There was no sense of organization, but I suppose the dead don't complain.

Unknown to me, a veteran Homicide detective had stripped and climbed into an empty chamber before the newbie arrived. As the ME droned on for a while about the process, including a catalogue to track which corpses he placed in the long, refrigerated chambers, he mentioned that a new John Doe had arrived. So new, in fact, that the ME was waiting for the rigor to pass to do the autopsy. He told the rookie detective, however, that this was a formality since the decedent had been shot in the forehead at point-blank range, leaving gun-shot residue clearly visible around the small-caliber entry wound.

Make-up, of course, had been applied carefully to the detective beforehand, to simulate both the entry wound and the GSR. Becoming more enthusiastic, the ME declared this a teaching moment and directed the new detective to bend over the corpse to look for the GSR. At that moment, the corpse became alive and, with a feral scream, reached up with both arms to pull the detective's head down to him.

At first I gasped, then joined the others howling with laughter. The detective almost fainted and ran toward the door, cursing everybody.

The next day PT was off, and I had pulled his usual 1 and 2 beats at the lower end of Georgia Avenue, stone ghetto. Black officers generally got the beats and cruisers there because they could "relate well with the community." The truth was that, not only did we see each other as blue; so did the community. In fact, some citizens viewed black officers as traitors in the racially charged atmosphere after James Ray assassinated Martin Luther King in 1968.

A foot beat can provide a break from the constant demands of the radio. It's not possible to notice and appreciate small details such as interesting shops from a car. The Kennedy Street beat, for example, featured an African restaurant serving unusual and authentic foods; some were quite good. The owner liked to complain about kids running in to demand a "monkey sandwich."

But it was 1:30 a.m., and nothing much was open except a few bars slowly beginning to empty before closing at 2:00 a.m. The beat covered sixteen blocks, and I had decided to complete two four-hour circuits. After pulling the bottom box, I turned to walk north, suffused by an intangible unease. Pilots who don't trust their instincts don't live as long as those who do. I stopped and looked around slowly.

Leaning against a street lamp with three of his groupie admirers was Big Red. I suppressed a momentary flash of panic. He was giant, ugly, and menacing. A shock of dirty, dull red hair was parted on one side by a scar left from a grazing bullet. The right side of his neck bore multiple scars from an earlier fight to the death with beer bottles. Now, he was on parole for robbery and almost killing a cop with his own stick.

"You lost down here, Honky?"

"This is my beat tonight," I replied in a measured voice.

"That means you got to take care of trouble when you find it – don't it?"

"That's what I'm paid to do."

"Well, Honky," as a single nod to his friends closed off the sidewalk. "Looks like you can't even finish walkin' your beat without me sayin' it's okay."

Smiles and glances among the groupies confirmed the smell of fresh blood. The game continued.

"That's fine," I responded evenly. "You say it's okay, and I'm sure your friends will step aside."

"It ain't okay, you pig motherfucker!" screamed Big Red. "Take off your badge and gun and fight me like a man."

"Not a chance. I'm paid to wear this uniform – all of it."

Red came off the streetlight and headed right at me. I pulled out my revolver, cocked it, and pointed it at his massive chest. He stopped just in front of me. He stunk worse than an alley dog with sewer breath.

"You wouldn't dare shoot an unarmed man."

"You don't give me any choice. Besides, I have a throwaway gun in my left pocket. Everybody knows about you, Red. Nothing your friends might say later will amount to shit – and you know it. Either way, you'll be dead with a bullet through your heart."

"You're bluffin'."

"Cops have a saying you ought to know about."

"What?"

"It's always better to be tried by twelve than carried by six. Are you getting my message? I know for a fact that I'm goin' home tonight. You got to decide if you're goin' home or to the city morgue."

Red stared hard at me and the revolver. I watched his eyes and never moved. If he intended to lunge at me, his pupils would dilate slightly and his eyelashes would rise, signaling an attack. The longest minute of silence in the world finally passed.

Red stepped back and laughed.

"Let him pass; this Honky motherfucker ain't worth any blood from a soul brother."

I was bluffing about the throwaway. I was not bluffing about what I needed to do. I was going home that night.

Chapter 9

Business Problems

Barranquilla, Colombia, April 1969

The lab had been operational for three months now. Through the hard work by Sterling and Gonzalez, two steady streams of base had been arriving for processing into pure cocaine hydrochloride. If one stream became a little weak, enough was available to keep operations at, or near, full capacity. Gonzales had paid the local police to keep the lab under 24-hour protection. Located in the eastern part of the city, slum dwellings—seemingly crushed against each other—surrounded the lab. Amidst the squalor, beauty existed in a few hardy weeds and flowers that needed no care. Some worked at the lab; most knew about it; all kept their mouths shut.

From the lab, a short drive west on *Avenida Centenario,* then south on *Avenida Boyaca,* took you to *Aeropuerto Ernesto Cortissos,* a modest international airfield at the southern edge of the city.

On the south side of the airport, Maria, a young woman in her twenties waited for a black van to pick her up. They drove her to a far end of the parking area where she undressed from the waist up. Handlers placed body packs of cocaine around her front in an artful simulation of late-term pregnancy, even the artistic touch of a slightly protruding belly button. Next, they taped a special bra securely to the undersides of her breasts, and all around the back. Only women with small breasts were selected. The handlers filled the front of the bra with slightly damp cocaine and molded it to produce normal-appearing, large breasts. Then, Maria was vacuumed, given a new maternity outfit, and groomed to look like a middle-class traveler going to Miami to visit relatives for a few days. Her fee was two-hundred dollars, with the promise of three-hundred more after a successful flight – a princely sum in east Barranquilla.

In Miami, two of Marcus Sterling's men greeted her as a "relative." From the airport, she was whisked off to his packaging facility. There, the process was reversed. Removing the damp cocaine from her bra and breasts was done with a brush and finally with a special vacuum while she stood on a large black sheet. Maria remained in the facility as a "guest" for a few days, until it was time for her to leave. On the return trip, an armed escort "helped" her with the suitcase, normally containing about a half-million dollars.

If the cash were all hundreds, then the added weight would be only eleven pounds. Sterling and Jones, however, could never convert that much cash into all large bills, so the suitcase was heavy. Bribes in Miami ensured that the suitcase was processed just like all others, with the important exception that it was not somehow lost. All understood that a body floating in the Miami River was the price for betrayal.

Business was good. Tyrone Jones used only a handful of distributors who operated under a no-adulteration rule. He wanted to build a solid base of satisfied consumers and secondary distributors. Although he couldn't enforce the rule down the line, everybody knew that Jones' people had the best product. He had not underestimated the demand. Cocaine went out the door as fast as flights to Miami arrived.

Then the flights to Miami stopped coming in.

Zoila was being prepared in the usual way in a corner of the parking lot at *Aeropuerto Ernesto Cortissos*. A little younger than most, twenty at best, she had long pretty hair, a comely face, and was of indigenous ancestry. She had very small breasts and dark skin, a *morenita*. The lighter-skinned handlers teased her about her skin color and breast size. As in many countries in Latin America, skin color is a proxy for social class. Nervous from the start, she did not take the teasing well. She was a good Catholic girl who had two children to care for, and a husband who dumped her for another woman. She needed the money.

After landing in Miami, her apprehension soared. She began to sweat. The U.S. Customs line seemed so long to a girl who had never traveled more than twenty kilometers from her home. Finally, she presented her passport and visa to the Customs agent, who was a Latina. At first, she was relieved. The few phrases in English that she had been taught were long forgotten.

"What's the purpose of your trip?"

"To visit relatives in Miami." The agent paused and looked up at her. Her accent was uneducated, and yet she had money for new clothes and an expensive outing of only a few days.

"When is your baby due?"

"About six weeks."

"The father must be proud. What type of work does he do in Barranquilla?"

"He's looking for a job." Zoila knew immediately that it was the wrong answer; she was not working.

"So, you're relatives here paid for the trip?"

"Yes, my uncle; he's Cuban."

"What business is he in?"

"I'm not sure."

"So, your Cuban father married an Indian in Colombia. What tribe?"

"Wayuu."

"How did your parents meet? Here in Miami or in Colombia? And what business was your father in to take him to the northern jungles?"

Zoila, sweating profusely and scarcely able to answer, felt paralyzed. The agent picked up the phone, speaking in English, said, "I've got one for a secondary inspection. She's pregnant, very young, beyond nervous, and her background, clothes, and reason for coming, don't seem to add up. Thanks."

The agent told Zoila to go with the two men who came out of a side door, which she hadn't noticed. They were big Americans with short hair and grim appearances. The handlers could only watch from behind the line. The raw fear made her knees buckle.

"Are you all right?" one of them asked. His Spanish was excellent. "I'll have a nurse check you over before we ask a few questions."

After walking inside, Zoila unleashed a torrent of remorse.

"I didn't want to do this. I have no husband and two children to feed. They gave me two-hundred dollars, and said I would get three hundred more when I returned. I hate this stuff; it's ruining lives in my neighborhood." She tore open her blouse and packs of shaped cocaine fell to the floor. She ripped off her bra and yelled, "Take it!" spilling more unpackaged cocaine.

The stunned agents sat back in their chairs and watched Zoila sob. They were not about to touch her. Fortunately, the nurse arrived and took in the situation.

She led Zoila to a bathroom, cleaned her up a little, and found a blouse for her.

As she calmed down, it became apparent that she was only a classic mule. She did not know the men at the Colombian airport; she supplied one first name heard in conversation – useless. She knew nothing about what would happen to her here, only her return ticket date. The U.S. Customs Service, however, had uncovered some extremely useful information: a method. This discovery explained how nearly pure cocaine was entering east coast cities, especially Baltimore and Washington. Zoila was carrying about 3.3 kilos of cocaine. A retrospective check of records showed similar flights and passengers for about three months – which corresponded with coke's appearance on the streets. This new information was cabled to all U.S. ports of entry in the southeastern United States.

Chapter 10

The Weight of Responsibility

Barranquilla, Columbia, March 1969

"What?" screamed Gonzalez into the phone.

Mindful of his temper, Sterling replied evenly that, "My two men were there and watched the whole thing until they pulled her into secondary. The Customs bitch was all over her with questions we never prepped the mules to expect. She got nervous and couldn't give good answers."

"I'm going to kill her whole family here. Get a hit man to take her out in Miami when those bastards have finished squeezing her for information."

"Alvaro, listen. Cops investigate murders, especially up here, and most especially a mule caught with a full load. More important, she knows nothing about our operations or us. We were very careful about that. We don't want to attract attention."

Alvaro's cat went flying across the room. Somebody had to pay.

"Alvaro, I already talked to Tyrone, and..."

"How did he react?"

"He considers it a business setback and wants a little time to think about new options for transportation, now that every pregnant woman from northern Colombia will be grilled trying to enter the U.S."

"A fucking *setback*? He considers it a fucking *setback*? Does he ever get upset? Hey, it was only 3.3 keys and our entire transport system."

"Tyrone is smart and calm. We need that right now. He thinks we should discuss using freighters out of Cartagena."

"Stupid idea! First, we have competition there. We're not the only geniuses to figure out that coke is the future. Second, it's too damn far for overland transportation. Even with armed guards—speaking of drawing attention to ourselves—an ambush is possible. Third, we can't bribe in a way that insulates us. The product will always be worth far more than bribes. Too much temptation. Fourth, too many people will know too much. We need to maintain control. I want a farm to arm operation."

"I'm impressed, Alvaro. Are you taking lessons from Tyrone?"

"Fuck you and Tyrone. I'm going to get drunk. Tell Tyrone what I said and see if the Professor can do better on his second try.

"Also, we need an interim solution. I suggest we use 'swallowers' to keep moving some product. Tell Tyrone that each packer can carry between 700 to 900 grams. The mules generally want about two-thousand dollars to take the risk. You know, one condom egg ruptures and they die. We can work out details later."

"Thanks, Alvaro."

"Fuck you, Marcus."

Tyrone thought of himself as a businessman. He owned two nightclubs on Fourteenth Street and a motel on New York Avenue, the northeastern gateway to the city, an area known to accommodate visiting male businessmen and tourists. All were good cash businesses, ideal for laundering the proceeds of his drug business. Also, he paid two pimps to keep the motel and nightclubs supplied with working girls. He chose his pimps carefully and enforced two ironclad rules: (1) No girls abused; and (2) No girls under eighteen. He even stopped by the businesses to interview the hookers from time to time. Not all of this was because he was a kind person. He had killed a few people, but took no pleasure in their deaths. Sometimes, death was necessary to protect his interests. Long ago, Jones delegated compliance enforcement to others.

Right now, however, Tyrone was tired. He asked his assistant and one of his bodyguards to wait in the outer office with the receptionist. In addition to all of the demands of running his legitimate businesses, the drug distribution network, and keeping the IRS satisfied, he now felt like a babysitter for his two partners. Alvaro had good connections, good ideas, and some business acumen; but he was a loose cannon prone to violent and impulsive decisions. Marcus's forte was logistics; he paid attention to details and could implement a plan, and even improvise as necessary. Tyrone knew, however, he was the smartest of the three, and the burden of overcoming this setback would largely fall on him, perhaps with help from Marcus. Alvaro was right about freighters out of Cartagena, but he offered no constructive alternative. Crossing the large expanse of open sea in small boats was out of the question. Using swallowers was just an interim solution.

Tyrone's heroin came from Sicily and Brazil, by well-established routes, packed within legitimate merchandise. From the freighter, selected teamsters moved it onto cars or trucks and later drove to a safe garage for recovery. Unknown to U.S. law enforcement, the Sicilian Mafia was now operating in the U.S., with three of the five La Cosa Nostra families in New York. Tyrone had contracted with the Bonanno family for exclusive heroin rights in Baltimore and D.C. However, he could not piggyback on their heroin routes. Besides, the Mafia had shown little interest in cocaine. Soon-to-be-legendary drug trafficker Frank Mathews had approached the Gambino and Bonanno families to explore a partnership for heroin and cocaine, but the mafia turned him down. Not long after, Rolando Gonzalez would sell Mathews his first kilo of cocaine for twenty-thousand dollars. Mathews was doing well and could become a problem later. Right now, however, Tyrone had a more urgent concern.

They had used scheduled airliners before, and it had worked

well for marijuana when baggage handlers at both ends were bought and paid for, usually with a combination of product and cash. This had become more risky of late, as the U.S. Customs Service had expanded the use of dogs. To lose some weed was one thing, but to lose cocaine because a mixed shipment of both of them tipped off the dogs was quite another. They remained in the marijuana business because of high demand, steady revenue, and a plentiful product grown in Colombia.

Could a small plane make a direct run into Miami from an airfield near Barranquilla? Too far, not enough fuel. It was over one-thousand miles from Barranquilla to Miami. Moreover, Miami or any port of entry was far too risky. With enough fuel, could they make a long trip to somewhere else in Florida undetected by the U.S. military? Although Tyrone did not know much about general aviation (GA), he had driven past small airports all around Washington: Woodbridge; Beacon Hill; College Park; Bowie, and Leesburg to name a few. Therefore, Florida must also be full of these little airfields.

Wait. The U.S. military, by law, had no role in civilian law enforcement. The military would relegate a small, slow aircraft to the trash as a civilian problem. So, it was back to Customs. What did they have? Not much besides fast boats.

Tyrone hit the intercom and asked his secretary to call Marcus. He wanted to know what Marcus thought of using small planes, and whether they should talk to Jorge Ortiz, one of several pilots from Batista's old Cuban air force doing odd jobs for Marcus. If they agreed it was feasible, then they would broach the subject with Alvaro.

Chapter 11

A New Plan

Miami, Florida, May 1969

With the pressing need for a solution, Marcus agreed to a meeting with Ortiz. Tyrone agreed to take the next, direct Eastern Airlines flight to Miami. In the meantime, Marcus would put Ortiz to work on a plan, with an emphasis on details and feasibility.

The next afternoon Marcus picked up Tyrone at the airport. Although amateurs about aviation matters, they outlined the basic issues in the car: (1) range and fuel; (2) payload, how much could it carry; (3) avoiding the attention of law enforcement; (4) loss percentage as a function of the number of trips due to crashes or detection; and (5) silencing any surviving pilots who might want to cut a deal with the police. This last topic would not be discussed with Ortiz, but concerned Tyrone. The unspoken consensus was captured pilots were dead men walking.

Tyrone spoke no Spanish, but was quietly amused when he heard Marcus and Ortiz talking in the rapid, clipped manner characteristic of Cuban Spanish. Ortiz was of average build, prematurely balding, and probably a few pounds heavier than during his air force days under Batista. Although nicely dressed in a *guayabera* shirt and the regulation black pants, Tyrone thought he had some rough edges buried under the smooth pleasantries in his excellent English – which was fine with Tyrone.

Ortiz had done his homework. He agreed with their assumption that no light plane would have the non-stop range; unless you used an extremely risky method of loading the back with a row of three or four twenty-five-gallon fuel tanks and jerry-rigging a fuel pump into the main tanks as they burned off fuel. He could obtain such accessories.

"First," said Ortiz, "a big problem is payload reduction. Aviation gas weighs six pounds per gallon, thus a max range flight with an extra hundred gallons knocks off six-hundred pounds from the useful load – more than one-half of any GA plane available. Second, accidental fuel starvation is a common occurrence because of pump malfunctions between tanks. If this happens, the pilot must trim his aircraft for best lift over drag ratio, set the autopilot on heading hold, and climb into the back and sort things out before the plane glides into the ocean, maybe five or ten minutes depending on altitude. Flying low, you're dead." Marcus asked him if he had ever done this before. "No," he replied. "That's why I'm here talking to you today."

Ortiz quickly read their faces and said, "I have a better plan and a plane to do the job." Both men unintentionally sat up a little straighter in their seats.

"The trip should be divided roughly in half, with a refueling point at Matthew Town on the Great Inagua Island in the southern Bahamas. The pilot departs from an airfield west of *Barranquilla* heading north for five-hundred-twenty-five miles, crossing the western tip of Haiti, and east through the Windward Passage for another one-hundred-seventy-seven miles to Matthew Town. Although a small field, it has fuel. The total trip is just over seven-hundred miles. Next, the flight heads west over the northern Bahamas then directly to Valkaria, one mile west of the Florida coast but far south of all the space activity near Cocoa Beach. The final leg is about six-hundred-and-fifty miles.

"For this proposal I recommend the purchase of two or three Piper Comanches, specifically the PA-24-250 with optional long range fuel tanks. With the rear seats removed and one pilot, the plane can carry up to five hundred pounds of product. At 65 percent power, which is not a conservative setting, it has a thousand-mile range at a speed of one-hundred-fifty-four knots or about one-hundred-seventy-five miles per hour. The extra range gives the pilot a fuel cushion if he has to dodge storms or gets off course. The planes cost approximately thirty-thousand dollars each. What do you think?"

Both men looked slightly stunned. Tyrone finally spoke, "Marcus, I commend you for your selection of an advisor on this problem. And you, Jorge for putting all of this together in less than twenty-four hours."

Trying to appear modest, Ortiz said, "It wasn't that hard. I pulled out some World Aeronautical Charts and looked for planes with fair speed and good range. Even if these are not night flights, we need instrument-rated pilots who can avoid the disorientation caused by flying over open water in poor visibility. I know of one other qualified pilot who might be interested. May I ask what it pays per trip?"

The obvious question caught Marcus and Tyrone by surprise. This was supposed to be a feasibility meeting, not a done deal. Tyrone finally offered, "The pay will be excellent considering the risks. We need to talk to our other partner and get back to you on this. You fully understand the sensitivity of this matter, correct?"

"I swear on my mother's grave to speak to nobody."

As they parted, Tyrone heard Marcus say, *"Entiendes que sera´ su propia tumba si decides hablar de este asunto."*

"Si, comprendo."

Tyrone decided not to ask. He heard something sounding like tomb or death and considered that Marcus was adding some emphasis to his warning.

On the way back to the airport, the men talked over the merits of the proposal and how to handle Gonzalez. They thought it had great potential for moving cocaine in quantity and a few kilos of marijuana. Ortiz had estimated five-hundred pounds of product per trip, better than they had expected. In addition, it would minimize the use of swallowers, a method nobody liked. They decided it was the best plan; but who would talk to Gonzalez?

Tyrone was blunt about Gonzalez's prejudice against blacks, and he acknowledged his manner of superiority also irritated to him. Accordingly, the burden fell to Marcus to convince Gonzalez. They compared notes in the terminal building and agreed on how best to present it to him.

The next day, Marcus called Tyrone with the good news. Gonzalez liked it. Now, they needed to buy three planes, using three straw purchasers, and do a trial run.

Implementation

The three straw buyers bought the planes with cash and delivered them to Miami. Marcus paid each buyer three-thousand dollars for his services and told them to disappear. Ortiz planned a trial run, without drugs, in daylight to anticipate problems and evaluate the plan. He quickly thought through the three basic forms of navigation, critical for a long flight over water. Navigation by landmarks was out, except when near major landmasses such as the Bahamas or the Windward Passage between Cuba and Haiti. The trip required a lot more of dead reckoning, but between ground-based navigation aids, no other option existed.

During his practice run, Ortiz jotted down altitudes and headings. Basically, the pilot flies low near land and high over open water to pick up navigation signals out of Barranquilla, and later from the vortac at Guantanamo,[5] which also had Distance Measuring Equipment (DME).

While taking on fuel in Matthew Town, Ortiz began chatting with the lineman – who was quite taken with the gleaming new Comanche.

"Do you work at nights as well?" asked Ortiz.

The young man replied that two linemen pumped fuel during the day and evening, but lived nearby and would respond to night radio calls on the local frequency.

Ortiz pressed a little harder. "How late?"

The movement of the young man's shoulders and face answered his question.

"May I ask how much you make an hour?"

"A buck seventy-five."

"Do you have a telephone where you live and near where you sleep?"

"Yeah, don't use it much."

"Sometimes I, and a few co-workers in my company, have to deliver handmade, spare parts at unusual hours to another company that operates around the clock near Miami. Obviously, we need to count on getting fuel here to finish the trip, another six hundred miles. We can't spend the night here. If I called you from Barranquilla to say that one of us is leaving, would you go to the airport, listen to the radio, and be ready? It takes about four-and-half hours to fly here from Barranquilla."

"How much extra would you pay us?"

"Well, what do you think would be fair for getting you out of bed late?"

"Maybe twenty dollars." Which was more than he had hoped for.

Ortiz puffed up a little and said, "This is a time-sensitive business we operate. We can make or lose a lot of money based on our ability to supply these parts when needed. Because delays could be so costly, I will give you and your friend one-hundred dollars for late-night refueling. If you both show, to avoid arguing, then it is fifty dollars each. A deal?"

"Yes, sir!"

"Now, I need to jot down your name and phone number, as well as your friend's name and number if you have it."

"Yes, sir. I can give you both."

"Please don't brag to your friends, or I may need to reconsider our exclusive arrangement."

With the deal sealed, such as it was, Ortiz departed for the last

640 miles. Soon, he could pick up several coastal navigation aids. Twenty miles out to sea he dropped down to two hundred feet and reduced his speed a little, while crossing the coast. Valkaria airport was easy to find. Although physically exhausted and tired of pissing into a bottle, Jorge Ortiz was elated. He had flown a dream plane more than thirteen-hundred miles with one fuel stop. He called Marcus: "It was easy."

Chapter 12

The Crime Beat

Washington, D.C., July 1969

"Pull to the right, stop the car, turn off the ignition, and put your hands on the top of the steering wheel," said the imperious voice through the loudspeaker mounted in the grill of the cruiser. Mike Jansen had pulled over a drunk driver at 2:30 a.m., no doubt trying to find his house after the bar closed. The case required a pile of paperwork and at least two court appearances. Mike would be in court most of the morning, try to get some sleep later, and begin the next shift.

D.C. did not permit the results of breathalyzers as evidence, so the drunks had to urinate in a bottle back at the station. This was not always easy. I was doing paperwork on a stolen car and prohibited weapon in the basement when I heard Mike having trouble with his lockup. I listened to the following conversation between them.

"How 'bout filling this bottle for me?"

"Fuck you."

"Hey, you really *are* drunk."

"I ain't drunk."

"Doin' some tastin' but not drunk, huh?"

"Yeah."

"Well the only way to *prove* you ain't drunk is to piss in this bottle."

The drunk eyed the bottle with suspicion. "So, this will prove I'm not drunk."

"That's right. Just fill it about halfway."

"But I gotta piss bad."

"Fill it halfway, and I'll take you to a bathroom."

"Okay."

With the drunk feeling relieved, Mike used the desk next to me to start filling out forms.

"What do you have?" he asked.

"Operating a stolen car and possession of a prohibited weapon," I replied. "This knife is seriously ugly. Watch this." I held the nine-inch knife in front of him and pressed the button. The blade shot out of the shaft with such force that I almost dropped it.

"Holy shit! I've never seen anything like that."

"The kid here is seventeen with a juvy record as long as your arm. Says it will pierce a two-by-four board, and I believe him. All you need to do is hold it against the ribs near the heart, press the button, and walk away. I called Homicide to see if they have any unsolved cases fitting this M.O."

We worked in silence for a while, with the usual questions for the lockups. I finished before Mike and turned to go.

"I'll see you in court in the morning. Just another night in paradise."

We locked eyes and smiled.

Unambiguous Language

Fate sent me to the 6200 Club twice on the same evening. Preacher and I had the power shift – 6:00 p.m. to 2:00 a.m. The 6200 Club was the secondary lesbian bar in the precinct, and a hangout for lowlifes of all species. I enjoyed working with Preacher; he never got rattled and was supremely skilled at breaking up what criminologists call, "the degenerating cycle of violence." It's sort of a game in which each side understands the rules and decides how much to up the ante until violence is inevitable or one effectively surrenders and tries to walk away, which is not always possible. Without realizing it, many cops play this game during confrontations, almost guaranteeing a violent outcome.

Preacher would break the rules by saying or doing things that didn't fit the pattern expected to unfold. The most famous story about him involved a group of Renegade outlaw bikers partying in a house, shooting out streetlights, and raising hell generally. Preacher's appearance also fitted his personality. He was partially bald, wore wire-rimmed spectacles, always seemed slightly pale, and was a little thin and soft spoken. A photo adorned the bulletin board of him and Brinson standing next to each other with Brinson's huge hand resting on his shoulder. In contrast to Brinson's grim face, Preacher was smiling. Brinson towered over Preacher with a tattoo visible on one of his bulging biceps. One photo summarized their different styles.

Two cars were dispatched to the disturbance. Preacher walked to the other car and told them he wanted to try to quiet them down alone first. All warned him that these were thugs, outlaw bikers, most of whom had to "roll their bones" (kill an enemy biker) to become "patched in" to the gang. He listened, told everybody not to worry, took off his cap (against the rules), and knocked on the door. When a pair of bikers opened it, he asked if he could come in.

"Hey, the fucking police want to join the party." Then, the door closed. In a few minutes, the music was turned down. The door opened briefly with Preacher pointing to a shot-out street light and laying his hand gently on the shoulder of one of the bikers. The officers waited anxiously outside. Finally, he emerged, returned to his seat, and said, "We're 10-8 (back in service), party quieted."

Later, of course, other officers interrogated him as to what happened in the house. Preacher initially told them, "I want to chat with you boys, but the music is too loud, so please turn it down a little." They offered him a marijuana cigarette and a beer. He thanked them, put the joint in his shirt pocket and set the beer next to him. Guns and drugs lay in plain sight all over the living room – which he pointedly ignored. With the stereo down, he reminded them of "how our mothers raised us to be polite and not to destroy others' property."

"It's okay to party," he said, "but try to be respectful of your neighbors. They may be upset by too much noise." Preacher looked for someone who might be the boss and said, "Let me show you something outside."

He anticipated the "fuck-you" response, gently grabbed him by the outer ear like a wayward child, and led him to the door, lecturing him on foul language and good behavior along the way. This was greeted by shrieks of laughter from the other bikers. Pointing to the shot-out streetlight, he said, "The taxpayers—and that's all of us—must pay four-hundred dollars to replace it." When they turned to come back in, Preacher said that most stared at him, speechless. So, he wrapped it up with an agreement from them to quiet down. He thanked them for their time and hospitality, and left. One of them yelled, "Goodbye, Preacher," and that's how he got his nickname.

Pressed by one of the more hardline cops about ignoring all of the crimes committed or in plain sight, Preacher raised his voice a little. "Do you think we're going to change those people? Probably none of the crimes would have resulted in jail time, and if they did, jail for them is just part of their life. Also, they were well-armed. How do we justify the bloodshed, probably on both sides? They are who they are. Our job is to contain their depredations. The dispatcher sent me to quiet the party, which I did. Perhaps some of them actually listened to me." There were no further questions.

Later, Preacher and I were eating at the 6200 Club. Unlike at the Zombies, the food was edible. We carried a radio in with us, hoping to stretch the time to eat. Cops eat too fast; it is a matter of survival. Two-man units can't go out of service for food. If there were a real emergency and nobody answered, then we would take the run and leave. So far, we had been lucky.

For 7:00 p.m., the place was mostly empty. I noticed Big Carol with two of her girls in a back booth but paid no attention. I was hungry. About halfway through my meal, Preacher says, "I have a better view of your friend. You might want to take a look."

"Shit, Preacher. I thought you couldn't see with those glasses. Let me wolf down a few more bites, and I'll talk to her."

I walked slowly back to her table, watched the flurry of activity, greeted Carol, and told the two girls to hit the road.

"Empty your pockets, Carol, and I mean everything."

"Jake, I got four years of backup time for CDW[6] and selling. I can't go back inside, too many enemies there. If you bust me, you know they'll revoke parole."

We sat staring at each other. Slowly, Carol emptied her pockets: Dexedrine tabs; "buck action" heroin caps; a small bag of white powder, and about two-hundred dollars, in mostly tens and twenties.

"How much are you dealing?"

"Not much. Just a little to my girls."

"Are you packing? If you are, I'll bust you."

"No, no. I quit carrying."

"Let's go to the men's room to continue this conversation. Now."

As the door closed, exasperation filled my voice. "Goddammit, Carol, you've really put me in a bind. Didn't you see me and Preacher?"

"Yeah, but I needed the money, and I didn't think..."

"You sure as hell didn't think," I shouted. She was right about a parole revocation and time back in the slammer. Street people know the going rates in the court-and-correctional system better than most lawyers. If I busted someone like Big Carol, then it would cause ill will between the police and the patrons of these already tough bars. The lesbians would consider the bust as a hummer[7] or worse as a double-cross in light of my special relationship with Big Carol. I began to wonder why I left the food.

"Okay, Carol, I got a deal for you on a take-it-or-leave-it basis. If I flush this crap down the toilet where it belongs, then I want two things in return. One, no more selling here or in the Zombies. Go to Bobbie's house or whatever. Two, you owe me a big one, payable on demand – anything, anytime, anywhere."

Sweat poured off Carol's face.

"Thanks. Part two could be really rough, but I'll take it. Deal."

"I want to keep the cocaine because it's related to another issue. I'll say it came from a CI who can't be compromised. It won't come back to you."

As I watched the last buck action cap disappear beneath the swirling water, I mulled over the reality that life on the streets requires a scorecard. Experienced officers understand the targets of police attention as law violators can sometimes negotiate their position with direct assistance or information on more serious crime. Trading down, as it's known, doesn't appear in police General Orders. At most it's an entry in a pocket notebook.

"How come you didn't bust her?" asked Preacher as we went back into service, easing into the evening traffic.

"I'm learning from you," I replied.

The night seemed to pass slowly. Tomorrow, I intended to call Detective Lieutenant John Roberts about the cocaine. Tonight, it would stay in my locker, a serious rule violation. We wrote a few traffic tickets and separated a married couple who wanted to kill each other, just the bread and butter of routine police work.

At 1:00 a.m., I thought, "Just an hour to go."

"Scouts 63 and 64, a robbery shooting, 6200 Georgia Avenue, outside the Club. Look out for a black male, medium brown skin, twenties, about six feet, short afro, wearing a long suede coat. Last seen running west on Rittenhouse. Code one. Homicide responding, 0110."

"63 responding."

"64 also responding."

We were in 64 and close; it was a detailed lookout.

"Preacher, I've got a hunch. He could run north on Twelfth Street, with lots of houses on both sides. On the other hand, he could duck up into the cemetery next to the Methodist church. I think he's going to the cemetery – no cars, no lights. I'd like to hike up there. Do you want to stay with me or check out Twelfth Street?"

"Let's maximize coverage," he replied. "Get out here; I'll light up Twelfth Street. Be careful, Homicide is responding."

"You, too."

I turned around my cap, so the cap plate would not reflect light, and climbed up to the cemetery. The clear skies and full moon provided good light. I recognized him, walking slowly among the tombstones. The description was dead on. I circled behind and toward him. Then, I stepped on a dry stick. He half-turned toward the sound, and began to run.

"Halt, police. You're under arrest!"

He responded by turning to fire two rounds at me. I heard the bullets whiz past me; one sounded like it hit a tombstone. Now, we were running at full speed through the cemetery. I screamed, *"Halt, police or I'll shoot"* one more time with no effect.

It was my turn to use deadly force. To shoot a man in the back. I was furious at this killer for making me do this. I qualified Expert every year; I wouldn't miss. Without thinking, I screamed as I took aim, *"Hold it, motherfucker, or I'll blow your ass away!"*

He stopped and tossed down his gun. Out of breath, I raced up to him and knocked him down to the dirt, face up. Astraddle his chest, I grabbed his ears and began to pound his head on the clay, constantly cursing him as I gasped for air and pounded some more.

"Stop," he said.

I stopped, and we stared at each other panting. Sirens wailed in the distance. Somebody probably found my empty cruiser with the car door open.

"Did you hear me the first and second time I said 'Stop'?'"

"Yeah."

"And the last time?"

"Oh, man. You stopped with all that 'Halt police' shit and said you'd blow my motherfucking ass away. I knowed you meant it."

"You bet your life on how I told you to stop?"

"Yeah, I guess."

I hadn't even searched him for other weapons. I rolled him over cuffed him and pulled out a second gun. The cemetery was filling with cops, so I yelled my position saying everything was under control.

Preacher was the first to find me. He had put out a 10-33[8] after hearing gunfire. Sergeant Townsen walked up and began to upbraid me.

"Goddammit, Stone! Why didn't you just plant the motherfucker? Preacher here reports two shots fired, and they weren't by you, correct?"

"Correct."

"I'm going to write you up for exposing yourself to hostile fire and not returning fire to protect yourself."

Lieutenant Dominik had been listening and walked toward us. "You okay, Jake?"

"Yeah. A little rattled, but okay."

"Back off, Joe. Don't write him up for anything."

"But he..."

"Do you see this white shirt with gold bars?"

"Yes, sir," was the subdued reply.

Lieutenant Dominik gently pushed me away from the crowd. "Tell me what exactly happened."

"It was a lesson in communication. During the chase, I told him twice to stop. After he shot at me, I drew a bead on his back. The light was good. I couldn't have missed, but it was so hard to shoot a man in the back. I was putting pressure on the trigger, maybe two pounds or more, and then I just screamed at him, *'Hold it, motherfucker, or I'll blow your ass away!'* He stopped and tossed down the gun. I beat his head on the ground a few times, and he told me he had heard me the first time, but the last time he said, 'I knowed you meant it'."

"You did a good job, Jake. Townsen is old school. Do the paperwork and go home."

Chapter 13

High Times

Barranquilla, Colombia, July 1969

With production at near maximum, Alvaro was in one of his rare good moods. All three Comanches, which were about two and one-half with downtime for maintenance, continued to bring cocaine to the waiting trucks in Florida. High-performance planes were maintenance hogs. Not that Alvaro worried about his Airframe and Propeller logs being inspected; he didn't want to lose a load over the ocean because of mechanical problems. Pilots could be replaced. His new Maserati had arrived in Cartagena. In a couple of days, he would hit the straightaway on the *autopista* going west toward Ensenada, followed by the curves as it hugged the coast.

The flights had not encountered any problems. He and Marcus were a little concerned about the arrangement Ortiz had made with the two line boys in Matthew Town. While the solution was creative and plausible, and while the boys had sworn an oath of secrecy, Alvaro and Marcus understood the boys would eventually tell everybody. The extra money, a hundred dollars, seemed to strike a balance between flashy and motivational, ensuring fuel service to his planes at all hours.

The *gringo's* demand for cocaine seemed insatiable. Tyrone sold from Richmond to Philadelphia as fast as they could deliver it. The Professor sold no product in Miami and was adamant about two things: (1) keeping the lowest possible profile; and (2) avoiding conflict with potential rivals. For example, they used a small airfield south of the *autopista*. A marijuana dealer, who plied his product to tourists in the Lesser Antilles, owned it. Alvaro and Marcus had met him to discuss joint use of his private airstrip. He seemed pleased to be contacted first and asked to work out a business arrangement, especially since cooperation was somewhat unusual among drug dealers. The airstrip already existed; additional money for three extra planes was gravy. An agreement came easily.

Yes, life was good.

Chapter 14

Narcotics Division

Washington, D.C., July 1969

"Detective Lieutenant John Roberts, please. This is Officer Jake Stone calling…Yes, he knows me… No, and I don't want to speak to the sergeant. It's a sensitive matter we have discussed before... Thank you." Finally, the secretary dialed his line.

"Hello, Jake. Why are you calling the powder people?"

"I'd like to give you a bag of something, if you're interested."

"Quite interested. Do you have enough time left on your shift to go out of service and come to headquarters?"

"Yes. I'll make a landline call to Lieutenant Dominik for permission, then I'll see you in about twenty-five minutes."

"Great. Thanks, Jake."

Headquarters is located at 633 Indiana Avenue. It is both easy to find and to get lost in if you don't know where the special units are: Robbery; Auto Theft; Homicide; Narcotics; and the shadowy Intelligence Division, among others.

"Nice to see you, Jake," said Lieutenant Roberts. As I pulled out the bag of powder, Roberts asked if I had a copy of the 252 (arrest report) with me.

"No. It's complicated."

"Let's go to my office," said Roberts with a hard edge to his voice. I began to second guess the decision to break the rules. It was evidence – kept overnight in a locker. No paperwork or chain of custody. I promised Carol that I wouldn't serve her up on this. Like all police departments, however, regulations exist with consequences for disobedience.

"You cut a deal on your own, and you're not planning to tell me about it. Right?"

"Yes, sir."

"You know you're in deep shit, right?"

"Yes, sir."

"Take a seat and start talking."

"Sir, I use a confidential informant with backup time. She is the most reliable and useful CI I've ever worked with."

"Let me hazard a guess: Big Carol in the Zombies."

I was thunderstruck. How could he know?

"Well, the look on your face tells me I'm right. And if I had been wrong, your next stop would be Trial Board. We know all about Big Carol, her criminal history, and your friendship with her. Why do you think they call us detectives?"

I knew he wasn't sending me to Trial Board, but Roberts wasn't showing his hand. He just sat back, studying me.

"We are also working Big Carol. It's an ugly business, but we live on information more than street cops. You happened to tap one of our best informants, and we tolerated it because she helped you mostly with non-narcotic crimes."

So, where is this going?

"Speaking of Carol, I have some very bad news, Jake. Early this morning, the Zombies' manager found her by the trash bins with two in the back of her head, bound and gagged, with a canary in her mouth."

We looked at each other. The bastards discovered her working both sides of the fence. I was sad and angry at the same time. Except for a few buck action caps, she didn't deal heroin. Only the new cocaine crowd could be this brazen and cold.

I finally spoke, "What else do we know about the murder?"

"It's really early. She was helping us with the cocaine problem, and they probably assumed that she was the leak. Homicide is handling the case and may want to question you about her friends, habits – anything that could be helpful. I'm sorry Jake."

I nodded my head. Maybe Slim Jim was right.

"Jake, on a related matter, we are sure that cocaine is being distributed through an older, existing heroin network. Unfortunately, we have no idea who the big dog is. Hypothetically speaking, would you be interested in helping us root out this problem?"

"Sure, especially after the execution of Carol. Can you tell me more?"

"No. I want you to go back to your regular duties. FBI agents will be asking neighbors, the mail carrier, and others questions about you over the next few weeks. It's similar to the background investigation you had to become a policeman, just a little more thorough. You cannot discuss this with anyone. If someone asks, say it's a routine reinvestigation for your normal police work."

I approached Mike in the locker room after the shift. "Got time for a beer at Gordy's? It's usually quiet at this time."

"This sounds serious," said Mike.

"Yeah. Ten minutes?"

"See you there."

We found a corner booth. I recounted the lunch I had with Preacher and the arrangement with Big Carol. I also confessed about keeping the cocaine and the subsequent conversation with Roberts. I said nothing regarding her death – too soon.

"He cut you a break after all that?" exclaimed Mike.

"Yeah. And it gets stranger. He knew I got the coke from Big Carol, who is one of their CIs. They even have a file on our so-called special relationship. He or his boss requested the FBI to do a reinvestigation of me for a national security clearance, which means they'll talk to you. I asked him to tell me what this is about, and he said no. He did say there is a cocaine problem in the city, and hypothetically would I be interested in helping? Finally, he made it clear that this conversation never happened. So, I can't share details of future developments with you."

"Jesus, Jake. Do you look for trouble or does it just gravitate to you? I sometimes think you're an adrenalin junkie."

"Aren't we all? Maybe some are worse than others."

Both of us drank our beers in silence.

"What now?" asked Mike.

"I'm to return to my regular duties and wait for a call, I suppose."

"Jake, they're going to ask you to go undercover, which is voluntary. You have two problems with that. One, is a lovely wife and solid marriage. Two, being a cop for a long time has made your face too familiar in too many places. Think about the number of times you've testified in court. This undercover crap is for fresh-faced rookies."

"I hear you. Since when has anybody needed a national security clearance to work undercover?"

"Yeah. That's true, Jake. I don't know."

Regular Duties

"Scout 62, a shooting, Willie's Liquor Store on Kennedy Street; respond code one; an ambulance has been dispatched, 1412."

"Scout 62 is 10-4," as I flipped on the light bar, rotated to yelp, and listened to the four barrels open up on the interceptor engine. Expedite driving is dangerous; too many people with slow reflexes, who freeze, or don't know left from right. I frequently drove with the outside speaker on and the mike nearby to give specific instructions to motorists.

Less than a mile to go.

A small crowd gathered on the sidewalk near the store. Standing nearby was a uniformed special police officer, we call them SPOs, hired by local merchants tired of the robberies.

"That's Johnson," said Grabowski, my partner. "Looks like he planted another one."

"You know this SPO?"

"Yeah, he never misses. Kills a holdup man down here about twice a year. He's armed and dangerous. Why don't these assholes get the message?"

The ambulance had not arrived. I carried the first-aid kit through the milling people to the wounded youth. He was conscious, but had lost a lot of blood. Johnson had shot him three times in a running gun battle as he tried to escape. Two of the wounds were minor, one round, however, had nicked the brachial artery above the elbow. Fresh oxygenated blood was pumping out with each heartbeat. If I couldn't control the bleeding, then his life would end in a few more minutes. Years ago, I had watched an SPO die of a minor-looking wound which had severed the femoral artery in the leg. Book learning comes alive on the streets.

He was going into shock from the blood loss. His condition left me no choice. I put on a tourniquet two inches above the wound and marked the time. Nerves and muscle below the tourniquet will be severely damaged if it remains in place more than thirty minutes.

The kid asked Grabowski, who was behind me, "Am I going to make it?" First-aid 101 emphasizes reassurance of the victim. Trauma and hemorrhagic shock are the leading killers of men under forty-five in this country.

Grab was slowly shaking his head from side to side.

"No way, kid."

The ambulance soon arrived, and I gave them the information. Later, I would go to the hospital to interview the kid and make sure his room was under guard. SPO Johnson, pleased with his work, told us what we needed for the report.

Grab asked me if I wanted to join him for lunch next door in Fast Freddie's Pig Pen (ribs and wings). I begged off and said I'd get a sandwich in the African restaurant across the street.

"Scout 64, take the school crossing at Fourteenth and Upshur, 1510."

"Scout 64 is 10-4."

"Scout 64 drop your partner and remain in service as a 10-99 unit."

"Scout 64 copies."

Grab gave me a hard stare. As a wagon man, he was a bit short on interpersonal skills.

"Sure, I'll take it. But don't leave me there holding my dick after the children are gone."

"Deal."

The regular crossing-guard had left sick halfway through the one-hour post. Elementary school kids are fun and curious about everything.

"How many bullets your gun got?"

"Six," I said.

"How many bad guys you killed?"

"None."

"Why not?"

"Never had to."

"What's *Expert* above your badge mean?"

"Means I'm a good shot."

"What's the big, shiny key for?"

"You see that blue box across the street? Inside is a telephone only for police. And this key opens the box."

"Oh."

The Power Shift

Time passes faster when you are busy. Sometimes I volunteered for a couple of weeks on the power shift from 6:00 p.m. to 2:00 a.m. The most serious criminal activity was concentrated in these eight hours; so two officers manned most of the cruisers. Tonight, my partner was "Country," who had received some minor injuries in the Zombies' fight. He was a laid-back, West Virginia boy whose seemingly endless local expressions amused all of us. When one of us did not understand something he said, the response was usually, "Why do they hire people who don't speak English?"

The sun had just set and, so far, the workload was relatively light.

"Scouts 62 and 64, a shooting at Cousin Nick's, Fourteenth and Jefferson; respond code one, 1845."

"Scout 62 responding."

"64?"

"64 responding."

"Use caution, witnesses report a large number of choppers outside."

As Country and I rode up to the front of Cousin Nick's, Pagans were pouring out the door and onto their Harley choppers. The use of "Jap Scrap"—their nickname for foreign motorcycles—is forbidden amongst bikers. A few had ape hangers, handlebars so high I wondered how they turned corners. Their colors, with blue letters on a white background and a red border, were visible under the sodium vapor street light above Nick's. The fully patched Pagans wore the God of Fire patch under the top rocker of their blue denim vests. I watched with contempt as they rode into the night. A violent outlaw motorcycle gang, they have ties to traditional organized crime. Income sources include the production and smuggling of drugs, extortion, arson, and weapons trafficking.

Country turned to me and said, "What's the plan?"

"Nothing until I hear the siren from Scout 62. Then, we go in, talk to Nick, and look for dead bodies."

After 62 arrived, we climbed the three steps to Cousin Nick's and walked inside with our revolvers out and hanging down loosely. I had been to Nick's quite a few times before. In the center was an old wooden dance floor, surrounded on three sides by booths and assorted tables. The smell of gunpowder was heavy in the air; I thought I smelled a little cordite, dating the ammunition to the late 1940s, probably old military surplus.

Nick pretended to tidy up the bar. Two customers lingered in a corner booth, a hard-looking pair who stared openly at us.

"Nick, where is Dog?" I asked.

Dog was a German shepherd that weighed at least one-hundred pounds and had been trained to attack. I enquired once if he had a name, Nick shrugged and said, "Dog."

"He's tied up in the back," replied Nick.

"Okay, Nick," I said. "What happened a few minutes ago?"

"A couple of patrons got overexcited about something, and they decided to leave."

"First, Nick, I will lock you up for obstruction of justice unless you tell us what happened. Second, we are going to search for bodies after your truthful answer."

"Most of the Pagans were doing speed and alcohol at the same time. Of course, I didn't actually see any speed, but I just know the signs of a long run."

"I'm sure you're a qualified expert," I deadpanned. "Go on."

"Two guys began shouting across the room about money from some load. One pulls out a pistol and fires at him. The other shot back as people hit the floor. I fired a twelve-gauge over the head of the first guy, you know, to emphasize I don't tolerate this shit in my place. I also threatened to put Dog on anybody who pulled out another gun."

Bullet holes ringed the area above all booths on three sides. Nick and his shotgun were infamous for "maintaining order."

"I should lock you up for discharging a firearm in the city."

"Officer, we've talked before. I know, for a cop, you're okay. Please don't bust me on a hummer."

"All right, Nick, but we need to look around," I replied.

"Go ahead. Let me give Dog a treat and check he's tied down real good."

A brief search revealed no blood, no bodies. I asked the others if they had any objections to my writing this up as an "incident," rather than a crime. Nods indicated unanimous consent. I decided I would not bring Karen here for dinner.

The following night I drew a "reserve officer" as a partner in Scout 65. Except for a different badge and no sidearm, their uniform is almost the same as ours. I'm sure most mean well, but they are volunteers and poorly trained. Nobody wants to ride with them. Instead of answering the radio 10-4, we answered 10-99 with a reserve. The dispatcher had to decide whether to dispatch another car based on workload and the gravity of the run.

Four slow hours had passed with little activity. We had to help the morgue cruiser guy carry a stinker down four flights of stairs in one of those long wire baskets designed for corpses. Cops divide dead bodies into two categories: regulars and stinkers, the latter having been dead for a week or more. The worst words from a landlord are, "He always pays his rent on time. But I haven't seen him lately, and there's a bad smell coming from his apartment."

Unlike most law enforcement agencies, D.C. prohibited us from pronouncing someone dead at the scene, no matter how obvious death might be. The radio run was always for an unconscious person. The dispatcher, however, needs to know whether to send an ambulance or the morgue cruiser; thus, a timely status report after arrival was essential. The not-so-secret code for this was to say that the person was *very unconscious* – dead in other words. Another tool to manage limited resources.

The manager let us inside and subsequently ran down the stairs, followed by the reserve officer who puked going out the door. The morgue guy gave me a stony stare – the unspoken issue was who gets the top (easier) and who gets the bottom (harder). The decedent was an obese, older man, about two-hundred-twenty pounds. After some haggling, we agreed to switch at the halfway point and rest for one minute. We rested for more than a minute.

I returned to the car and snarled, "The job would have been a lot easier with two on the bottom."

"Sorry, I know."

"I've got some paperwork to do. Go find the manager for information about notifications. Be quick. I don't want to sit here all night."

He was quick, and I filled in the holes in my report.

We went back in service with little chatter on the air, almost too quiet. Sometimes the dispatcher gave cars returning to service three, or even four, radio runs at the same time. The people who complain about slow police response do not understand how crazy it can be at times. They want *their* problem solved right away.

"Scout 65, report of four suspicious subjects walking south from Madison Street on Kansas Avenue. Caller reports all four are armed, and one may be wanted for homicide; Respond code two, use caution, 2215."

"Scout 65 is 10-4" – a mistake. I should have said, "With a reserve officer." I drove east on Madison Street with no siren, only lights, which I planned to kill shortly. I considered correcting my error. Business had picked up, however, and all of the other cars were busy. I turned right on Second Street, then into an alley toward Kansas Avenue. I killed my lights and drifted toward the intersection with Kansas Avenue. Nothing. I waited a few minutes, still no sign of activity. Although finding nothing was typical of most calls of this type, the call had been quite detailed.

"Scout 65 is 10-8, nothing found." Despite being in service and available for radio runs, I decided to circle around. If they were watching me, then they would see the cruiser driving south on Kansas and west on Longfellow, away from them. I circled to come up Second Place and down Madison for another look. As I eased through the same alley, they almost walked into my car.

One bolted and the reserve officer chased him. We looked at each other; all of us were surprised. The game was on.

"Kinda late for a stroll, got some ID?" I said casually. Two handed me driver's licenses. In front of them appeared to be an open athletic bag, set down by the one in the middle. I left the car door open as I read the names and birth dates to the dispatcher.

"So, where you fellows heading tonight?"

The one in the center replied, "We repair small appliances and electronic equipment like eight-tracks, and we're on our way to do a job. Our car is right here," motioning with his head to a late model Buick with PA tags. A quick glance inside revealed what appeared to be stolen electronics. I was stalling, waiting for an ID from dispatch, and I sensed they were looking for an opportunity to flee or take me out. The dispatcher said words no cop wants to hear.

"Scout 65 is your outside speaker on?"

Without taking my eyes from them, I backed three steps to reach the control and turn it off.

"Scout 65 is on inside only with the volume turned down."

"65 are they driving a Buick with PA tags?"

"65 affirmative."

"We're talking to the FBI on another line. One is wanted for the murder of a state trooper, one for other homicides, and all are wanted by the FBI for interstate flight" (to avoid prosecution).

"Officer," said the one in the center. "We are being cooperative; we've shown you ID; we need to leave now for our job. Look, we have the tools. They're right here in this bag. I'll show you."

I let him reach into the bag, my brain reacting a split-second slow. His movements were deceptively smooth and natural.

I jerked my revolver out of the holster and pointed it at his chest. "You're a dead man," I yelled, "unless you *slowly* pull out your hand with the fingers spread wide apart. I want to see each hair on your hand as it comes out. The rest of you are dead if you move."

His hand came out a little too fast for me, but a glimpse revealed it was empty.

"Now, kick the bag over to me."

With a single glance, I observed four handguns, including an expensive .357 Magnum – standard issue for Pennsylvania state troopers. I suspected they might carry other weapons concealed.

"All of you slowly drop to your knees then face down on the concrete. Hands on top of your heads."

"This is hurting my face," whined one.

"The bed in the D.C. Jail will be more comfortable, I promise."

The sirens sounded closer, and the knot in my stomach was easing a little. Three professional killers almost whacked me, and one remained at large. Fearless Fosdick, who left me to chase one, despite having no weapon, arrived panting through the alley.

"He got away from me."

"No shit. Go sit down."

Several cars arrived at the same time; two almost collided.

Brinson leaped out of his car and said, "What do you need?"

"Help me cuff and search them."

"Any of them give you trouble?" Brinson asked through clinched teeth.

"Please don't break bad on me, Brinson. The entire world will be here on this one. In fact, I see blue grill lights, and two guys in trench coats arriving. There must be a secret FBI store which sells them the same coats."

Brinson didn't answer, too busy looking for weapons and making sure that their joints got a little extra pressure.

Soon the quiet, dark street became transformed into a surreal scene awash in blue and red lights from cars parked at all angles. Glancing up to ponder the last few minutes, I thought that Kafka, in his twisted worldview, would have enjoyed this. Abruptly, my brief reverie was broken by a voice I didn't recognize.

"Are you the officer in 65?"

I rose up and saw it was Deputy Chief Pyles.

"Yes, sir," and I saluted – a custom often overlooked within a chain of command where people work together on a daily basis. Lieutenant Dominik stood next to him.

"Damn fine job, Officer Stone. Those are some dangerous bastards. The FBI and my Tactical Unit are interviewing the reserve officer about the foot chase and other evidence regarding the fourth fugitive. The lieutenant here will put a letter of commendation in your official personnel file for this important collar. Congratulations on the good work."

Lieutenant Dominik gave me a half smile; he had heard these congratulatory remarks many times before. Because the most serious charges were federal or out of state, Chief Pyles informed me not to object when the Assistant U.S. Attorney recommended extradition in the morning. I was hoping for no turf issues. Sitting in the court's police waiting room for hours while other cases are called is a bureaucratic form of torture.

Paperwork finished my tour of duty. I went home, held a sleepy Karen for a few moments, and set the alarm for an early court appearance. For me, the case was closed.

Chapter 15

Filleted Princess

Washington, D.C. July 1969

"JJ, this is Tyrone with a problem. I want you to go to the safe house on Swann Street and recover the coke from a dead swallower. She was carrying about 900 grams in eggs. One of her handlers is with her now."

"Why can't he do it? I hate that chore?"

"JJ, it's too much money and temptation. I trust you and know you'll do a good job. When you are finished, wrap her in a blanket and toss her in a dumpster at least ten blocks away.

"JJ?"

"Okay, Tyrone. Please give the next one to somebody else."

"We are implementing other approaches to increase our volume and eliminate this method. Nobody likes it. Do it, and bring the washed product to me. I need to answer another call."

JJ slouched up the steps to the safe house, which looked like all the other row houses on the small street with an alley in back. The handler greeted him. He had stripped her, put a heavy blanket underneath her, and piled her clothes in the corner of the room. Mr. Jones had told him not to do anything else until JJ arrived.

JJ regarded the young woman. She had long brown hair, not black, and fair skin. He examined one of the hands for calluses; they were soft. Why did such an attractive, middle-class lady take this risk for two-thousand dollars, he wondered.

He could not delay this any longer.

Removing a switchblade from his vest, he made two long incisions from the bottom of the rib cage under each breast down to bone on either side of the groin. JJ took care not to cut too deeply. He made the last incision crosswise at the top where the two other incisions began, creating a flap. He braced for the stench, but she had not been dead long. Rigor was just easing. He reached inside and pulled the intestines from of the body.

He became queasy, and had to stand and walk a little. The handler sat in a chair in the corner facing away from her. The room had almost no furnishings except a foldout bed, two chairs, and ancient wallpaper, possibly original. A sole overhead fixture, aided by daylight coming through dirty windows, provided enough light for this job.

Back on his knees, JJ found the area where the containers of cocaine had clustered. He carefully slit open the intestines to remove them, one or two at a time. One was crushed – the cause of her death. Pressing along the intestines in this area, moving his hands from top to bottom, revealed more canisters. The total seemed less than 900 grams. He pulled the intestines further out and began squashing them, finding a few more canisters. An accidental look at her comely face gave him the chills. "Enough," he thought.

JJ carried the canisters to a sink to wash them and put them into a bag for Tyrone.

The handler helped JJ wrap her up in the blanket, shove her into the car, and search for a distant dumpster.

"Scouts 65 and 67, report of a dead, naked woman, mauled by dogs, in the alley at 1450 Clifton Street; code two, Homicide is responding, 1422."

"Scout 65 is 10-4."

"Scout 67 is 10-99."

Mike and I were the first on the scene. I asked the small crowd if anybody had seen or heard something unusual. Nobody had – the usual answer. I approached the corpse, careful not to disturb possible evidence, and noticed that dogs had chewed up one foot. As I inspected more closely, I jumped back into Mike, who was standing behind me.

"Mike! Dogs didn't do that. She was butchered by hand."

Brinson in 67 and a Homicide cruiser arrived together. Johnny Yates from Homicide stepped out and said, "What do we have here?"

I pointed out the linear incisions and the intestines, apparently pulled out of the body. A slight shiver ran down my back. Johnny, who is normally loquacious in the worst cases, set his jaw and merely said, "I'm calling Narcotics."

Brinson and Mike did not approach the corpse, said nothing, and stared at the remains of a young woman.

"Johnny," I said. "Why Narcotics?"

Half looking at her, he replied, "She's a drug swallower, she overdosed, and they filleted her like a dead fish for the drugs she carried. Notice some areas of the intestines were cut open by a knife. Dogs didn't do that; another type of animal did."

"Have you seen this before?"

"I've been doing police work in this city for eleven years, and this is the second dead swallower in three months. The first was cocaine. My money says the ME will confirm cocaine on this one as the cause of death."

Johnny took some photos; we uncovered the blanket in one of the trash bins along with a small bag of women's cloths. The morgue cruiser parked next to a Narcotics detective who quickly put on the rubber gloves with white powder favored by the morgue drivers. Brinson announced he was going back into service and drove off. I should have done the same as Brinson, but I remained morbidly curious about the intentions of this detective. In a few minutes he found an egg, presumably filled with cocaine. He set it down next to the intestines and snapped a photo. The egg went into an evidence bag, and the gloves into a dumpster.

"Let's go, Mike. I've seen enough for a lifetime. I'm glad the slick suits are dealing with this."

"Yeah," said Mike. "Let's hope we never get another one."

As we drove off, I flashed back to the taunt by Slim Jim. *You can never win. We gonna out-slick you at every turn.*

Chapter 16

Double Cross

Miami, Florida, August 1969

"He did *what*?" screamed Alvaro Gonzalez into the phone.

Sterling was ready for this reaction. "He flew to Nassau, sold the plane and its contents to a prearranged, unknown buyer. Next, he bought a commercial ticket for Madrid."

"What are we going to do about it?" asked a simmering Gonzalez.

"I have dispatched two teams of two men. One will go to Nassau to find out who these thugs are, and try to get our money and drugs back. The other two will go to Madrid, find the pilot, interrogate him, and kill him. He probably thinks he's safe in Europe and will be on a spending spree, which will be noticed."

"Have you told the Professor yet?"

"Yes. He approved the plan."

"Why am I always the last one to be informed or consulted?" complained Gonzalez.

Marcus was taken aback by the sudden need to be diplomatic with Alvaro. It never occurred to him that this loudmouthed killer had feelings.

"I'm sorry, Alvaro. Because you recruited this pilot, we thought you might feel better if we had an action plan in place."

Shifting the subject, Alvaro said, "I'm not impressed with many of these former Batista pilots, and some of the other ones I can find here. It was a Cuban pilot who became lost, landed at the wrong airport in Florida, and had to ask for directions. If it weren't so stupid, it would be funny. Now this double-cross. American pilots are better trained. What if you and Tyrone investigated along the coast for some upstanding, but crooked pilots who we can count on not to get lost or rob us?"

"Great idea, Alvaro. I'll talk to Tyrone and call you back."

"How fortuitous," thought Marcus. Alvaro had come up with the same plan he and Tyrone had discussed before this last incident. There had been several minor screw-ups. No single problem, rather a collection of them suggesting pilot incompetence.

Chapter 17

Intelligence Division

Washington, D.C., September 1969

We were on day work. The routine of petite larcenies, lost tourists, auto accidents, and a few robberies seemed somewhat predictable. Working as Acting Sergeant, I was reviewing some paperwork completed by other officers earlier when Lieutenant Dominik approached me with a sober face.

"The captain would like to see you."

"Now?"

"Now would be fine." I didn't ask why because he wouldn't say even if he knew.

Two brief knocks were answered, "Come in.

"At ease. Officer Stone, you have an appointment tomorrow at 9:00 a.m. with Inspector Schmidt of the Intelligence Division in his office. Arrive alone and don't be late."

"Sir, do you know what this concerns?"

"No. He led me to believe, however, you may know more than I do. Since you work for me, kindly stop by tomorrow and tell me what is going on. Dismissed."

"Yes, sir."

I turned on my heels and barely remember closing the door. I suddenly felt like the victim of a planned seduction. Detective Lieutenant John Roberts had mentioned that U.S. Customs seizures of cocaine had risen by more than three-hundred percent from 1967 to the middle of this year. The Narcotics Division had bumped this issue up to the Intelligence Division. On the other hand, perhaps an invisible partnership between the two divisions always existed. An inspector headed the Intelligence Division, aided by one captain, three lieutenants, and about twenty-five men and women. No one outside the unit was sure what they did. They were deeply involved in the periodic, and large, anti-Vietnam war protests and various groups considered violent by the FBI and D.C. Police. Among the well-known names are the Black Panthers, Weather Underground, Student Non-Violent Coordinating Committee, and Students for a Democratic Society, to name a few. Their bomb-making abilities and plans for disrupting otherwise peaceful marches in the nation's capital concerned the Intelligence Division, the FBI, and the CIA, whose involvement was an open secret.

As a member of the Civil Disturbance Unit, I received some of this information secondhand. For example, the Intelligence Division once told the Civil Disturbance Unit that they did not believe radicals would attack the South Vietnamese Embassy. Consequently, commanders assigned only six officers to guard the embassy during the protest. These groups, however, were not drug importers, just consumers. The Intelligence Division was clearly multi-mission. Their plans for me would wait until 9:00 a.m.

The Offer

"Good morning, Officer Stone. I believe you know Detective Lieutenant Roberts," began the Inspector in charge of the Intelligence Division. "I'm Ray Schmidt, and this is my second in command, Captain Roy Wilson. I oversee a staff of about twenty-five persons. Also with us today is Floyd Wainwright, FBI Special Agent in Charge of the Miami field office.

"We would appreciate your help in eliminating the primary source of cocaine that is poisoning our city, as well as our sister cities north to Philadelphia and south to Richmond. Emergency room reports show this cocaine has caused numerous deaths because its users are not accustomed to its high purity. Like heroin, when it comes from one of the authorized distributors, it has a brand name. In this case, it's *Orbit*. Your friend from the rainy car chase was a secondary distributor who had not yet cut his product for resale. Equally disturbing is the rise of gangs at the low end of the distribution chain, with each gang claiming its own turf. Homicides are rising because most inter-gang disputes are settled by gunfire."

"May I speak freely?" I began. The room, the entire staff area, was inside – windowless. Maybe the rumors about their wide-ranging and semi-legal tactics were true. The word *windowless* rattled inside my skull as I prepared to continue. "Since my conversations with Lieutenant Roberts, I speculated that I was being groomed for something, but never given a clue as to what it might be, an unusual approach in dealing with a beat cop."

"Although necessary, we apologize, for the approach. You are no ordinary beat cop. You are college-educated, a commercial pilot, a martial arts expert, honest and, according to interviews with superiors, resourceful in dealing with difficult situations. In addition, you were honest before you married Karen. A stack of hundred dollar bills will not turn your head. Detective Lieutenant Roberts told you, the FBI, at our request, completed a full-field re-investigation, and they have granted you a national security clearance of secret. Later, there are agreements to sign. Accordingly, some of what I'm about to tell you is classified. I also want to allay a possible concern you are being railroaded into accepting any assignment. After our discussions today, you may decline the offer and return to your regular duties without prejudice. Fair enough?"

"Yes, sir."

Of course, having gone to so much trouble, they might redefine *regular duties* as a year of picking up cigarette butts in the warehouse district while walking permanent midnights. I decided not to share my cynical thoughts.

Lieutenant Roberts began to speak. "The President recently signed what's called a PDD, or Presidential Decision Directive, which defines the flow of illicit drugs into this country as a threat to our national security. How efforts will be coordinated across the U.S. remains to be determined. He is, however, aware of our local problem and asked the Chief to take all necessary measures to address this regional surge in cocaine. We thought we had a victory when we tightened the laws and prescribing practices of physicians on amphetamines. Cocaine, however, quickly filled the gap, and availability grows on a daily basis. We know that the supply comes from a well-coordinated, multinational group – not a collection of amateurs smuggling in a few keys from South America. We have squeezed dry our informants and lockups.

"We think we know the following. The big boss here sends drivers to Miami, loads a truck or station wagon, and drives the cocaine to this area. We cannot stop that. Rather than bring a large load into the city, we suspect the vehicle drives to a house in a nearby, but rural, part of Virginia, or maybe Maryland. Cars with mixed plates, not all DC, come at random times to pick up their share. These are the primary dealers, who later put the Orbit sticker on their product. We did arrest one of them who made it clear that talking to us was a death sentence. We told him if he did cooperate, we would reduce charges. He hardly reacted. He said he was probably a dead man, and we could play any game we wanted. The secondary and tertiary dealers are almost as afraid. They give us a little something to ease their pain, but their information often conflicts with what we get elsewhere. In short, few facts are reliable. We do not know who is pulling the strings here. Thanks to some good work done by the FBI and CIA, however, we believe we know who the Miami connection is."

I reacted, "Does the CIA have law enforcement authority on domestic cases?"

Inspector Schmidt breezed past the legal realities. "They do indirectly because it's defined as a national security matter.

These drugs are not coming from within the United States."

Roberts continued, "We believe this is the same organization that was using young women and packing them with three or four keys so they appeared very pregnant, complete with large breasts and butts. The shaping was done skillfully and successfully until an alert agent began to ask basic questions one mule couldn't answer. She cooperated but knew nothing. The flight was from Barranquilla to Miami. Retrospective interviews of U.S. Customs agents by the Bureau of Narcotics and Dangerous Drugs, we call them the BNDD, revealed others who remembered young, pregnant women taking the same flight. This random catch told us nothing about them, but it took away their system. For now, they have adapted and are using swallowers. This is an interim method because it cuts into their volume.

"Then we got what appears to be a break. Agents from BNDD have been suspicious of Marcus Sterling for some time. Tax returns from his business did not seem to square with his wealthy lifestyle. BNDD Miami believes Marcus Sterling, a real estate agent, is the intermediary in this farm-to-arm operation. He never touches the product, but he is in charge of logistical issues, which are, in this case, getting the cocaine into the United States and ultimately into our area. At first, we focused on seaworthy ships taking the drugs from Barranquilla to a remote expanse along the coasts of Puerto Rico. There, the bad guys could lower a fast boat for a beach delivery, which puts the drugs in the United States and Customs out of the picture. This method has been used by other narco-traffickers. Problems for them include the distance and cost. From Barranquilla to Puerto Rico is seven hundred and seventy miles of open sea at maybe fifteen knots. Storms in that area can be severe. A sturdy boat would be expensive and subject to boarding by the U.S. Coast Guard and later the Customs Service.

"Finally, with the help of the FBI, we leaned on selected baggage handlers for Eastern Airlines because they had been compromised before. We found no reason to believe commercial flights were bringing cocaine into Miami. For a while, we were stumped. A Mexican route was out of the question. In fact, they could not move product any further west than Cartagena. Agreements backed by firepower dictate which routes are open to whom.

"BNDD continued to investigate. A fair number of persons who purchased Sterling homes had been in and out of prison for drug-related charges. In addition, he corresponds with another Cuban in Coleman Prison, in central Florida. As you may know, prison staff opens all correspondence before being passed onto, or from, any inmate. BNDD had asked for copies of the correspondence between Sterling and Jesus Ramirez, doing federal time for drug trafficking. Until recently, the letters talked about old times and seemed harmless. Last month, however, Sterling said he had sold property to some orange and fruit growers who needed agricultural pilots. Maybe they could talk about it further. Sterling's real-estate transactions do not include any agricultural businesses. He is seeking pilots. You can tell where this is going. Do you want out or do we continue?"

I was curious. They had a plan, but it wasn't 'Drug dealer needs pilots' in some help-wanted ad.

"Go on," I said.

Roberts continued with the lead. "We believe they are using general aviation aircraft to fly the drugs from Barranquilla to Miami."

"Whoa," I reacted. "That's probably over one-thousand miles if you cut across the center of Cuban airspace. I don't think so."

"We know," said Captain Roy Wilson who spoke for the first time. "I flew F-4 Phantoms for a year in 'Nam before taking this job. We are quite sure they pass through the Windward Passage between Gitmo on the west, and Haiti on the east to refuel somewhere in the Bahamas. Among the seven hundred Bahamian islands, a few have airports with fuel. This is a sketchy picture because they run a tight ship, with everything on a need-to-know basis and employee loyalty beyond question. With the exception of Sterling, we do not know any of the other principals and are relying on informed conjecture – which is an oxymoron. I suspect they have been using ex-Batista pilots, some of whom have not flown for nine years. Such a limited pool may be the reason they are looking for younger, better-trained American pilots who can be trusted.

"We want you to fly for Sterling."

They said it! Fear and excitement mingled together, creating a powerful turmoil within me. This was mad, yet heady stuff. I felt a visceral pull to be in the middle of it. Maybe the deaths of Carol, the swallower, and many unknown to me were not in vain. Others could fill out dog-bite reports.

"We, and the agencies we work with," began Inspector Schmidt, "have the resources to place you deep undercover, with a new identity as a pilot who was busted on federal charges for flying marijuana from Mexico into Texas. The cover includes having served most of your four-year sentence in El Reno prison in Oklahoma. Afterward, the Bureau of Prisons transferred you to Coleman prison in central Florida prior to release on parole. You requested Florida because you want to live with your half-sister in Miami as part of the pre-release plan while you look for work. Your half-sister is an undercover FBI agent working on another assignment. Her name, for this operation, is Jamie Hudson. She will be your liaison with us and the FBI, as well as helping you regarding any needs you may have."

"Will I actually be imprisoned in Coleman? How do I meet this Jesus guy? What can I tell my wife about this?"

"Yes," continued Schmidt. "You enter Colman as a regular inmate for one month. Only the warden will know your identity, and you will share a cell with Ramirez. We can say little to Mrs. Stone for the protection of both of you. Captain Wilson plans to visit her, emphasizing the importance of this unique assignment and the necessary isolation. He will give her his direct phone number, although he cannot say much except that we are in contact and you are okay.

"Doing time requires specific skills to maintain your cover. All inmates can smell a *fish* or new inmate a mile away. Having served more than three years in El Reno, you must act like this is only a transfer. Each federal prison has a thirty- to forty-page *Admission and Orientation Handbook* for inmates. We will give you one for El Reno and one for Coleman, along with some other reading material written by former inmates and guards. After you have read all this thoroughly, a veteran federal prison guard will coach you for a few days here in a D.C. hotel. He has done this before for federal agents, and the process includes some realistic role-playing."

I began to feel overwhelmed. So much for heady stuff. I can't be made as a fish because that blows my cover – a death sentence for an undercover cop in prison.

Lieutenant Roberts spoke, "There's a little more about the admission process you need to understand. Each prison has two types of Special Housing Units, better known as *the hole*. They are for administrative or disciplinary segregation from the general population. They all look similar: an eight by ten feet concrete cell, with bunk beds, one metal desk, and sink-toilet combination. Food is bad and comes in on a tray pushed through a slot in the door. We cannot break procedure. You will spend four or five days there until they decide what to do with you. That, of course, will be to bunk with Ramirez on the low-security side of the complex. The hole can be profoundly stressful. The guard will teach you some methods to help manage those few days better."

I lost it and blurted out. "I'm going to put up with all of this prison crap, make friends with a thug, fly drugs from Colombia through the Bahamas into the U.S. using airplanes with no maintenance records, over open seas notorious for severe storms, learn who the bad guys are without being able to speak Spanish, and not get killed in the process? Is there anything else?"

Inspector Schmidt spoke, "When you put it like that, it sounds..."

"Don't patronize me! It *is* crazy."

An awkward silence hung in the air. Nobody moved or talked, and heads dropped imperceptibly so eyes would not meet.

Captain Roy Wilson broke the silence. "The odds in warfare are often poor. You have faced extreme danger, but only for short periods. All of your points are well-taken. This assignment will be extremely dangerous. You will be under and alone except for contact with your FBI housemate."

"Why," I asked, "isn't BNDD doing this?"

"It's my turn to speak candidly," said the inspector. "They are a new agency, poorly resourced, and have little credibility within the brand-name federal law enforcement community. They have a few pilots who are quite visible in their jobs. They would be made and executed trying to go undercover. Also, we have information that their intelligence side has been penetrated by at least some of the drug cartels."

"The FBI," I offered, looking at SAC Floyd Wainwright.

He responded, "The authors of the Harrison Narcotic Act were unsure if an outright ban on heroin and cocaine would be constitutional, thus it is a tax code provision. Accordingly, the FBI's view is this is a problem for local police and Treasury agents, who seem more concerned with moonshine. We are willing to help, but not take the lead. Because of the scope and international dimensions of this case, however, we will make our resources available to you. Before you ask, the CIA is working with us on this regarding information gathering. Of course, they are prohibited from leading any domestic law enforcement initiative."

"Your willingness to consider this assignment is deeply appreciated," said the inspector. "You may not need the money, but you will receive a special hazardous pay rate, a substantial bonus at the end, and an automatic promotion to sergeant. We ask that you give us an answer within two days. Unfortunately, you cannot discuss this offer with anyone. You can call Captain Wilson or me with any further questions."

Inspector Schmidt rose to stand, signaling an end to the meeting.

"No need to wait," I said. "I'll do the job. How do we begin?"

Everyone got out of their chairs, smiled, and pumped my hand in what seemed a spontaneous gesture of both relief and good will. A tense meeting suddenly had become more cordial.

"I'll be your primary point of contact in the Division," said Captain Wilson. "We have an arrangement with the Justice Department and the U.S. Marshals Service, under which they will swear you in as a Special Deputy U.S. Marshal. In short, a federal agent, not a D.C. cop freelancing. Your undercover identity is James Sixkiller, a traditional Cherokee name. We thought you would enjoy that. We checked, and no Oklahoma Cherokees are in Coleman. With the help of FBI and CIA experts, we constructed Sixkiller's life. Where you were born. What happened to your parents, everything. Coordinating with the Bureau of Prisons, we will insert this identity into BOP's record system. Come back tomorrow, and we have prepared a complete, tabbed notebook: biographical section; juvenile and adult rap sheets; *Admission and Orientation Handbooks* for El Reno and Coleman; selected articles from former prisoners on prison survival; a summary about Jesus Ramirez; a more complete intelligence overview covering much of what we've discussed today; information about Jamie Hudson, your FBI housemate; and a list of critical phone numbers, including ours. The notebook carries a 'Secret' classification, but is paragraph marked. Before each paragraph a code will appear in parenthesis as (U), (C), or (S) or unclassified, confidential, or secret. Even though it includes unclassified material, keep in mind all of this is sensitive and for your protection. We cannot allow you to carry the notebook out of the Division. One of the secretaries will set up a desk to study and make phone calls. How long do you need to become familiar with the notebook?"

"Three or four days," I guessed. "Also, my captain made it clear to me he would like to know what's happening."

"I'll take care of the problem," replied Inspector Schmidt. "I have known him for years and can smooth things over a little. We are detailing you to Internal Affairs (IA) for one year. That is your story to co-workers. Everyone understands that cops from IA don't talk about what they're doing or where. The re-assignment will help insulate you from pressure by the curious or pushy about your whereabouts or work. As of tomorrow, however, you begin here. After one week here, you meet the famous trainer we call Jerry for a few days of counseling and role-playing. Jerry is a former prison guard who has received special training in helping to place federal agents undercover. For you, Jerry has no last name, and he can be very intense to work with. Meanwhile, we will make the necessary changes to insert you into Coleman. Come in late tomorrow if necessary."

A few more handshakes, and the meeting ended. I couldn't help but make mental notes of these three people. To some extent, my life would depend upon their diligence and honesty with me. I was pleased the inspector named Captain Wilson as my primary point of contact. His penetrating blue eyes conveyed directness and integrity. They told me he understood what I had committed to do. He would be an ally if things unraveled. The inspector had a job to do. Although he was a politician-bureaucrat responding to pressure from the Chief, and indirectly from the President, he needed me to succeed. His motives were a bit different, but he was also in my corner. Roberts was likable and a little inscrutable. I believe that cops who work narcotics too long become cynical. They believe no real victory is possible. The best outcome is "to make a difference." I was more wary of him.

I thought about why I accepted this assignment. Partly it was the right thing to do. Maybe my work can help alleviate the pain on the streets. Personally, the mission appealed to the darker side of me drawn to danger, fear, and conflict. I complained about the seduction, but saw it coming. I didn't know what "it" was going to be. The edge is normal for me. My worst fear was getting too old to enjoy the fear.

Gordy's

"Mike!" I gestured across the locker room for him to come over. My area was empty, and the next shift had headed up for roll call.

"I got stuck on a run," said Mike. "What are you doing still loitering around here? Time to saddle up and go home. By the way, I didn't hear you on the air until this afternoon."

"Yeah. That's why we need to talk. How about Gordy's in ten minutes?"

Mike regarded me somberly and said, "Sure."

We found the same corner booth as before. It was my dime. We ordered beers, and Mike sat back to contemplate me, a friend of many years.

"I passed most of the morning with some new acquaintances from headquarters. They'd also invited an FBI SAC from a major city to join the discussion. I've accepted an assignment lasting from four to five months. It's dangerous and will take me far from this area."

Mike continued to sit back, look out the window, and drink his beer.

"Why? Don't you get enough adrenalin with people trying to kill you here?"

"It's the right thing to do."

"That's so lame, especially because you always understate danger. You couldn't resist, could you? Well, you are who you are. I'm going to miss you – you stupid son of a bitch. Can you call?"

"I think so. I have a favor to ask."

"You need a will? Ask a lawyer."

"Would you call and visit with Karen occasionally? She's not going to handle this well. Maybe take her to dinner and a movie; she likes you. I'm trying to think of ways to decrease her sense of isolation."

"Sure. But, I wonder if having me around will make it better or worse."

"I see your point. Try it and notice how she reacts. If it doesn't seem like a good idea, just ease back to her comfort zone."

"Jake, remind me of why we became friends."

"You found somebody crazier than you to hang out with."

"Good luck, and please return."

"Thanks. I will. Remember, while I'm gone, you are the thin blue line."

Smiles, another beer, and lighter conversation concluded the evening.

Karen

Karen's reaction could have been worse – maybe. There is no way to dress up a bombshell, so I did not try. I told her the Chief of Police had handpicked me for a lengthy and *somewhat* dangerous assignment. I added that the purpose of the FBI re-investigation was to give me a national security clearance of secret because of the importance and nature of the work. I told her the job involved a lot of travel, and I might be out of contact with her for long periods. I emphasized that I would call, but could not disclose my location. Watching her trying to keep a stiff upper lip almost killed me.

"How long?" she finally asked.

"About four to five months."

The stiff upper lip gave way to some sniffling as I held her tightly. I told her I loved her and reminded myself this scene has been played out so many times before in other houses, for other reasons. The expectations, however, were different. She married a cop, not a soldier. Accepting this was asking a lot of her, and I hoped she would not pull away from me emotionally to save herself. I worked a dangerous job, but at least I returned home every day.

"How dangerous is it? Tell me the truth."

"The Chief picked me because I have the talents to achieve our goal. My ability to read and remember almost everything will be important. They have created a new identity for me, and I become this different person based on the details of his fictional life. All of these efforts are in cooperation with other relevant governmental agencies to ensure that this ends successfully."

She was studying my eyes and body language for additional information.

"I'll tell them no tomorrow if this might ruin our marriage. That's more important than anything."

"Would you do that?"

"Yes," I said without hesitation.

"No. You will always be my husband. On the one hand, I'm proud they picked you for this. On the other hand, I'm afraid. I can tell you're downplaying the danger involved. This is your nature, a man who loves living on the edge. I knew that when I married you. This is a big one, however, long and dangerous. I guess I'll learn how tough I am."

I didn't know what to say, so I held her again.

"Let's go upstairs," she said. "I read about a new position I want to try. We need to make the most of our remaining time."

And she led me upstairs by the hand.

Jerry

The Intelligence Division had booked a suite with two twin beds for prison training in a local hotel. Jerry and I arrived about 4:00 p.m. on Tuesday. He was a taciturn, fit, black man around 50. The door had barely closed when he said, "What's your name?"

"Jake Stone," I said.

"*Wrong*! It's James Sixkiller – you never heard of this guy Stone."

"Where and when were you born?"

"Stilwell, Oklahoma in 1944."

"Why are you inside?"

"I got caught after I landed in Tulsa with a planeload of Mexican marijuana."

"What kind of work did you do in El Reno?"

"I made furniture for government offices." He grilled me until we broke for dinner, where he continued to call me Sixkiller. A common saying exists about prison guards with twenty years of experience. They have one year of experience, repeated twenty times. Jerry was an exception. With his sharp intellect, he had memorized my new identity to ensure that I didn't trip up.

Over the next three days, we covered a dizzying array of information and slang known to all experienced cons during daily conversation. What are the basic prison types and characteristics: minimum or Federal Prison Camp (FPC); low security or a Federal Correctional Institution (FCI) with a double fence perimeter; medium security could be an upgraded FCI or part of a high security U.S. Penitentiary with double or triple fences with electronic detection systems. Some penitentiaries have high walls, and all have the highest staff to inmate ratio. In addition, about five other administrative facilities exist for special purposes, such as medical or temporary detention.

Jerry emphasized knowledge needed for daily life. Know that a *call out* is an appointment; get used to being counted five or six times a day and night. Become familiar with the staffing in your unit, this determines where you live and who your team members are. Each unit has an overall manager, a case manager, a counselor, and a secretary who manages inmate schedules. Understand the role of a basic correctional officer, or guard, also known as screws, hacks, and other uncomplimentary titles.

The overview covered the use of phones by inmates; dining etiquette; regulations; prohibited acts and the disciplinary process; money and the commissary; pat downs and searches; visitors (Karen can't come); health care; cell and job assignments; permitted and standard work clothing, including approved colors; emergencies; authorized personal property by category, and more.

Even though this was only a transfer from another federal lockup, they still need to decide where to put me and what assignments to give me. This process takes about five days while I stay in administrative segregation or the hole. Jerry told me to bring two soft-cover books, as hard covers are not permitted; practice deep breathing for stress relief; do whatever exercises are possible in the confines of the hole; such as pushups, squats, and jogging in place. Accept the offer of one hour of recreation five times a week. Do not talk to other people unless spoken to; respond with minimal, polite answers. Although designed for two, this small space houses three or even four. The pecking order of who gets which bunk bed or uses the toilet first is based on length of time there.

I ended up with a list of Basic Dos and Don'ts:

- Do not lock eyes or stare at another prisoner. He may perceive it as sexual interest or a physical challenge.
- Do seek out other Indians. Because of an old law,[9] a disproportionate number of Indians are doing federal time. So, I shouldn't have any trouble finding them. Jerry

emphasized that race is everything in prison. It dictates gang composition, your friends, and who might help you if necessary. Jerry explained most prisoners will consider a few Indians irrelevant to a gang scene dominated by Blacks, Latinos, and white supremacists.

- Do carry yourself well and with confidence, but keep a low profile.
- Do protect your personal space, while respecting the space of others.
- Do not be seen as friendly with guards. People will suspect you of being a snitch.
- Do be careful with everything you say. It can be misconstrued.
- Do not get sucked into a debate about anything.
- Do watch the hands of the persons around you, especially in unsupervised areas such as a corridor, bathroom, or even in general population. Shanks are everywhere. A rapid hand movement will signal an attack.
- Do not allow anyone to call you a "punk" or "bitch" in front of others. These are special words in prison and require an immediate physical response. The guards understand and will not bring disciplinary charges. This response marks you as someone not to be taken lightly, an important asset.

"Well," said Jerry after three days with a cheerful smile on his face. "Are you ready to be a successful inmate?"

"I prefer to go home," I replied dourly.

"Think of the time as shock treatment to prevent you from slipping into a life of dissipation and crime."

I smiled at his calculated cynicism.

Chapter 18

Insertion

Central Florida, September 1969

I had several more discussions with Inspector Ray Schmidt and Captain Roy Wilson, who emphasized that I should say only "Roy" or "Ray" during phone calls because all prison phone conversations are monitored. Accordingly, I memorized a dedicated number in the Intelligence Division used only by two cleared secretaries to answer incoming calls. Also committed to memory were certain codes for the status of things, both inside and outside prison. The secretary who answers the phone says "Hello." After chatting for a minute, she passes me to Roy or Ray for a coded conversation. The (false) names of the two secretaries were on my list of approved contacts as friends.

The insertion began after Karen and I bought tickets to Orlando, and drove an hour east to Cocoa Beach for a vacation. The beach and oceanfront room proved wonderful, but our conversation and behavior were strained at times. We tried to enjoy the moment, but both of us were watching the calendar. No amount of denial allowed us to remove the sword of Damocles.

For the most part, we managed pretty well until the blacked-out sedan rode into view. Karen stiffened at the sight of the car and the two men in dark suits and sunglasses who got out. She gave me a long hug and kiss, and urged me to be careful.

I was ambivalent about doing this to her, and for what? More drug kingpins will replace these, assuming the plan is successful. If I am destined to die young, her loss is my fault. I volunteered and turned away to face the agents. Although clueless about what a convict was doing at a beach resort, they were good at following orders. Turn James Sixkiller and his folder over to the

U.S. Marshals for a routine transfer from the Orlando Federal Court to Coleman Prison.

Karen returned to the room and made herself a cup of tea. Her trembling hands tried to put the cup back into the saucer. Jake was gone and so was the stiff upper lip, replaced by tears.

I had to be strong for Jake, she thought. *He needs to face these unknown dangers without thinking I might not be able to handle the stress. Facing fear of the unknown is worse than fear of something tangible. I have no idea where he is going and what he will be doing. I hate to admit it, but I am also angry with Jake. He realized this was a major blow to us, and he did it anyway. I did not marry a soldier, and he presented me with a fait accompli. Maybe I'll go to the library when I get home and review literature that addresses the lives of women married to cops and soldiers.*

The Hole

Receiving and Discharge was the first stop for photos, fingerprints, and a written psychological evaluation to look for security-related problems. Later, guards would handcuff, shackle, and take me to the hole. What nothing can prepare you for was *the sound*. No other sound exists like a heavy prison door, made of casehardened steel, gathering momentum on its rails, and slamming against the wall and latching. The impact is so intense that, for a second or two, you can hear the high frequency harmonics from the steel as it recovers from an impact that vibrates your bones. It also does what no speech can do. You are inside and powerless; freedom is on the other side of that sound. I pushed from my mind Dante's *All hope abandon, ye who enter here!* Only the Warden knows...

The hole, eight-by-ten feet, had four stacked bunks and three other inmates, eliminating the prospect of sleeping on the floor. No mail, one shower each week, bad food, one phone call every week, beds made prior to 8:00 a.m., and six "official" counts per day including one at 3:00 a.m. and one at 5:00 a.m. This was life for only a few days. My *cellys* seemed well-behaved, except for one Florida cracker named Bo. He didn't like Indians and called me "nickel." The other cellys were Reggie, a quiet, muscular young black man, and a Mexican farm laborer who spoke no English. I tried to follow the advice of Jerry. Exercise proved to be difficult, but possible. The sweltering heat and body odor made the sense of confinement overpowering. Sharing one toilet did not help. The noise in a prison during the day is nonstop and numbing: conversations; commentaries; insults; obscenities; and opinions are constantly ricocheting across and down corridors until quiet hours begin at 9:00 p.m.

Bo began decompensating from the stress after two days. He wasn't sleeping and complained that somebody was inside his head telling him strange things; worse, he became angry and aggressive. He repeatedly shoved Reggie and me, and said we were out to get him. On the third day, he pushed Reggie and added, "Nigger, get out of my way." Reggie decked him with a professional-looking straight left and a right hook, knocking him out and breaking his jaw.

The guards came, including one Latino to interpret and obtain statements. We told the same story. Gleeful screams from all sides shouted, "Fight in the hole!" The guards took Bo, conscious but incoherent, to the infirmary. They gave Reggie a *shot*, or a write-up for fighting, which was resolved in an interview with the lieutenant without any sanctions.

Reggie and I talked a little the following day, while I kept to my script with few improvisations. He was doing twenty-to-life for kidnapping and raping a white woman, convicted by an all-white jury. He considered himself lucky. An old interracial union called the United Packinghouse Workers of America helped get him a good lawyer, based on his steady job in a packinghouse in Jacksonville and clean record. The woman had convictions for prostitution, and the alleged, so-called kidnapping consisted of

Reggie driving her from a strip bar to his apartment for consensual sex. His hobby was amateur boxing in a nearby gym. Surprisingly, he was not bitter. "I'll get out someday," he said quietly, "instead of being fried in the chair."

Transfer

After six days the guards finally came for me. Sweating and stinking, I wished Reggie good luck. After a *pro forma* interview to review paperwork, I was scheduled for a Mandatory Release rather than to a halfway house. Having lost my good time in El Reno, because of alleged participation in a prison riot, I had to serve most of the full sentence, which expired in less than three weeks, plus two years on parole. A photo I.D. to be carried at all times, a nine-digit code to access the phones, locker number and, most importantly, the cell assignment followed the interview. Laundry was next, where I received green shirts, pants, shoes, work boots, towels, washcloths, a pillow and pillowcase, sheets, and basic toiletries: plastic razors, toothpaste, and two rolls of toilet paper. Then, I was escorted to my housing unit and shown the bulletin board where mandatory appointments, or call outs, are listed for each inmate there. Usually, call outs are to see a doctor, visit a counselor, and so on. The guard asked me if I could read. After nodding my head, he gave me a set of rules and told me to study them carefully. For example, non-institutional clothing may be worn after 4:00 p.m., on weekends, in the recreation yard, and at breakfast and evening meals. Also detailed was the disciplinary process.

Cell Mates

Finally, he took me to my cell, where I met Jesus Ramirez. The guard gave us a brief, if somewhat awkward, introduction and locked the door. I remembered Jerry's advice to defer to any prior cellmate, and he had probably enjoyed the short period with no celly.

His first question was blunt but not hostile, "Who'd you piss off to do so much time in El Reno?" I smiled while reminding myself he was enjoying the fact that he already knew I transferred from El Reno. Ramirez was in his early thirties, about five-foot-eight-inches, very muscular, a little darker than most Latinos, *un Moreno*, not unusual among Cubans. Lifting weights was almost an obsession with many inmates. It works off stress and makes them stronger both for self-protection and to cope with an environment that has stripped them of power.

"Let me think," I said. "The Customs Service, Border Patrol, BNDD, FBI, and the FAA. I believe that's all."

It was his turn to smile faintly.

"We've got time," always a bad prison joke. "Tell me what happened."

"I'd been working with a Mexican drug and immigrant trafficker. All of the northern border states are lousy with airstrips a few miles inside Mexico. I got five-thousand dollars for each round trip."

Ramirez shifted slightly on his bunk when I mentioned airstrips.

"Standard procedure was to climb to only three-hundred feet and cross the border in a remote area, steer for a nearby Texas airstrip, climb as if you were leaving the traffic pattern, and squawk 1200 for visual flight rules." A frown told me he was not a pilot, and an indicator that I must explain further.

"Almost all aircraft have a transponder inside which lets air traffic controllers see you, but not talk to you. Codes other than 1200 are used for formal flight plans."

"Why do you want them to see you at all?" A fair question.

"Because they *can* see what's called a skin paint without the transponder; the flight may have come from the airport near the Texas border or, without a transponder, may have originated in

Mexico. The idea is to obey the rules as much as possible in order not to attract attention. My destination was Lawton, Oklahoma, carrying three-hundred-fifty pounds of marijuana and two illegals. I made the required calls for an approaching aircraft and landed without incident. The general aviation section of smaller airports normally has some remote areas where you can offload, refuel, and file a false flight plan to return to a border airport. As I taxied around the corner, the whole world was waiting for me with guns and flashing lights."

"How did they know?" asked Ramirez.

"A Border Patrol agent with field glasses wrote down my tail number as I crossed the border at three hundred feet – bad luck. Then he got a supervisor to call the FAA and put an electronic 'V,' for violator, tag on the plane. So, when I popped up near the Texas airport to look legit, the FAA tagged me. They can follow a 'V' across the country, and the pilot never knows it's there.

"For that reason, some smugglers hop across the border and land on a dirt strip owned by a trafficker or cooperator. They may scare a few cows and piss off ranchers, but they'll offload and be back in Mexico in three hours. Ranchers, however, have shot down a couple of these planes. Other ranchers will report a suspicious pattern to Border Patrol, who keeps the area under surveillance. At a real airport, for example, a truck driving away on a paved road looks normal, in contrast to a fast-moving dust cloud in south Texas."

"Well," he said. "You succeeded in pissing off just about everybody, but I don't understand why the FBI had a dog in this fight."

"The plane was stolen."

This time Ramirez laughed aloud.

"Why aren't you doing two-hundred years?"

"I had a good lawyer. He got a lot of the bullshit charges dismissed, even the airplane, in return for a plea to 'smuggling with the intent to distribute.' I would have been out by now except for the riot in El Reno. I was in the wrong place with a bad crowd, and they stripped me of all my good time. Quite a few of us were involved, and the warden and assistant regional director made the punishment decisions. If we were there, then we did something wrong. But I'm out of here in nineteen days."

Even if it is ten years away, any inmate can tell you the exact time of his mandatory release and next parole-hearing date. Chalk marks on the wall.

"What's your story?" I asked.

"Not as interesting as yours. I'm merely a drug smuggler who got busted in Miami with two keys of heroin."

"I didn't realize much heroin comes into Miami," I said.

"It doesn't. I was doing a favor for a friend of a friend. The dealer in Washington had excess and called my associate in Miami, who specializes in weed. 'Can you find a buyer for these keys?' he asked. While we're not heroin dealers, we know who they are. Unfortunately, the one we approached had already been caught and flipped. After we consummated the deal, six or seven feds plus Miami narcs were all over us."

"How much more time you got?"

"I look good for parole in eleven months. Been keeping my nose clean and head down. Problem is Parole Board decisions are hard to predict. They may give weight to my prison record and say, 'He's been a good boy here, time for release'; or they may focus on my criminal history and say, 'He's a typical recidivist who should stay locked up.'"

Both of use remained quiet for a while, listening to the incessant sounds of a prison.

Ramirez broke the silence. "It's almost time for the 4:00 p.m. stand-up count. After the count clears, we have twenty-two minutes for dinner followed by open movement and recreation until dark. I'm going to the Commissary, if you're interested and have money. Remember not to talk when they come by."

Prison is about structure and repetition, which makes it clear who is in charge of your life. We listened to the sound of two guards making their way down the corridor. As they passed by our cell, we stood by the bunks. Both looked inside, and moved on to the next cell. This process repeated itself until the count cleared and the cell doors opened simultaneously.

"After being in the hole for six days, I'm going out into the yard and get some exercise, maybe see if they have a sweat lodge."

"I need my smokes," responded Ramirez. "Do you want anything?"

"No thanks."

Doing Time

I knew they had no sweat lodge. The Indians here had insisted on igneous rocks instead of river stones; many tribes insist on the spiritual tradition after dark, but the yard closes each day at dusk. Also, the tribal members couldn't agree among themselves about its construction because of the different traditional cultures. In some prisons, the Indians had banded together to surmount these problems, but not in Coleman.

I needed to make my first phone call to the Intelligence Division. The prison allows fifteen minutes. Both prepaid and collect calls were permitted. For my short time, we agreed on collect.

"Hello."

"Will you accept a call from James Sixkiller?"

"Yes, I will."

"Go ahead, Sixkiller."

"My first conversation with the real world. How are you, Fran?"

"Fine. How long were you in the hole?"

"Six days. No shower. Really ripe. Was dreaming about dancing with you."

Laughter. Both of us were playing this by ear. Guards monitor all calls.

"I'm glad it was only a dream," she said. "But keep up the good work."

"Hey," I said. "I've only got fifteen minutes. Is Roy or Ray around?"

"This is Roy. If you're dreaming about me, we can cut this call short. How are you doing?"

"I'm okay. My cellmate isn't an asshole, a big plus. Some guy named Ramirez, a smuggler like me. Interesting story. Says he was importing and selling weed in Miami. His friend or partner in Miami has this buddy in D.C. who specializes in heroin but needed to dump two extra keys, kind of like car dealers who advertise overstocked, low price. Asked if he had a Miami contact who would buy it. Although he doesn't deal heroin, the big shots are acquainted with each other. Problem for Ramirez was he approached a dealer who had been busted and flipped. No good deed goes unpunished, right?"

"James, not much time left. Do you still have your half-sister's number? She might like to hear from you since you're invading her space soon?"

"Yeah. I got it. Say hi to Ray for me. I get three hundred minutes a month, so staying in touch shouldn't be a problem. I'll call her tomorrow about this time, okay?"

"Yeah. I'll call her and let her know this is a good time for you."

"Thanks, bye."

"Less than three weeks. Stay tough."

After getting out of the way of other prisoners who wanted to make calls, I went over the conversation in my head. The first call he made would not be to my FBI "half-sister," but to Karen with an upbeat report, just short on details. "Not an asshole" means Ramirez was comfortable talking to me, including his criminal background. A bonus was the information that Marcus Sterling is cozy with a major D.C. heroin dealer. Ramirez was amiable, but I sensed he was being careful, maintaining his distance. The words of Jerry rang in my ears: Trust no one in prison. He would definitely talk to Sterling before approaching me. I reflected on the fact that bad things happen to bait.

Later, I walked out into the yard to look for a gathering of Indians. About six or seven stood together, talking, smoking, and joking. As I approached, one yelled out, "Hello, Sixkiller." Several laughed.

"How did you get that name," said one.

"I earned it," I deadpanned.

There were no introductions made the way the white people do. They were passing the time telling raunchy, racist Indian jokes, and I just joined in.

"How do you kill a Lakota warrior," said one, not waiting for a reply. "You catch him drinking water and slam the toilet seat on his neck."

Contagious laughter was followed by other bad jokes. The most offensive jokes about a tribe usually come from a tribal member. I was certain that some were Miccosukee and Seminole, Florida tribes. Others had high plains and southwestern features. BOP tries to keep inmates within two hundred miles of their home. Accordingly, those from distant tribes were being punished. I listened and told a few jokes, trying to assess the cohesion of the group. If they had a sweat lodge, for example, their leaders would become apparent. They seemed content to pass the time. Finally, one asked me, "What are you in for?"

"Smuggling drugs."

"Didn't you know that is illegal?" said another to laughter.

The conversation turned to Indian country discussions and legal battles over tribal sovereignty issues, and grew more serious and bitter. The American Indian Movement had been founded only a year ago. All speculated what role it might play in the future. Many Indians are well-versed in Indian history and law. After all, whites wrote American history, which omits or glosses over the crimes committed by whites against Indians, especially in the hundred-year period from 1790 to 1890. My own parents, born in Oklahoma at the turn of the last century, were not U.S. citizens until enfranchised in 1924. They were only Indians without a vote and few rights. One older man, probably Kiowa, had memorized the most notorious words of the Supreme Court in a 1903 case. Indians are "an ignorant and dependent race that must be governed by the Christian people" of the United States.

At dusk, the yard began to close, and we trekked back to our units. One tall Indian in his thirties caught up to me and said, "I'm Jim Hightower. We know you're short time, but there are more of us, and we're here for you."

"Thanks," I replied. I was isolated and grateful for the offer of support, even if it was only companionship.

He accepted an invitation to head over to the gym with me, which consisted mostly of weights and minimal exercise equipment, treadmills and a couple of stationary bikes. I needed the exercise, not only because of the hole, but also because of the stress from the sense of walking on eggshells.

The gym crowd was tough. The skinheads and Chicanos were heavily tattooed, and some of the blacks were hulks. All moved carefully around each other to avoid conflicts. A guard entered and looked around repeatedly. It struck me as odd how a single shared interest forced them to get along, sometimes being polite to each other. Outside, organized crime groups of different ethnic backgrounds and former enemies occasionally sit down to make peace for money and a lower profile. Dead gang members in restaurants and streets draw a lot of law enforcement attention.

Hightower and I worked out in silence for more than an hour, always mindful of the clock. Recreational activities ended at 8:30 p.m. with the final institutional count at 9:00 p.m. Despite a few stares at the two Indians in the weight room, the workout was uneventful. We headed for the showers and began to talk. I asked him if he knew Ramirez.

"Yeah. He's a loner, knows how to do time, and avoids the other Latinos for the most part. Rumor is that he has some bad-ass connections on the outside. Last year a Cuban was shanked by another Cuban, reportedly on orders from Ramirez."

"What happened to cause Ramirez to put out a contract?"

"The dead Cuban liked to brag a lot about being a big shot in the Miami drug business. The grapevine says he started talking a lot about going back into business with Ramirez and his partners when he got out, and he had met a Colombian boss. Ramirez is keeping his head down and should be out in a year. He didn't need this loudmouth."

"What does a prison contract cost?" I asked.

"I hear about three-hundred dollars. Life is cheap here."

"What happened to the killer?"

"Nothing. Latinos encircled the victim. None of them saw anything. Be careful with your cell mate." Advice I intended to heed.

Ramirez and I stood by our bunks waiting for the final count at 9:00 p.m.

"Are you still working as a grounds orderly?" he asked. All inmates are required to work at some job.

"Yeah. The unit manager told me I had too little time left to train for a new assignment."

"We call your job 'picking up cigarette butts and polishing rocks.'"

I laughed. "That pretty much describes it."

"The laundry isn't bad. I could have asked for something else, but my priority is not to make any waves. Here they come."

After the guards passed, I sensed the end of our conversation and climbed into my bunk with a book. I had already called Jamie, my "half-sister." She was either a good actress or truly amiable, maybe both. We had a foolish conversation about nothing much. She warned me not to expect my "new wife" to do any home cooking. Food often arrived in white boxes with Chinese letters. I was looking forward to meeting her and getting out of prison.

Days passed under the rigid structure of prison life. Breakfast begins at 6:00 a.m. All meals revolve around rotations based on your unit. Sick call at 6:30 a.m.; work at 7:30 a.m.; lunch rotations begin at 10:30 a.m.; work resumes at 12:30 p.m.; the commissary closes at 3:00 p.m.; yard recall at 3:30 p.m. for the 4:00 p.m. stand-up count; commissary reopens and evening meal rotations begin; pill line at 7:45 p.m.; recreation recall at 8:30 p.m.; final institutional count at 9:00 p.m. The routine has a numbing effect, leaving no doubt about who controls your life.

In one of my conversations with Roy, I found a way to mention "Colombia" as a tourist destination for surfers. Despite the discovery of the "pregnant" women method, Intelligence was not sure if the current influx of cocaine was from the same group using new methods. If I developed information on which one of four Latin American countries was the original source, not leaf but product, I was to mention the country in an innocuous context. Possibilities included one of the Andean countries through Mexico, direct to Colombia, or refined in Colombia. Claiming to be a big deal was not the real reason for shanking the Cuban. Rather, he linked Ramirez and a Colombian boss in the same sentence.

After about ten days, Roy asked me if I had seen any interesting birds while out in the yard, a code for anything from Ramirez about working with somebody outside, no matter how indirect. I joked that scarecrows with machine guns staffed the towers. An awkward silence followed. Both of us understood the odds of a contact would decrease after my fast-approaching release date.

Release

Ramirez and I were standing by our bunks for the 9 p.m. institutional count, a ritual now too familiar. After the guards were well along the corridor, I was looking through my books when Ramirez said, "Got a minute?"

"Maybe two or three," I replied.

"One of everybody's parole conditions is to seek and obtain lawful employment. I was just curious if you had anything lined up?"

I surprised myself at being so casual, since I knew that something was coming. "Nothing really. I'm going to live with my half-sister for free until I get work."

"Very generous of her. What does she do?"

"An interior decorator. Not exactly my field. I still have a valid Airframe and Power Plant license, so I can repair planes, but not fly them. They took my commercial license."

"What kind of planes have you flown? Is that the right question?"

"I had single and multi-engine land certificates. I've flown just about all of the single engine planes out there."

"I have a friend," began Ramirez, "who is looking for an agricultural pilot. It pays extremely well for Ag flying. If you're interested, he can contact you at your sister's house next week. He knows you've lost your license, but respects your experience."

"Flying again. That would be fantastic. But I still need legit work."

"We know. So, he can set you up as a mechanic at a small airfield near Miami, and you can pay your sister instead of freeloading."

We both smiled at the mutual arrangement. I was filled with joy and fear at the same time. I had to put the thought that this scumbag was doing me a favor out of my head, although in some ways he was. The investigation can proceed to the next level with a tighter focus. The next day I told Roy that I had seen a red-shouldered hawk from the yard.

I had gone through most of the pre-release motions. I met my parole officer (an FBI agent familiar with the situation and able to cover for me on required reports). And I met with the occupational counselor regarding employment. Both agreed that working as an aircraft mechanic would be feasible and help prevent my recidivism and a life of cycling in and out of jails. Of course, my half-sister would help provide a stable home environment off the streets. I said goodbye to Hightower and my Indian friends, and I gave Ramirez a sheet of paper with my sister's phone, name, and address. Although he took the paper gracefully, I was certain he already knew that much and more.

As the prison door slammed shut behind me, I noticed that this time, the sound was beautiful.

Chapter 19

Under and Outside

Miami, Florida, October 1969

Jamie picked me up in a blue Plymouth. The Intelligence Division had shown me her photo before entering prison. We hugged like family, and I dumped my few belongings into the trunk. A two-hundred-and-sixty-mile drive lay in front of us. I felt a little nervous, something I put off as strange, especially since being liberated from a wretched experience. How big was the bonus they promised me? Jamie was quiet, nothing like the bubbly young woman on the telephone. She was attractive but not flashy. About five-foot-six-inches, long, light brown hair with bottle-blonde streaks, lovely figure, feminine, but somewhat plain. Of course, she was also undercover so her attire and presentation had to fit with her job. Jamie broke the silence.

"I'm going to take you shopping. I saw what you put in the trunk."

I laughed, "Not suitable for an ex-con pilot."

"Not suitable for anything except wash rags."

"I'm offended," I replied solemnly.

She answered with a gentle laugh.

After a few more miles of bad road in silence I said, "Tell me about crime in Miami."

"We call Miami an open city. It's not controlled by any one of the twenty-four La Cosa Nostra, or LCN, families like New York, Cleveland, New Orleans, Buffalo, and so on. The crime rate rose dramatically since arrival of the Cuban Exiles. We are watching, for example, Jose Miguel Battle, who controls a group of thugs who call themselves *The Corporation*. By the way, I now have permission to tell you about my activities. I argued that the living arrangement with knowledge on only one side would be awkward and possibly dangerous. Back to crime. How about kidnapping, bribery of public officials, extortion, and bombings for starters."

"Bombings?"

"Oh, yes. Freelancers or made men from the Bonanno family in New York commit most of the serious crimes if Santo Trafficante, the Tampa Mafia boss, sanctions their activities. He considers Florida his territory for LCN operations, and the families generally respect that."

"You mentioned bombings," I said.

"Three months ago, the FBI arrested a guy named Henry Kiter, who was extorting Delta Airlines for three-hundred-thousand dollars. If they didn't pay up, then he would blow up a departing Miami flight. He was not affiliated with any group, just homegrown pond scum."

"Can I ask what your undercover role is?"

"By training, I'm an accountant. I keep the books for one of the major players in Miami, and I'm part of an FBI team that's trying to gather intelligence on organized crime in a disorganized city. So, how was prison?"

"Don't give up your day job for a life of crime. I was in Coleman for less than a month, a very long month. I could never understand why some prisoners released after a long sentence deliberately violated parole to go back inside. But now I can. They have stayed so long that the rigid prison structure becomes part of their life, not to mention three-hots-and-a-cot plus medical care. I heard that old Appalachian moonshiners liked to be caught occasionally. A short sentence was ideal to get their teeth and other medical problems taken care of before they went back to work again, a perverse safety net."

Miles of flat land passed in silence and short conversations. Around Vero Beach I said, "Shall I spell you on driving?"

"Do you have a license?" she asked, turning toward me with

a smile.

"It's a perfect forgery of an Oklahoma license, done by the FBI's finest."

"Works for me, Sixkiller," as she pulled off the highway.

Approaching Miami, I asked Jamie if the Intelligence Division had kept her up to date on new developments while I was in prison. She seemed informed about the Colombian nexus, the heroin dealer in D.C., and the general situation.

"Other than my half-sister, are you going to play any role in this?"

"Actually, SAC Wainwright, the U.S. Attorney, and your inspector are discussing that right now. Undercover work is highly unpredictable. Until they reach a consensus, I think the answer is that I have a passive support role, which protects both of us. Of course, if you get your dick in a wringer, we will help. In addition, it appears that my current assignment is about to close down. The U.S. Attorney expects to issue warrants in a month or two. For sensitive or classified calls to Washington, I have a new STU-1 secure phone in case someone puts an illegal tap on mine. The house is swept and the regular line is checked weekly, but I use the STU-1 for sensitive or classified matters. That is the long answer."

"Thanks. What happened to the bubbly, silly girl I had telephone calls with?"

"Oh, I can do that too."

"So, who's the real Jamie? I don't mean your name, but the real you?"

Miles passed without an answer.

"How long have you been a D.C. cop?"

"A little more than three years, counting prison time."

"Funny. Have you changed?"

"Older cops seem to fall into two categories. Those who are cynical, burned out, and waiting for their twenty years to be over. As a rookie, I once asked an officer how many years of service he had on the force. He replied, 'I can retire in eleven years.' And there are those who manage to maintain perspective. They take some joy in knowing that, from time to time, they improve the quality of life for the people. Camus concluded one of his essays by saying that one must imagine Sisyphus happy."

Jamie gave me a long look. "So, you're content with the struggle, rolling the stone up the hill?"

"Yes. If that changes, I'll leave."

"It's hard being a female FBI agent in Hoover's Bureau. He and Clyde don't care much for women. Away from Washington, I can be more feminine, but in general, austerity rules. I suppose I was naive when I joined the Bureau. The violence and cruelty people are capable of was only an abstraction. Now I need to handle its reality. Basically, I'm the girl on the telephone who now has a more serious side with tougher skin. Does that answer your question?"

"I think we'll get along fine," I said.

Endless flat roads, cattle ranches, and orange groves seemed numbing to someone accustomed to hills. Finally, we turned onto the Sunshine State Parkway, which would lead us to Miami in approximately one hundred miles.

"Tell me about Karen," said Jamie.

I answered with superlatives and felt slightly foolish after I noticed her smiling.

"Too much information, huh?"

"Not at all," she replied. "Do you know what most men say when asked by a woman about their wives?"

"Um, I'm going to find out."

"Well, the answer is: 'She's okay' or 'She's nice;' like they were talking about a bag of used golf clubs. No wonder she loves you, a macho man who can wear his heart on his sleeve when he wants to. Personally, I consider you an endangered species. That's praise, by the way." She beamed a smile at me and punched me in the leg.

"Do you have a steady boyfriend?"

"Used to. He didn't like my job. He didn't like this or that. He wanted me to be somebody else. Familiar story, right?"

"Yeah."

"What did you do before becoming a G-Man?" I asked.

"I was a military brat. We moved constantly within the United States as well as to Germany and Korea. My mother could not handle the constant dislocations, and I wanted to attend college in the United States, so eventually we moved back. Before college, it was nearly impossible to have lasting friendships, and I think it turned me into a loner. Finally, I could make friends who wouldn't disappear with the next set of reassignment orders. I wanted to become an FBI agent, and they were recruiting accountants. So, I have an accounting degree.

"Your job is tough on relationships. Karen had a hard time with this assignment. Did she tell you not to do it?"

"No. It was close. I would have declined if she couldn't have handled it."

"Female to male friend. She can't handle it. She didn't say no because she loves you and understood how much you wanted the job."

I looked over at Jamie. She was right, of course.

"You know how to make a man feel good."

"Love is always a balancing act. After you return home in one piece, you owe her big time. A romantic vacation would be my recommendation. She already has all the things money provides."

"Thank you. I'll do that, except I don't feel so macho right now. My ass is hanging out in the breeze without a lifeline. I don't like the part of waiting around some indefinite period of time for some unknown thugs to appear with some unknown offer of employment. Do I sound paranoid?"

"Actually, you sound like you have a firm grasp on reality. Welcome to the undercover shakes. You'll need the vacation just as much as her."

We got off the parkway and turned south on Twenty-seventh Avenue, left on Seventh Street, and left again on Seventeenth Court. Near the end of the street was a pink, stucco rambler with a Spanish tile roof, a two-car garage, and a yard that needed watering and care. The house was L-shaped with large overhanging eaves, vented for natural cooling. As we walked in I noted the family room, three bedrooms, one converted to an office, and a functional kitchen. Well, this was home for a while.

"I want a short nap," said Jamie. "Afterward, let's go shopping for you and eat dinner." Jamie noted my look and added, "You stink and have nothing to wear. Take a shower while I nap. I have an extra pair of jeans and a shirt that might fit you – my old boyfriend's. You should look like a reputable gangster, and when was the last time you ate real food?"

"Yes, Mom."

"Also, I have a thousand in cash for you as well as a Sig model 210 with some extra clips, and various holster styles."

"You can be my date anytime!"

"Yeah, well maybe when you smell a little better."

I called Karen on the secure line. She squealed with delight to hear my voice. Then she paused. "You sound terrible," she said. "Are you hiding anything from me?"

"No, except I haven't slept much lately. I'm in a quiet house now and plan to rest for a few days."

"Please call me whenever possible. I guess you can't say anything about where you are."

"No. I'm so sorry. Did Roy or Ray come by to see you?"

"Roy did. I liked him. He was nice, yet kind of somber at the same time, like his eyes had seen a lot."

"Yeah. That's Roy. I trust him. How are you and the family?"

"Fine. I bought a dog. It was actually Roy's idea, but I wanted one anyway. I got him from one of those places where people moved or something and need to give away their pet. He's so sweet."

"Tell me about our new roommate."

"Well, he's only three and is a German shepherd who weighs more than a hundred pounds. The vet said he has stopped growing."

"Jesus. What do you feed it?"

"A lot. I call him *Wuffe*."

"That sounds like a girl's name for a hundred-pound dog. Karen, I need to do some errands, but I'll call when I can. If you don't hear from me for a week or so, don't worry. It means I'm working. I will be able to return to this house for breaks, okay? I love you, take care. Feed Wuffe. Bye."

"Bye, Jake. I love you too."

After we hung up, I thought, *Jake is my real name. Jamie has seen my profile, but always calls me James. Protocol; stay with the script. I don't know Jamie's name. I'm growing accustomed to strange.*

Contact

Jamie and I were famished and ate dinner first. Later, I decided an Indian gangster in Florida wore black alligator cowboy boots, Levi's jeans, a black leather belt with a suitable silver and turquoise buckle, and western shirts. We actually found a western store that looked like it opened during the last century.

The old man was a little crotchety. "You ain't no Seminole. You make a wrong turn about a thousand miles west of here?"

I laughed, said "Yes," and told him that I was from Oklahoma.

"You like this heat and humidity?" His ribbing was good-natured.

"I plan to return home after I finish my business here," I replied.

Since I didn't know how long I had to wait for my business partners, I also bought a few books.

We drove home; I showered and slept hard. I never heard

Jamie make breakfast and leave for work.

Two days passed followed by a loud knock on the morning of the third day.

"Sixkiller?" One Cuban and one American stood in the doorway. The American did the talking and obviously was a boss. Jamie didn't help them with their clothes shopping. The Cuban was dressed in black except for white socks. The boss wore some ill-fitting beige pants and a Hawaiian shirt that concealed the bulge under his left side.

"Maybe. Who wants to know?"

"Ramirez sends his regards. Says you're expecting us."

"Right. Let me leave a note for my sister. Am I returning here tonight?"

"Probably."

I left a short message for Jamie and slipped the Sig into the small of my back. The three of us walked out to their car; the Cuban got in the back.

The American spoke first. "We are in the drug-smuggling business. You've just done four years and are on parole. If you're caught again, you'll be an old man when you leave prison. I want to make certain that you don't have no second thoughts. If you do, you can step out, and we'll drive off with no hard feelings."

"I appreciate your directness. I'm in. Smuggling drugs is what I do. What's your name?"

"Tony."

"How about him," motioning to the back seat.

"He is called No Name One, one of two professional enforcers we keep on the payroll full time. No Names Three and Four are part-time employees. We point out the targets, and the enforcer kills them using whatever plan works best for him. Number Two is sometimes called Napalm Josey because he likes to fire bomb homes and kill everybody. He says he gets off on the screams. We leave the methods up to them."

"Handy to have around," I replied.

"The boss is also Cuban and maintains two companies of professional soldiers who will assist in the next invasion of Cuba. A former U.S. special forces colonel trains and leads them. He keeps them ready since we don't know the timing of the next opportunity." We drove in silence for a bit.

The American continued, "I made arrangements for you to meet with the head mechanic at Opa-Locka Airport. His name is Sam Slaughter. You need to go by later, talk with him, give him a copy of your driver's and mechanic's license, and discuss likely jobs. He understands that the primary reason for your part-time employment is to keep the parole officer happy so you can work for us the rest of the time. Also, we are going to meet Marcus Sterling who is in charge of logistics, and is a principal in this operation. Be respectful and don't ask too many questions. Follow his lead."

We pulled into the parking lot of a real-estate company in North Miami. After climbing one flight of stairs, I looked at an office door that read "Ex-Pat Realty." Underneath in Spanish Sterling had written with slightly larger letters *Volveremos* ("we shall return"). After walking past some cubicles, we arrived at the end door and knocked.

"Enter," said the voice from within.

Marcus extended his hand to me and said, "James, finally good to meet you. You seem to be an interesting character, and your former cellmate gives you high marks. Fortunately, I can access the BOP database and did a little reading about you."

I couldn't tell whether the latter remark reflected concern, or should be accepted at face value. It didn't matter now; I had made the leap.

"What did you do before your connection with the Mexican trafficker?"

"I worked for one of those small regional carriers, which pay nothing, and I supplemented my income as an aircraft mechanic. I also worked a great scam with a car dealer. We approached

Mexican illegals who had no documentation and offered them for cash, a car, tags, insurance cards, and a good-looking Oklahoma driver's license."

"Did you get caught?"

"No, a cash only business."

Abruptly changing the subject, Sterling began, "Here is what you need to know, James. You will pick up a mixed load of cocaine and marijuana from an airfield about thirty kilometers west of Barranquilla, Colombia. The airplane is a Comanche PA-24-250. Are you familiar with that plane?"

"No," I replied.

"No problem. I will ask one of our experienced pilots to make the first run with you. Will that be sufficient?"

"Perfect," I said.

"From Barranquilla you refuel in the Bahamas and fly to a small airport on the coast of central Florida. Mr. Ortiz will explain the details. A truck will be waiting to help offload the product and drive it north. You, or another pilot, return the empty plane, depending on demand and personnel considerations. You won't get stuck in Colombia. Somebody can drive you to the international airport in Barranquilla to rest in Miami for a while. Based on experience and the difficulties possible en route we don't want tired or hung-over pilots flying. Do you drink, James?"

"Rarely and not to excess."

"Excellent. Do you have questions?"

"What is my fee for each trip?"

"Five thousand at loading and five thousand after offloading at Valkaria, a small airport on the Florida coast."

"When do I start?" I asked.

"First, take care of the paperwork with Sam Slaughter. We stay in business because we don't make careless mistakes, James. Details are important. No product comes into Miami, and this is a legitimate real-estate company, in case you decide to relocate here permanently. Later next week you and Jorge Ortiz, our most experienced pilot, will take a commercial flight to Barranquilla. Verify with Tony that the number you gave Ramirez is still the best number to reach you. A Comanche is sitting at the small airfield waiting to be loaded."

Tony dropped me off at a Hertz place, where I rented a red Ford Galaxie with a 390 cubic inch motor and a four-barrel carburetor on top. I picked this car to because it was fast and flashy. Jamie was home when I returned.

"Nice wheels," she smiled. "So, you're taking me to dinner?"

"Sure. You must know a good seafood place around here."

"Absolutely. Give me five minutes."

That's women speak for fifteen to twenty minutes. I put away the Sig and settled in front of the TV. Live footage from the carnage in Vietnam. I changed channels.

We found a quiet booth in a nearby seafood joint. Jamie wanted to share an appetizer, marinated alligator chunks on sticks. She told me it tasted like chicken.

"Next time," I said. I picked the Grouper, and she ordered Red Snapper.

"You seem a little moody," she observed.

"I had company today. An American gangster named Tony and a Cuban they call No Name One. There are four of these thugs, all hired killers. I met with Marcus Sterling who gave me the basic details. He was cool, all business. Next week I fly to Colombia with another pilot to do a run to a small airport north of here. From there the product goes toward Washington by truck."

"That's great news. Call Roy when you get home. I'll brief my people and the BNDD liaison."

"That brings up another point. Sterling casually mentioned he had access to the BOP database and had done some reading about me. Obviously, my cover was airtight because I got the job instead of a bullet. BNDD is only a year old. They brought in many people from the former Federal Bureau of Narcotics and added new hires, all of whom should be properly vetted. Many carried their clearances over from the old FBN, a potential weakness. In addition, BNDD issues a provisional clearance to some employees because the FBI cannot keep up with the high demands for clearances from so many agencies. Supposedly, those with provisional clearances do not have access to sensitive information. I'm concerned that the practical need for manpower might force some managers to bend the rules. If you were a drug trafficker, what would be your highest counterintelligence priority?"

"Penetrate BNDD," responded Jamie without hesitation.

"BNDD has been helpful," I said. "For example, they made the connection between Marcus Sterling, Ramirez, and the smuggling enterprise. I don't trust all of them. I'm going to ask Ray to sanitize the information we give them, and marginalize them from this point forward. This narco-group is so successful because they are both smart and ruthless. Does that request sound paranoid?"

"No, actually. They don't have a need to know the type of details which can get you killed. Let them contribute on a more strategic than tactical level, so they will perceive their supporting role as consistent with your justifiable concerns."

"Well put. If Ray balks, can you talk to the Special Agent in Charge here?"

"Actually, this is supposed to be a Headquarters op, but he will support you on this. We have our own concerns about BNDD. Unfortunately, drugs are not an FBI priority." We talked shop and more personal things until late. The call to Washington could wait until the morning.

As we walked toward the house, Jamie was brushing casually up against me. I was probably imaging things since female contact seemed a long time ago.

"It's dark now," she began. "Remember the drainage canal that runs along the side yard?"

"Yeah," I said cautiously.

"It is full of alligators."

"Gators? How big?" I walked a little closer to the canal to squint through the darkness.

Jamie snuck up behind me and grabbed me around the lower legs.

"Aaagh!" I fell backward and crosswise on top of her while she laughed aloud.

I rolled to one side of her and said, "I'll get you for that. Are there really gators there?"

"I saw an eight-footer sunbathing close to this spot a few days ago."

"Then what are we doing here?"

"Having a little fun." She kissed me gently on the forehead and ran a hand down my side, letting it come to rest on my hip.

"This is dangerous," I said.

"Yeah," she agreed. "We'd better get away from the canal," shamelessly playing with my words.

We were still smiling as we entered the house and flipped on lights, heading for the living room. I turned on the tube and sat in a Lazy-Boy. She scooted up between my feet, asking for a neck and shoulder massage. While it was only a massage, I found it slightly erotic. I sensed that she did too.

Chapter 20

Smuggling Drugs

Twenty-seven-Thousand Feet Over the Atlantic, October 1969

Jorge Ortiz and I had seats together in a mostly empty Pan Am DC-8 jet doing a daily milk run from Miami to Barranquilla, to Bogota, and back to Miami.

"I'll summarize a few important things about the Comanche," offered Ortiz. "Obviously, we bought the PA-24-250 with the extended range ninety-gallon tanks. Gross weight is twenty-nine-hundred pounds. With ninety gallons of fuel, the payload is six-hundred-seventy pounds. Subtract out the average hundred and seventy-pound pilot and you have five-hundred pounds of cargo. But the cargo area is placarded at two-hundred pounds, so we removed the back seats, which give us more space and the ability to shift the center of gravity (CG) forward."

"How can I do a proper weight and balance check prior to flight with these changes?" I said.

"Well, you can't exactly. So, I did some test flights adding weight with dumbbells and other known weights at different moments in inch-pounds to determine an approximate CG at four hundred and four-hundred-fifty pounds."

"Jesus. That scares the crap out of me."

"Being scared tells me you're well-trained. I explained this to three pilots; two hardly reacted to this trial-and-error method. The other one freaked out and wanted to quit."

"What happened to him?"

"Well, he had seen too much, knew too much, and met too many people. One of the No Names arranged a fatal accident."

Returning to the original subject, Ortiz asked me, "Have you ever taken off in a plane only to discover you had an aft CG problem?"

"Once, as a favor I ferried two fat helicopter pilots back to their home base. They had no baggage, so I thought: I'm within weight, but maybe toward the aft CG corner. Later, I calculated my CG limit and was lucky to have survived."

Ortiz continued, "The plane can land at max gross weight and needs less than fifteen-hundred feet to land with 32 degrees of flaps. Therefore, if you sense a CG problem, make one-half standard rate turns to return and rearrange or remove cargo, and keep your speed up making those gentle turns. The landing strip is twenty-five-hundred feet and paved – almost commercial grade."

"How large is the cargo door?" I asked.

"Twenty inches square. The marijuana is in bales of fifteen-by-eighteen-by-forty inches and weighs about fifty pounds, so it fits through the door. We have to arrange them by climbing over the seat. The other product is more compact and dense, and rides in stacks behind the pilot. Usually we take off with less than four hundred pounds of cargo and 15 degrees of flaps. You've flown Pipers before, so be careful when low on fuel about uncoordinated flight maneuvers that might uncover the fuel outlet in a tank. It is always kind of scary when the engine stops. Piper also recommends burning the aux tanks dry before switching to the main tanks. Finally, to prevent inadvertent gear retraction on the ground, you must move the handle aft before moving it upward. Now, you are an expert."

"Do you have a proper Pilots Operating Handbook[10] (POH) for me to study?"

"We can drive over to the strip when we arrive, and I'll take it out of the plane for you to look over tonight, but I want to leave early tomorrow so we don't have to dodge thunderstorms in the dark, a mistake we made during an initial run."

I still had questions, but studying the POH would help a lot.

The Trip

One of Ortiz's men picked us up, and we drove directly to the private airstrip about thirty kilometers west of Barranquilla, where two Comanches were parked. One was down for maintenance.

In the nearby motel, I studied the POH, a process I'd done for many planes. Fatigue finally took its toll. I slept hard until the phone rang with a wakeup call. I understood nothing she said, except it was time to get up.

Ortiz and I drove to the strip in silence, drinking coffee. The airstrip looked better in daylight. No numbers were painted on the ends, which indicate compass direction if you add a zero. For example, runway 27 faces 270-degrees or due west. Ortiz said this runway was approximately perpendicular to the coastline, thus accommodating nocturnal winds from the differential heating of the land and sea.

I insisted on weighing each bale, but the coke was in one-kilo bricks.

"This weighing shit is going to slow us down," groused Ortiz.

"Yeah, well it might mean that your load arrives intact along with two pilots," I said, being in no mood for estimates.

"Also, does either of your assistants speak English?"

"I do," said a man called Juan. "I or one other worker who speaks English will help you on trips when you come alone."

"Thanks," I replied. For a reason just beyond my reach, I was in a foul mood. Maybe it was the long, boring trip with Ortiz, almost thirteen-hundred miles with a fuel stop in a plane that tops out at one-hundred-fifty knots. Alternatively, I learned nothing here except the name of one laborer. I shrugged it off to do the preflight inspection and oversee the cargo layout. The more dense cocaine was toward the front, behind our seats, and the bales were in back. The procedure seemed to work out better than I expected.

"Three-hundred and fifty pounds," beamed Ortiz.

"We are still over gross with two pilots."

"You gringos worry too much."

"Being careful keeps me alive."

"Okay, let's get out of Dodge," said Ortiz. "That's right, isn't it?"

"Yeah, if you like cowboy movies."

We got in and began the checklist, leaving the door open for ventilation.

"Fuel selector on right tank, mixture rich below three-thousand feet..."

"What are you doing?" demanded Ortiz.

"I'm trying to start the goddamn plane. Here's an old west saying for you from Jessie James: 'Who's robbing this train anyway?' I read the POH, and you don't start with aux tanks. You switch to aux after altitude. Finally, I talk to myself when reading checklists so I can compare what comes out of my mouth with what I'm doing physically."

Ortiz slumped back in his seat with two helpful comments. "The book says rotate at fifty-six knots. I recommend sixty-five knots plus 15-degree flaps because of the weight. I've had the nose wheel bang down on me trying to get off at fifty-six."

"Thanks." We had agreed that Ortiz would navigate and only assist with piloting duties. He had made this over-water run before, and we intended to fly low near the shore, which minimized reception of available navigation aids. Since international flight is illegal without a flight plan, we planned to stay at about a thousand feet until over the ocean to avoid detection. The Navy would pick us up on radar at Guantanamo, but we were drug runners, not a military threat.

"I'm setting 20 degrees on the heading bug," said Ortiz. Fly that until you pick up the 12-degree radial off the Barranquilla vortac. The heading should work for about twenty-five miles to give us a wind correction angle, then we just dead reckon until we pick up a crossing radial off GITMO's vortac. Better to fly over Navassa Island on western Haiti than get in Cuban airspace."

"Time off is 8:50 p.m.," I began. "Mixture rich. Prop., forward. Three greens on the wheels. Fuel pump on. Flaps at 15 degrees. Full power. Oil pressure green. No warning lights. Coming up on sixty-five knots. Rotate. Positive rate of climb. Retract gear and flaps. Level off at a thousand feet. Power back to 75 percent. Turning right to intercept the 12-degree radial. Trim off excess control pressure.

"Now, not much to do for the next three hours until we enter the Windward Passage," I said to myself.

Ortiz reached behind his seat, "We try to think of everything for pilot comfort. Here's a one-liter mason jar with a top for used coffee and drinks."

"Thanks."

The hours over open water with no features were grueling. We calculated a wind correction angle and stayed on that course. Ortiz had put in the GITMO navigation frequency and turned the volume up in hopes of hearing the Morse code identifier. Soon, we heard a faint pattern of dots and dashes.

"The needle is unstable," I said. "What do you think of popping up to three-thousand feet to get a bearing, and then drop back down?"

Ortiz didn't respond immediately. "Do it. Better to piss off the U.S. Navy than the Cubans by getting too close. Port-au-Prince radar can't see this far west."

Unfortunately, we were too close. The wind had shifted direction, pushing us westward toward Cuba. I dropped down to five-hundred feet and, after a quick calculation, flew almost due east at full power for 15 minutes, then back to one-thousand feet.

"We're crossing the 120-degree radial," said Ortiz. "Let's fly a wide DME arc until we can see Haiti off to the right. Crossing 110 degrees, 100 degrees. I see Haiti on my side. We're okay. Turn right to 15 degrees. No, make it 18 degrees for wind. That should take us close enough to Matthew Town on Great Inagua to pick up the non-directional beacon at the airport north of town, another hundred-and-fifty-five miles. Time now is 1:10 p.m. They'll be open for fuel, but if one of our boys takes care of us, we give him the hundred dollars."

An hour later, we were on the ground. It felt so good to stretch and walk around. The runway was lined on either side with white sand and salt, beyond which lay nothing but the scrubby, low brush that could tolerate this environment. The economy of the island is based on massive salt deposits, a main supplier to Morton's Salt. The base operator's office and fuel truck were on the far west end of the runway. One of the boys was taking care of us. The plane doors were locked, and a tarp lay on top of our cargo. We walked in, bought some peanuts and candy, and used the bathroom.

"I see your Comanches here often," said the booming island voice from behind the counter. He looked fit, in his early fifties, and of mixed racial origin.

"I appreciate your business, but how come you don't buy one of those fancy jets and fly direct?"

I decided to answer. "The fancy jets are several million dollars we don't have. We operate on a narrow profit margin, so these planes cost about three-thousand dollars and burn a lot less fuel."

"Well, better for me you stop in regularly. Nice to see somebody other than salt cargo planes. Looks like fuel is just under two-hundred dollars; let's call it fifty cents for the nuts and drinks and two-hundred dollars for the whole thing."

We climbed back in and set the heading bug for 340 degrees. Only six-hundred-and-fifty miles to go. This time the Bahamas lay in front of us. A direct course would take us over Nassau and into big trouble. The plan was to skirt the land masses on the north side, then turn west to 290 degrees after passing Great

Abaco Island. From there it's only a hundred miles to Valkaria airport.

We dropped down to two-hundred feet about fifty miles offshore, to penetrate the military air defense identification zone that lies off both coasts of the United States. If military radar picked us up, the operator would conclude the sole aircraft was too slow to be military, and thus a civilian law-enforcement problem.

Soon the small barrier islands of the coast came into view. With the help of land-based navigation aids, I believed the airport was at our 12 o'clock, just out of sight. Although we listened to the local frequency, nobody was on the air. With the strong onshore winds we knew runway 9 would be in use.

Valkaria was a typical World War II military airport with long runways for that time, which roughly formed the shape of an overlapping, equilateral triangle. This was a variation with an additional north – south runway in the middle of the triangle. Four airstrips of about four-thousand feet attested to its value for the military during the war. Shore reconnaissance aircraft and anti-ship planes were launched from here for both the Gulf and the southeastern U.S.

"I got it at 11:30," Ortiz almost shouted. "Let's pull up to one-thousand feet and do right traffic for runway 9."

"Sounds good," I replied. I had already shoved in some power to bring us to traffic pattern altitude and looked forward to a smooth landing. I dropped the gear on the downwind leg of the pattern. All planes, big or small, normally fly a rectangular configuration before they turn onto the final approach. This explains how you sometimes see the airport out of your window in good weather and wonder why the pilot is flying past it.

"Shit! I've only got two greens," exclaimed Ortiz. One of the three wheels was not down and locked, a serious problem.

"Exchange bulbs," I ordered. "I'm breaking left and climbing to two-thousand feet while we sort this out."

"I switched them, and it's not the bulb," said Ortiz.

"Have you had this problem before in this plane?" I asked.

"Once it flickered for a while, and then gave me a solid green."

"I'm at two-thousand feet. Any objections to shaking the plane to make it lock?"

"No," said Ortiz. "Let's try that before the manual gear-extension procedure. Head a couple miles south, the alligators there won't report anything unusual."

"Are you ready?"

Ortiz nodded. I began a series of violent side-to-side oscillations to try to force the unlocked main wheel to move into place.

"Stop! It's green," yelled Ortiz. "Let's get this thing on the ground before I puke on your shirt."

Ortiz gave me taxi instructions to the backside of an old hangar where we tied down the Comanche. Two men and a truck were waiting. He had made an international call from the Matthew Town airport with an estimated arrival time. In fewer than ten minutes, the four of us had transferred the cargo. One man was Latino, the other a black American.

"Sweep out the plane. I don't any want drug traces," ordered Ortiz to the truck drivers.

I introduced myself to both men, but was more interested in the American. When I said my name was James, the black man looked briefly at me but did not smile.

"You two are *tocayos,* 'the same name,'" chuckled Ortiz. "Kinda like namesake. When somebody else has your first name, you have a special relationship."

I looked at James, but he turned away.

Motioning behind him, Ortiz said, "We always park a car here with keys under the mat. Although it's another hundred-and-fifty miles to Miami, Mr. Sterling doesn't want these planes near there. The airspace is too congested unless you file a proper flight plan, talk to controllers, and follow all the other procedures. So, no paper trail involving these aircraft. I'm going to ride a few miles in the truck, spend the night, and then get a commuter flight back to Miami. Besides, I'm tired of looking at you. But good job."

"No sweat," I said. "And you were getting uglier with each passing mile."

"Fuck you, and here's your money."

"Sweet dreams."

I rooted under the mat for the keys and cranked up the '67 Chevy. My mind was spinning with what I had and had not learned.

Race is a common bonding agent in prison and street cultures. Ortiz works for Sterling, and both are Latinos. Sterling, the logistics man, works with a production manager in Barranquilla, another Latino. For the trip north, however, it's a black American and a Latino. The distribution manager is sending one of his own to watch over the load. It wouldn't be unloaded in Richmond, too far south, or in Baltimore, although both cities contain potential users. Under the firm control of a black gangster, the drugs will be unloaded in a single, secure place in the Washington area. From Washington, he can route smaller amounts, at low risk, both north and south. So, the production manager is Colombian, the logistics manager is Cuban, and the distribution manager is a black American. He is probably a major heroin dealer who has also been in the business for a long time with an established distribution system. Is this a true triumvirate, or is one the boss of bosses?

They also keep their mouths shut. Ortiz gave me no information outside of what I needed to make the runs. If I had probed, it would have aroused suspicion. Plenty of opportunities existed to talk about the operation. Also, I need to warn Ray to resist the temptation to send a couple of FBI agents to Matthew Town, a small, gossipy place. Unlike our early guess, they do not land at or near Miami. This no-place airport on the central Florida coast is much safer.

I need to look up tocayo *in a Spanish-English dictionary. The black*

American had no accent and probably doesn't speak Spanish. Maybe I can use this word to strike up a conversation – or pull his chain one night at the airport.

Almost there. I'll be glad to see Jamie, and she'll be happy to see me, hopefully not too happy.

I parked the Chevy at Ex-Pat Reality, picked up my car, and drove home.

As I was fumbling with the house keys, Jamie opened the door and pulled me inside. She was wearing white shorts and a sexy tube-top. After briefly looking me over like some sort of patient, she hugged me hard enough to crack my back.

"There's another place on your back that needs to be cracked. May I?"

"Do you know what you're doing? I don't want to spend the night in an orthopedic ward."

She took my question as a "yes," and embraced me a little higher up. The bear-hug did feel good as did having her big, perky breasts pressed into me.

"Hey," I said. "Where's my forehead kiss?"

"Coming up."

The kiss was sweet and gentle – not romantic or erotic. I was actually looking forward to it.

"You appear like crap, taste like salt, and smell of sweat and oil. Was this the last place you bathed?"

"Stop equivocating! Are you going to let me in or not? By the way, you look great, and the answer is yes, my last bath was here. Sometimes Ray or Roy works late. I want to call on your line. Sit next to me if you can stand it."

"Roy! I just made a run. Shall I brief you now, or do you prefer to go home? How detailed? Everything. Okay, I will write this up tomorrow if Jamie can get a cleared courier from her office to carry it to D.C., so take light notes. She's here with me and says no problem on the courier."

I emptied my brain from my impression of Marcus Sterling, to the mechanics of their flight planning, to my preliminary conclusions driving home. I emphasized that I did not want any federal agents snooping around Matthew Town. I waited for his reaction.

"You filled in large information gaps with only one trip," Roy began. "I agree with the assessment that one black and one Latino driver was a control measure by the distribution manager. D.C. has about four large-scale heroin dealers. Absent any turf wars, we assume they have an agreement."

"Four questions," I said. "Who seems to be the most security conscious? Who reaches outside of the black stereotype user with an ambitious distribution network? Does one or two seem more prosperous than in the past? Has law enforcement focused their intelligence efforts on anybody for money laundering? Maybe we can eliminate at least one or two that way."

"That is a tall order, but I have some ideas. Tomorrow, I will task some analysts on your questions. We may need help from BNDD and the law enforcement side of Treasury. I plan to call the two FBI agents assigned to help me on this operation. Look, at the risk of being blunt, you're not the lone ranger. We have other federal agencies available to us."

"The FBI role doesn't concern me. I wish we had more help from them. For the reasons we discussed, however, I'm uncomfortable with BNDD's role. Moreover, as investigators, they are not as skilled as the FBI."

"Okay. We've had this discussion before. It's your ass, so I'll reluctantly defer to you. Let me think of something bureaucratically useful for them to do that keeps you isolated. If I come up with anything on the heroin-cocaine dealers here, I'll call. You sound grumpy and exhausted. Go to bed."

"I need to shower first or my housemate will put me in a shed next to the gators."

"Gators?"

"We live next to a drainage ditch full of them, and she eats them!"

"Yeah, better go shower. Goodnight."

"Goodnight, Roy."

"James, I'm so proud of you. What you are doing takes real courage."

"Thanks," I replied, somewhat self-consciously.

"Shower that scum off of you, and I'll give you a nice massage to relax tense muscles."

"Thanks."

After I toweled off, I pulled on a pair of clean shorts I used for lounging around the house and flopped down on my bed.

"Jamie," I called. "I'm ready to be relaxed."

She came in with a bottle of lotion, the same white shorts, but with a sheer negligee top. I stared; she looked so sexy, especially for a man who recently left prison.

"I'm glad you like the top," she said casually. "Now lie face down, and I'll work on your back, neck, and legs, then flip over for the front later."

Although she was quite skilled at the massage, the show wasn't very subtle. I thanked her, got a forehead kiss, but slept somewhat fitfully. I did not want a complicated relationship with Jamie.

The Hammer

Jamie gave the memo to the courier the next morning. I walked out to look for the gators, which I concluded were a myth. I had two more days off, then a solo run. The sun was behind me, and a reflected light briefly hit me in the eyes, then a sound from across the ditch. A moment later, a large gator crawled up the concrete slope toward me. I slowly backed toward the front steps, attributing the sound to the gator and forgetting about the light in my face.

I sat down in the Lazy-Boy to wonder if I was under surveillance. By whom? Nothing made sense. If Sterling had discovered my identity, I'd be in a dumpster with two in the back of the head. I didn't like coincidences.

For the next two days, I worked over at Opa Locka airport, doing odd jobs for the chief mechanic. Actually, my Airframe and Powerplant Mechanic's certificate had expired, but I had done enough A&P work that his assignments were easy. Working gave me time to think about next steps. One crazy idea was to take a commercial flight to Barranquilla, stay in a tourist hotel, and find a cab driver who spoke English. Then what? *Say, what's the name of the local drug kingpin?* I put the idea on rear burner. I also mulled over the apparent surveillance problem. Even if local law enforcement knew I was on parole, they have bigger problems to deal with than snooping around in bushes taking pictures.

The next day, I told Jamie about the surveillance matter. She was puzzled as well, but said she would inform SAC Wainwright. We said goodbye, and I headed over to Ex-Pat Reality to arrive by 8:00 a.m. I knocked on Sterling's door and was greeted with "Enter." No Names One and Two were standing in front of his desk. They frisked me roughly and removed the pistol from the small of my back, the first place they looked. I thought this might be my last day on earth. Nobody was smiling. Sterling took a single, typewritten page, turned it around and pushed it toward me. Complete with a correct address, it appeared like a formal letter to Marcus Sterling, President of Ex-Pat Reality. I read the letter:

Dear Mr. Sterling:

You have employed James Sixkiller as a pilot. He was an associate of mine in Oklahoma for years. Does he still carry a pistol in the small of his back? The only good thing I can say about him is he's a skilled pilot. Otherwise, he is a double-crossing, thieving, piece of human garbage that owes me more than ten-thousand dollars. Watch your back because he's watching it too.

Sincerely,
A Distant Friend

"Care to comment, James?" said the icy voice of Marcus Sterling.

"Yes. Was it postmarked in Oklahoma?"

"No. It was pushed under the door."

"That's because I have no associates in Oklahoma. I owe nobody money, let alone ten-thousand. I worked alone and was busted alone by a border patrol agent who spotted the tail number of my plane as I flew low over the river. That letter was hand-delivered by the same person who has been snapping photos of me from the bushes near my house."

"James, how did he know where you conceal your pistol?"

"From the photo surveillance. Finally, no low life in Oklahoma knows anything about you, least of all the correct address of your company. Somebody here has you in their cross hairs and is trying to set me up for whatever comes next."

Sterling said nothing during my rebuttal, but his body shifted slightly when I used the phrase "correct address of your company." His silence continued for a full minute after I finished, looking at me with a penetrating gaze designed to give him more information or break the weak. I returned his gaze without expression. It was his move.

"Number Two, return the pistol to James. James, make sure to phone the pick-up team from the Bahamas. Ortiz gave you the number, correct?"

"Yes, and I will call."

"*All* of you get out my office."

Marcus punched intercom for his secretary to call Tyrone in

Washington. Tyrone picked up on the third ring.

"Good to hear from you too. I need your advice." He read the letter to Tyrone, repeated what Sixkiller had said, and how he had reacted.

Marcus gave Tyrone time to think, as he would do if the roles were reversed.

Tyrone began, "I believe Sixkiller. He had all the right answers without knowing this was coming. That said; the only thing Sixkiller could be setup for is a load rip-off. We may have a problem in the pipeline similar to the Nassau double-cross."

"Tyrone, I trust our pilots and have confidence in all of them, even Sixkiller. Whoever is setting this up knows one of our pilots is a gringo, and if I were to guess, at least one Latino is behind this. Do you think this is coming from Barranquilla or here?"

"I can't say yet. Maybe even from my office, too many unknowns. Call Gonzalez in Barranquilla and tell him we need his help – which we do. His ego couldn't tolerate finding out second hand we're doing an internal investigation. Frankly, the only possibilities for problems from Barranquilla are the ground crew loading planes or Alvaro's big mouth. Thinking about it, I see this as more of a Miami problem. Why set up Sixkiller? Why announce their intentions? Marcus, maybe you are the target, and this is not directly related to drugs."

"I hadn't thought of that. The letter said to watch my back. What about the Matthew Town gossip?"

"I doubt it. How would they know your company's address?"

"Good point."

"We caught and killed the guy in Madrid," said Tyrone, "but he never gave up the dirt bags in Nassau. Everybody talks when tortured, so I don't think he knew their identities. I'll also bet the airplane is at the bottom of the Atlantic, and the drugs were sold overseas. Unless you personally are the target, my assumption is these same people are planning another trip to the well."

"It rises to the top of my list."

"Are any of the four No Names trained investigators?"

"Yeah. Number Three was a small-town detective sergeant. He actually attended the FBI National Academy program for cops, but didn't graduate for technical reasons," said Marcus.

"What about putting him with one of the other three, if any has an IQ above room temperature, explain the situation, and see what they come up with. I'll do the same on this end. Alvaro can check out his ground teams. Ask Alvaro to send someone he trusts to check their homes. Are they living a little too well? Bank accounts, and things like that. What do you think?"

"I like the plan. Tyrone, you always ask me to call Alvaro with bad news."

"It's not exactly that. You have the right knack in delicate situations, especially if we suspect Latinos of screwing us. You know he doesn't care much for blacks."

"Okay. Stay in touch. First lead requires communication among all three of us," said Marcus.

They hung up. Both feared the worst. Marcus pondered how to present the problem to all of the pilots. Their vigilance might save the day.

Rough Trip

I settled back in my seat for the two-and-a-half-hour flight to Barranquilla. Sterling believed me. In fact, I always flew the precious drugs and never had to ferry an empty plane back to Barranquilla. First, they would investigate internally for a problem. From the pilots' perspective, the most vulnerable times are loading and unloading the product. Perhaps, we should ask for more security at these two points. How ironic, asking one set of killers to protect you from another. *My enemy's enemy is my friend.*

"Welcome to Barranquilla" proclaimed the airport greeting in English and Spanish. My carry-on luggage consisted of water bottles and peanuts. If the Confederate army survived the 1863 siege at Vicksburg on fresh water and peanuts, I could reach Florida. Oh yeah, and the rinsed-out jars. Soon, I spotted Juan and another man, still carrying the "Sixkiller" sign. We drove west to the private strip where a truck was waiting with two men guarding it. They ambled off to watch from the shade.

"How much is in the truck, Juan?"

"About two-hundred-and-four kilos or four-hundred-and-fifty gringo pounds. I brought the scale because I know you worry about weight."

I was watching the sky as we loaded the plane. It was clear and unbearably hot and humid – so humid that visibility was down to only five or six miles in the haze. Two of the three ingredients for thunderstorms were present. Hot air over warm water is inherently unstable. Hopefully, no trigger was waiting to cause the air to rise rapidly and form thunderstorms. Orographic lifting is out because the sea is flat, but a frontal boundary could provide the necessary lifting for storms, colder air sliding under hot air. I weighed and loaded the cargo with the able help from Juan and his assistant. Finally, we put the tarp over the load. I asked them to stay with me a few more minutes while I performed the plane preflight, which gave me an idea.

"Juan, I saw a pay phone off the main road here. How much does it cost to phone Barranquilla?"

"About fifteen cents or twelve-hundred pesos."

"Can you give me twelve-hundred pesos to keep in the plane if I need to call after you leave today or some other day?"

"Sure."

Handing him a pen and paper, "Write down the office phone in case of an emergency. Thirty kilometers is a long walk."

I gave him a dollar in exchange for the coins and number. Juan was not trained to be security conscious. He wouldn't know that my knowledge of Barranquilla operations was limited to him and this truck.

After taking off, I followed the usual route. This time, however, I did not stay low and climbed to ninety-five-hundred feet, an illegal altitude, but so what? The entire trip was illegal. The altitude did three things for me. It guaranteed me five-hundred feet of vertical separation from anyone flying legally out here. It vastly improved my ability to use ground-based navigation equipment. Finally, it gave me a better chance of seeing and avoiding thunderstorms.

I was able to track the twelve degrees radial off the Barranquilla vortac further this time. At ninety-five-hundred feet the wind was pushing me to the east, so I steered due north to maintain my position on the radial, a twelve-degree correction. The high altitude allowed me to monitor center frequencies intended primarily for commercial traffic. They would issue extreme-weather alerts if necessary. Finally, I listened to the Kingston vortac, which had recorded weather. The time passed, and I was content with this new plan, too content.

"Attention all aircraft, Center Weather Advisory three Charlie, level-four and level-five thunderstorms, moving northwest to southeast at thirty-five knots in lines from Kingston, Jamaica to Santiago, Cuba, tops to forty-five-thousand feet, hail to two inches possible, wind gusts to seventy knots."

Damn! The mountains in Cuba and Jamaica, not some cold front, caused the orographic lifting! To the west, the distant sky appeared black with tinges of green. *Think fast, Jake. Storms like this chew up and spit out small planes. Haiti. I'll climb to eleven-thousand feet and cut right across western Haiti to outflank the lines. Center says the storms are moving at thirty-five knots, and I can coax about a hundred-and-sixty knots out of her at that altitude.*

I shoved the throttle and prop forward and leaned the engine out to twenty-five degrees rich of peak exhaust gas temperature.

Question: What is my relative angle to the storm lines? I turned right to a heading of fifty degrees, probably too much. Next, I tuned in a low-powered, non-directional beacon in western Haiti.

I was greeted with the sound of lightning instead of Morse code and quickly turned off the receiver. These beacons use the same frequencies as the AM radios found in most cars, rendering them useless in storms. The storms appeared to be growing or moving faster than thirty-five knots. Despite doing everything right, I seemed to be losing. At two miles high, Haiti should have been coming into view, despite the haze. I could see the coast at my 12 o'clock, but there was no time to congratulate myself.

"Unidentified aircraft over Haitian airspace heading fifty degrees; identify yourself or we will intercept you."

Screwed. Buy time. Lie. Say I'm sorry. I did not want to be intercepted by some World War II fighter with real guns.

"Port-au-Prince Center, this is a Cessna 310, squawking 7700 (emergency), at eleven-thousand feet trying to outflank these storms. We apologize."

In heavily accented English came the request: "Say tail number and intentions."

I just invented a tail number with a U.S. country code and a mix of five letters and numbers, adding that our destination is Nassau.

"We don't have a strip (flight plan) for your aircraft."

"Manley (Jamaica) gave me vectors east for weather, and they just released me. They're probably overworked."

"Cessna 310, proceed as filed."

"310 roger."

If they had sent up an interceptor and seen a single-engine Piper instead of a twin-engine Cessna, I would have been forced down or shot down. I'm not sure which was worse. Papa "Doc" Duvalier and his Tontons Macoutes were legendary for their violence and extreme torture methods. No pilot of a plane loaded with drugs would leave Haiti alive.

Watching the north coast of Haiti slide under me, I realized how much I had overcorrected. No wonder the Port-au-Prince voice sounded so clear. The Ile de La Tortue lay directly in front of me, about thirty-five miles east of Haiti's western tip. After turning left to a heading of three-hundred-fifteen degrees, I tried the non-directional beacon at Matthew Town. It rewarded me with Morse code and only a few crackles of lightning. Once clear of Haitian airspace, I shut off the transponder and dropped like a stone from eleven-thousand feet to two-hundred, where they could not see me.

Later, I climbed back to the traffic pattern altitude of one-thousand feet for the airport, the storms and Haiti lay behind me. But I had a slight tremble in my hands, probably from too much coffee. I saw one of the boys watching me set up to land. What did he plan for those hundred dollars?

"Glad to see you back so soon," said the fixed base operator. "Where's your partner?"

"Oh him. I pushed him out of the plane an hour ago for talking too much." While not very funny, he enjoyed the only joke he might hear that day.

"I'm Rupert Nevis. What shall I call you?"

"James. Pleased to meet you officially."

The line boy burst into the office and said, "It took seventy-eight gallons, Mr. Nevis." He gave me a long stare. I nodded my head.

"Well, at $2.44 per gallon, the total is one-hundred-ninety dollars plus a bottle of soda on the house. I'm sorry about the high price of avgas. The price would be higher if Morton Salt didn't come in regularly. You know how islands are. If we don't make it here, somebody has to import it, for a price."

I thanked Rupert for his hospitality, used the rest room, and grabbed a cola. I also called the pickup team. The line boy got his hundred-dollar fee for outstanding service, but I still visually checked the fuel and made sure the caps were screwed on tight. The air temperature and humidity had dropped a little, so visibility on the final leg would be much better.

After departure, I began ruminating over James who

answered the phone. He was surly about my being late. I explained briefly, with Rupert no doubt listening, it was a weather delay. He ended the call with, "Hurry the fuck up because I don't like long rides, I don't like Latinos, and I don't like standing here holding my dick because you had to run around a few raindrops."

So, he's another jerk having a bad day. At least I had some beautiful scenery on the way to Valkaria airport. From the extreme northwestern tip of Great Abaco, Grand Bahama lay off my left wing. The islands looked gorgeous in the setting sun.

At two-hundred feet and a hundred-and-forty knots, the barrier islands off the Florida coast slipped rapidly under me. I slowed up to make right traffic for runway 9. Later, I congratulated myself for a pretty landing after a jarring day. How odd that pilot skill seems measured by the landing. Despite having responsibility for many complicated tasks, the sideways look from another pilot is most likely to come because of a substandard landing. Down to business. I taxied to the truck.

Rodrigo and James waited. I greeted them both and called James *tocayo*, ignoring his bad phone manners.

"I ain't nobody's motherfucking *tocayo*. You can take that Spanish shit and shove it up your ass."

Rodrigo piped up, "It's not an insult. Relax."

"I don't have to like any of you white people or Latinos. I have to work with you because the boss said so."

"I guess you don't like Indians either."

"I don't like any of you motherfuckers who have never suffered the kind of oppression black people endured."

Stirring the pot some more, I said, "You blacks don't know anything about oppression; most of you survived slavery. Until 1890, the white government of this country starved, moved, and exterminated as many Indians as possible. All of the so-called Indian wars and relocations at the end of a bayonet reduced a pre-Columbus population of twenty-two million to one-million in two hundred years. Genocide was U.S. policy."

"I wasn't born then."

"Well my grandparents were, and they were beaten if caught speaking their own language in school."

"I work for a black man, an important black man, who wants to make sure these loads go where they're supposed to, not stolen along the way. A lot of shit can happen between central Florida and D.C."

"If Marcus Sterling and your boss thought I was a crook, would they let me fly off alone with a fortune in drugs?"

"I don't get paid to second guess Marcus and Tyrone."

His name, Tyrone, the D.C. connection. A slip because he's upset.

"You know, James. I landed here willing to overlook the rude crap you gave me over the telephone. But you had to start slinging mud again. I don't take shit from some ignorant truck driver whose only job is to babysit."

James screamed something and charged directly at me. I stood like I wasn't going to move; behind me was the truck door. At the last moment, I hopped to my right, dropped down and turned away from him so both hands were on the ground with my right knee in between them against my chest. The left leg shot out and sent him headfirst into the truck door. When he started to get up, I hit him with a roundhouse kick to his neck. He was out. I turned to Rodrigo and said, "Let's unload the plane."

Uh oh, I thought. He's up and still wants to fight. I stepped over to him and hit him with a left uppercut so hard I could hear the jaw dislocate and teeth shatter from the impact. He never moved, and we loaded the truck. Later, he was semiconscious as I buckled the seatbelt around his waist. Rodrigo regarded me oddly.

"I don't want him to get hurt in a crash," I replied to the unasked question.

We swept out the Comanche and secured it. Having found the keys to the same '67 Chevy, I was preparing to leave when

Rodrigo walked over.

"I will tell my boss James started the fight, and I overheard the phone call. Maybe better if you had killed him. He is a dangerous man, and now he is your enemy. He will try to kill you someday."

"Rodrigo, I appreciate you'll tell the truth about this, and I promise to watch my back."

Developments

At the first 7-Eleven along the road, I stopped for a big cup of ice water for my aching hand. Hatred for racism clouded my judgment, but I learned something useful. Hopefully, except for adding another enemy to a growing list, no damage was done to my relationship with Sterling. He will bring up the incident with me. In addition to the telephone number in Barranquilla, I had the first name on a short list of suspects in D.C.

The ice helped, and the drive to Miami did not seem to take so long, perhaps because it was more familiar now. I needed to talk to Ray or Roy, but it was after 9:00 p.m. when I parked in the driveway. Tomorrow will be soon enough.

Jamie was waiting inside with a big hug and a kiss to the forehead.

"Your hand is swollen," said the surprised and slightly accusatory voice.

"The black racist who meets me to unload the plane attacked me." I told her the story, including the two pieces of good news. She seemed a little subdued.

"James, let's sit and talk."

I climbed into the Lazy-Boy and she sat on the sofa next to me.

"This sounds important," I said.

"I suppose it is," she replied. "You're more than a friend to me. I am so attracted to you – emotionally and physically. If you asked me for sex, I would be in the bedroom and naked before you could clear the door jamb."

I laughed.

Pouting, Jamie said, "Now you're making fun of me."

"No," I lied. "It's a wonderfully clear summary. What an image!"

"I'm no home wrecker. Giving you a partially naked massage last week was wrong and selfish. It is so hard to accept there is something you want badly, but can never have. I tell you this because I love you. At first, I wanted a casual affair with a pleasant man staying in my house. That changed, however, as we worked together and my respect and admiration for you evolved. I realized that I had something valuable that I have never had before, a real friendship with a wonderful man who also shares my views on law enforcement as a unique brand of public service. Most outsiders don't understand our world. For me, this is a rare and important relationship, and I do not want a sexual undercurrent to damage the friendship."

She paused, then continued. "Respect for you will keep my lust in check. Please don't think any less of me. Also, it's not fair to Karen. I like the way your voice softens when you talk to her, and you're not afraid to say 'I love you' to her in front of another person. That is precious, and I'll do my part to support your marriage. Sometimes I think, 'Why couldn't he be a jerk like most men I know?' You know, one-dimensional. I get along fine with them. They put that requirement in my job description. I have never been attracted to an adult, male friend. How about you?"

"Me, neither."

"I'll try not to taunt you sexually anymore."

We both laughed, but we had moved to a different and more comfortable course now.

"The sexual attraction is mutual, and that's not going to change. The key is how we handle it. I love you, too, but differently from Karen. You are good to me, a wonderful person, and a new kind of friend. Thank you for this needed course correction."

"I've never had a male confidant. What are the rules?"

"Well, we keep our clothes on. I don't know. We make up rules as we go with the overarching goal of preserving my marriage, and not letting either one of us get hurt."

"Spoken like a true bureaucrat, but I think that's right. Maybe we could hold hands and eat popcorn in front of the TV," she mused. "And talk more. It's scary to open up your soul to another person who is not a spouse. I think many marriages fail because couples keep secrets and don't trust each other. I sense trust between you and Karen."

"Could we hold hands outside?" I asked.

"I don't know, but I could kick you, a sure sign we are true siblings."

We both laughed gently. Jamie kissed my forehead again, and returned to the sofa with her feet toward me.

"We need to do this right," she sighed. "Someday, I might meet Karen, and she will know in a heartbeat if we were lovers."

"Female radar," I offered.

"Yes."

I turned on the television to *Bonanza* and moved to the sofa, putting a pillow behind my back to prop me up a little. "Come here," half pulling her so that her head rested on my chest.

She put her hand over mine and whispered, "Thank you for helping to rearrange our relationship."

Chapter 21

A Family Feud

Miami, Florida, November 1969

"Roy! Yesterday was a good day for the white hats. Is Tyrone on your short list of distribution suspects?"

"Oh, yeah. Tyrone Jones, a.k.a. the Professor. Is he our man here?"

"It has to be him. He always sends down one of his flunkies to oversee the return trip to D.C. We had a little dispute after he started with his racial thing about hating whites, spics, and Indians. On the other hand, he worked for Tyrone, a very important black man."

"How bad was the dispute, Jake?"

"He attacked me, and I defended myself. I will put all of the details in the report for the FBI courier. Okay, I messed him up, probably broke his jaw. Rodrigo said he would tell Tyrone it was self-defense. I wouldn't worry about it. Did you read my recollection of the letter accusing me of scheming against Sterling?"

"What do you make of that?" said Roy.

"It doesn't seem to be a big happy family anymore. Sterling called me early this morning, which is unusual after a flight. I am sure he'll mention the fight, but my gut tells me he wants something else. His tone was cordial, but not too cordial, like I've been made. I'll call after the meeting. Oh, I almost forgot. I have what may be the office phone number of the boss in Barranquilla. This might be a good job for the BNDD boys. They could work with the local phone company to identify the number's owner. Later, photo surveillance and maybe a wiretap."

"Good job. Let me run the phone tap idea by General Counsel. Call me after talking with Sterling."

"Will do."

I called Karen who picked up right away.

"Guess who?"

"Are you okay?"

"Fine; I'm busy on this assignment. I've earned a couple of days of rest at the house because of the traveling. Part of my rest plan is to do some heavy reading, so I bought the new edition of *Playboy*."

"You're a bad boy, but please don't change."

"How are your projects going?"

"I'm negotiating a deal with a basketball star to help me. I felt so tiny standing next to him. Although it's quite exciting, there are so many details to resolve."

"I hope your negotiations work out. I love you and will call when possible."

"I love you too, and please be careful."

"I will. Bye-bye."

I drove my hot rod over to Ex-Pat Realty and was greeted by the usual *enter* after I knocked. Sterling was alone, no goons today, a good sign.

"You're probably thinking," began Sterling, "I brought you here to talk about the fight last night."

"I was sure you would ask me about it."

"Tyrone tried to sound offended but conceded that Rodrigo's account was convincing, and the other James is well known for his intolerance. Don't worry about it. Did he pay you?"

"No."

Using a key in his pocket, Sterling opened a drawer and counted out five-thousand in hundreds. Then he partially closed the drawer.

"I have never asked you to ferry a plane back to Barranquilla. Other pilots can do the ferry runs. After the Nassau incident, I am exceedingly careful about who flies the drugs. I trust you, Ortiz, and another pilot. This trust goes beyond not stealing from me. All of you are creative when put into a tight spot. After you reported a weather delay in your conversation, I checked the actual weather. The news reported monstrous storms along your travel route. I don't know how you got away and don't care much – you delivered. How do you like working for me?"

Here it comes. "Fine, sir."

"In private you may call me Marcus and knock off the sir stuff."

"Thank you, Marcus."

"You graduated from Northeastern University in Oklahoma with an accounting degree, correct?"

"Correct."

Marcus punched the intercom line and said simply, "Don't disturb me."

I had graduated from college, and taken quite a bit of accounting. My cover, including the accounting degree, was designed to invite my help on financial matters if the opportunity arose.

Marcus began, "What I'm about to say is not to be discussed with anyone. Clear?"

"Clear."

"I run a viable real-estate company. At times, company demands on my time require more attention than the business that puts real meat on the table. I suspect, but cannot prove, our Colombian partner is billing us for more kilos than he delivers. His invoicing system is convoluted, and I don't understand it well. Tyrone also suspects a problem. Is it true, for example, he always brings extra cocaine to the plane?"

"Always. His truck driver, Juan, says it's because I'm so irrational about weight that he can't predict how much to send."

"On average, how many one-kilo bricks are returned to the truck on your trips?"

"Four to six."

"Let's say five at thirty-thousand dollars wholesale; that's one-hundred-fifty-thousand he seems to be billing us for, which is never delivered each trip. This has also happened to Ortiz."

We exchanged looks. It was his show. I had nothing to say.

"He took my questions as an assault on his integrity, which is true. Glance inside my cash and drug business drawers. They are a mess. I don't know how much cash to move offshore. I can't prove he's cheating me. I need your help putting things in order with a special view toward establishing that Alvaro is defrauding us."

My mind immediately snapped to attention, *Alvaro* is the name of the Colombian boss.

"Will you help me?"

"Of course."

"James, how much time do you need to straighten this out?"

"If I don't fly and work for six or seven days, I should be able to give you preliminary findings."

"Will a thousand dollars a day be sufficient?"

"More than enough."

"By tomorrow at 8:00 a.m., I will move a desk into the corner of my office, and I'll give my secretary keys to my office as well as to the cash and records drawers. You will keep them afterward. She thinks she runs the office, but is not to have them. Here's a thousand in advance. Take your girlfriend or sister out for the night. See you in the morning."

"Thank you for such confidence in my work."

"Get out of here."

Data Mining

Jamie was at work. A secretary quickly handed off my call to Roy.

"Does Brer Rabbit like the briar patch?" I asked.

"That's what the book says."

"First, the minor news. The name of the Colombian boss is *Alvaro*. While not much, we are connecting dots now. Maybe the BNDD people can use the name in conjunction with the phone number. Second, Marcus and Tyrone think Alvaro is skimming about one-hundred-fifty-thousand dollars off every trip with shaky billing and accounting practices. He sends them a bill for thirty-thousand dollars for each kilo transported to Florida plus expenses. It looks like Sterling may be averaging five bricks shy per load, with Alvaro blaming the pilots because we refuse to carry more weight than is safe. Better yet, Sterling's records and cash drawer are a mess. According to him, the demands as a legitimate real estate broker are soaking up his time. At a thousand dollars a day, he wants me to clean up his drug records, estimate how much money, now in stacks of hundreds in his drawers, to move to offshore accounts, and prove Alvaro is cheating him. Is this a prosecutor's dream or what?"

"Oh yes. More evidence is always better. No prosecutor likes trials unless he is running for office," responded Roy.

"I need a miniature camera to photograph some of these documents when he's out of his office. I told Marcus that I could give him a preliminary report in about a week if I don't fly. He seemed content with the timetable. Can Jamie get a camera from the FBI field office or I could use some of this cash he's giving me to buy one and voucher it?"

"Let me call the field office before we start using drug proceeds."

"Hey, how big is the bonus? I'm making more down here."

"Please don't even joke. The temptation is always around the corner."

"Jesus, Roy. Take it easy. You're receiving all the cash with the FBI courier in a dated envelop marked 'evidence' with my signature written across the seal."

"I'm sorry. I had to watch a friend and great undercover cop go to prison. He told himself he would take the money only once for some need; then once became twice. The lure of fast money is worse than a heroin addiction."

"Don't worry. My new hobby takes up most of my free time."

"What's that?"

"Gator watching."

"We have mental institutions up here as well as jails. Goodbye, Jake."

"Goodnight, Captain. Gotta check on the gators."

Jamie promised to help if necessary. My college accounting courses were not enough, and her degree and experience were invaluable. Alvaro showed the five or six bricks as returned to inventory, but included an amount approximately equal to their value as expenses in various parts of the bill. The invoice layered and obfuscated the process to the point that the scam was difficult to detect.

Each night I returned with scraps of paper stuffed in my pants, plus what I could remember without taking the risk of writing it down. After two days, Jamie brought me a miniature camera, an enormous help. All of the information went into the daily log I kept in Jamie's safe. Later, I added the film. Both of us had the combination, and she had an FBI carpenter place it behind a wall panel with concealed hinges. If one of us were killed, then the other could retrieve the evidence. Gradually, we brought some order to the chaos. He had about two million in cash, most in fifty-thousand dollar straps. The drawer opened with such difficulty because one million in hundreds weighs twenty-one pounds. Stacks of smaller bills, mostly fifties, were tossed in back.

Sterling seemed to come in early each day. It was rare for me to be first. When the light was on, I knocked out of courtesy.

"Enter."

"Good morning, Marcus. I have mostly finished your task. Tell me when is a good time to talk."

"Now."

I explained, "You have about two million in cash and probably need less than one-quarter of it for domestic transactions. Put the rest into offshore accounts paying interest; moreover, having so much money here is a bad security risk. This is just an office, and your secretary or anybody else might have copied the keys."

"I've been considering a bank in George Town on Grand Cayman. What do you think?"

"That's fine. Use a code and numbered accounts so someone with your photo on a fake passport can't access it," I suggested. He agreed. I went on to explain a more orderly process for record keeping. Mostly, his head nodded up and down with an occasional "good" thrown in.

Finally, I came to what he really wanted to know. With help from Jamie on his accounting tricks, I walked Sterling through the systematic fraud Alvaro was using to conceal the disposition of the missing bricks. Raw counts of what went into the plane and was later unloaded would agree. Bricks returned to the factory from the airport truck were shown as returned to inventory. His billing process was so Byzantine, however, he added an amount roughly equal to the returned bricks into the bills as various expenses.

"So he *is* cheating me and Tyrone! How certain are you?"

"Totally certain."

His face was red when he picked up the phone.

"Shall I leave?"

"No. Stay here in case there are questions."

"Tyrone, it's Marcus. That bastard in Barranquilla is ripping us off. Sixkiller did an audit of my records and explained what he's doing. Yes, he's sure. The guy has millions, and he just wants to fuck us for a few hundred grand to prove he can do it, for whatever sick reason. What do you recommend?

"No! Too subtle for this moron. I'm going to call and confront him, and tell him to send us the money he ripped off, to send a simplified bill in the future, and if he doesn't like that, then I'm going to send a couple of No Names down to rip off his balls and bring them back for my dog.

"Tyrone, he's a total psycho. All he understands is fear and intimidation. Okay. I'll start soft before I work up to dog food. Thanks, Tyrone."

The subsequent conversation with Alvaro in Spanish was lengthy, but the tone was more placid than I expected. Sterling looked nonplussed when he hung up.

"Alvaro called it a prank, which is bullshit, and denied nothing from your audit. He promised to return the money and fix the billing process. What do you think, James?"

"I don't know the man. If I were to guess, he has a new plan."

"I agree, but for now we can only wait. Take a few days before your next trip. I want to see if anything changes. On your next trip, I'll order a No Name down with you for security. He will ride out to the airstrip and help count. Don't worry, however, he will return on a commercial flight, not sitting next to you."

We both smiled. Sterling was well aware of my distaste for his goons.

"By the way," added Sterling, "your parole officer stopped by Opa Locka Airport the other day and received a glowing report. Thank you for all of your contributions."

"You're welcome. You'll call me about the next trip?"

"Yes."

Chapter 22

Textbook Investigation

Nassau, Bahamas, November 1969

No Names One and Three had come up dry in the Miami area regarding the Nassau rip-off earlier in the year. Sterling had given them permission to widen their investigation to Nassau. They had tortured and killed the pilot in Spain, and remained convinced he really didn't know who bought the planeload of drugs. The only clues they had involved some Mexicans. Also involved was a middleman who dealt only in cash, but they did get a description. He had medium brown skin, about five-foot-nine-inches, a slight island accent, and wore Hawaiian shirts, a taboo in Nassau. One witness said he claimed to be from California.

The No Names worked the bars and night scene. Not surprisingly, they quickly became known and feared for their interrogation tactics. A nightclub bouncer readily recalled seeing such a person, as did a few waitresses and bartenders. Nobody could add any helpful information.

Number Three spoke up, "We're fishing in the wrong pond. We should be breaking arms over at the airport. That's where the plane landed. That's where the pilot turned over the plane to this middleman. Somebody saw something. Something else too. We shouldn't rule out that the middleman is actually the mastermind, or is at least wearing two hats."

Number One needed more time to absorb this. "So, this middle man walks around in different clothes when he's playing the middleman, and regular clothes, which ain't much here, when he's the mastermind."

"Right," said Number Three. "And suppose there isn't any

middleman. Or the real mastermind is out of the country pulling the strings."

"Yeah," said Number One. "We should start at the airport."

Walking up to one of the line boys, Number Three asked, "How long have you worked here?"

"Almost two years," as the nineteen-year-old looked at two men who were not here on vacation.

"Do you know much about the different makes and models of airplanes?" asked Number Three.

"Sure. I need to be certain what kind of fuel they take. Some pilots are in a hurry and don't tell me."

"Good. Did a Piper Comanche land here late in the summer?"

"I recall seeing a new one. I fueled it, and he pulled into that hangar over at the end."

Although a little vague, his description matched the dead pilot.

"Who knows all about these hangars? Like who owns or leases them?"

"The fixed base operator, Mark Hughs. His office is in the two-story building off to the side of the longest runway."

As they walked away, Number One said, "We introduce ourselves to Mr. Hughs, jack him up until he talks, and leave."

"No," replied Number Three. "This is a big airport. The guy must have connections with the police and pols. We gotta be careful. You still got your fake Interpol ID?"

"Yeah."

"We use the ID to appear legit and get his help. Let me talk."

"You always talk anyway."

Each airport with scheduled airline service also has a general aviation fixed base operator, the FBO, who serves the needs of everybody from corporate jets to vintage aircraft. As the men approached the FBO counter, they flashed their credentials, provided their seldom-used real names, and said they needed to speak with Mr. Hughs right away. Hughs came out presently and asked how he could be helpful. He was a balding, white man with a distinct British accent.

Number Three explained that the Spanish government had requested a follow-up investigation into the disappearance of the Comanche last summer. He stated an eyewitness had seen the plane enter the hangar at the end of the row. The plane took off shortly and disappeared. The Spanish police later arrested the pilot with a large amount of stolen cash.

"Who owns that hangar, Mr. Hughs?" asked Number Three.

"I own the hangar, but I'll check my records and ascertain to whom I leased it. Follow me." They did as they were told. This Englishman made them uneasy for some reason.

"My accounts show a lease for the month of August to one Rafael Gonzalez of Sonora, Mexico. May I assume that you are interested in this month?"

"Yes," said Number Three, almost too quickly.

"He paid in cash. I have never seen the plane, nor do I have further information for you. If you like, you may walk down and look around, be my guest. Good day, gentlemen," and he turned and headed back to his office.

A lone Hispanic male was cleaning the hangar. Numbers One and Three exchanged looks. After establishing he had worked there for a couple of years, the questions began politely enough. However, they could see fear in his eyes. Finally, Number One couldn't restrain himself and locked up an elbow.

"We don't have all day, asshole. After I break most of your joints, I'll start removing body parts." Number One was on top of his game. "Tell us everything about the plane? Who was here? Who paid the faggot pilot? Who took the drugs and where?"

"You're hurting my arm so much I can't think. Let me just stand and try to remember."

Number Three nodded his assent.

"I was cleaning the next hangar over when the pilot pulled in. With my ear to the aluminum siding, I could hear some of what they said. In addition to the Cuban pilot, who was counting money, were three bad men with heavy *Norteño* accents. The Mexicans debated whether to kill him and take both the plane and the money. They decided against murdering the Cuban because the airport was busy, and they feared being caught. One Mexican, who was also a pilot, kept saying, 'Too heavy.' Two had tickets to Mexico City. The Mexican pilot was going to fly the plane somewhere close, where they would unload and destroy it. Four or five small airports are less than an hour away. He fueled the plane recently, so that's why they couldn't kill him and all get in. I could hear only parts of the conversation."

"Have you seen or know anything about a Negro man, who wore Hawaiian shirts and spoke with an island accent?" asked Number Three.

"I noticed him reading the paper once in the FBO lounge."

"He was never in the hangar here when you were listening? No island accent?"

"No."

"They pushed the Comanche out of the hangar and the Mexican pilot gets in alone or with the Cuban," began Number Three. "Then two walk to the commercial side for a flight to Mexico City, while the others fly to some small island to off load drugs and destroy the plane. Is that right?"

"Yes sir."

"Did you hear any names?"

"Only nicknames and common first names which I don't recall."

Number One shoved him hard up against the aluminum and shouted, "What else?"

The aluminum made a terrible racket and a voice from the next hangar demanded, "What's going on in there?"

"Tell him you fell while cleaning."

The young man did what he was told.

Number Three sat on the floor shaking his head. "After all this time and work, we don't have shit. We already knew that our Cuban pilot sold us out to a group of Mexican thugs. At least one is probably in south Florida waiting for another chance to rob us. This American Negro is a ghost. Sterling will love this."

The Bad News

Sterling listened carefully to the report from his two investigators.

Then he instructed, "Forget the American, who probably is a Bahamian. I suspect his role was to arrange unloading the drugs and disposing of the plane at the destination airport. He worked for the Mexicans for a fixed fee or a percentage. We are most vulnerable at two points: the airstrip west of Barranquilla and Valkaria. From now on, one of you takes the commercial flight to Barranquilla, and at least one of you will arrive early to meet the incoming flight to Valkaria to do reconnaissance around the field prior to arrival. Carry extra clips; you may need them. I'll make the assignments. Inform the other two. Everybody is full time from now on. Any questions?"

Both shook their heads.

"Dismissed."

Walking out of the office, Number Three said, "He's not mad at us?"

"That's because we do good work," replied Number One.

Chapter 23

One-Way Ticket

Miami, Florida, November 1969

Jamie was making meatloaf and something when the regular phone rang. Only Sterling would call during dinner.

"Hello... Yes, your office at 8:00 a.m. All of the pilots? I'll be there."

"Is this the first pilots-only meeting?" asked Jamie.

"Yes. He said a follow-up investigation of the Nassau incident indicates Mexicans may be planning another rip-off. More tomorrow."

Sterling's meeting went as expected. An explanation of what little we knew. Then came the instructions: Be vigilant. One of the No Names would ride, armed, all the way to the truck in Barranquilla, returning by a commercial flight. One or two No Names would meet each incoming flight at Valkaria. There, he believed, the threat was the greatest.

"James," said Sterling at the end of the meeting. "Can you and Number Four ride to Barranquilla in the morning?"

"Sure," I answered, without much enthusiasm.

I had seen Number Four, but we had never spoken. We simply exchanged nods at the airport and boarded the same plane. I entertained myself with a novel during the flight. After passing through Customs, I saw Juan with his Sixkiller sign but no other assistant. Juan did not seem himself with a drawn face, nervous body movements, and sweating more than normal for the heat.

I stopped and looked around for Number Four. Two men, with a pistol thrust into his ribs, were escorting him away. I ran in the opposite direction, but three armed goons quickly surrounded me, removed my pistol and shoved their own in my back. I had the intruding thought that switching to an ankle holster would be more comfortable. Dealing with being kidnapped could wait a moment longer.

While the goons focused on me and Number Four, they lost track of Juan who fled to blend in with a crowd around an outside concession stand. Juan knew what fate awaited me. That night, he locked himself into a stall in the men's room. The next day he took the first flight to Miami and called Sterling as soon as he arrived.

Room of Horror

The goons said nothing to me except, "Do not resist," in heavily accented English. After walking to a blacked-out van, they pushed me roughly into a rear seat. One put a hood over my head and cuffed me behind the back. The fear meter went off the scale. I sat at the mercy of unknown thugs for an unknown reason. They said nothing. *Maybe I've been made,* was the only possibility I could imagine. In that case, a swift execution was my best prospect. But why here? Number Four is loyal, and he will not return to Miami on the next plane. Nothing made sense.

After about a twenty-minute drive, the van stopped. I heard the doors open; somebody grabbed me by the shoulder and pushed me from behind, first in one direction then another until I fell. Next they tied a noose around my neck, and led me inside what seemed like a large building, based on the noises and talking I heard that seemed to come from all levels. I flashed briefly to the constant din within the expanse of Coleman. Conversations were in Spanish; isolation compounded my fear.

A door opened, someone rammed me into a seat, and then removed the hood. In front of me was a Colombian man dressed in loud clothes, toying with his mustache. Behind his expensive leather chair lay a beautiful view of the Magdalena River.

"So," he began his rage barely under control. "This is the famous Sixkiller. The man who would dare humiliate me in front of my business colleagues. They think they are better than me, and don't hesitate to show their supremacy. I hired Mexicans to rip our own load in Nassau, and they still don't know what happened. For many months, I fucked them in their asses for hundreds of thousands of dollars, and they never knew it. Not until this college-educated Indian decided to do their dirty work. That's what's wrong with your ignorant country. Why do they let some aboriginal go to college? You should be doing manual labor for white people." Screaming now, his face flushed, pounding on his desk, "How dare you humiliate me, especially to that nigger in Washington?"

"What do you want from me?" I asked in a quaking voice.

"First, never speak to me unless I ask you. Second, always address me as *El Patron*. Third, I don't want anything except to hear the sound of your screams in the torture chamber next to my office. The screams help me relax and focus on work."

"Get him out of here. Follow the instructions."

"Si, El Patron."

My knees buckled briefly entering the room, littered with various instruments of torture: dental tools; truncheons; electric cattle-prods; and a large bucket with wires running to a rheostat connected to a wall outlet. Overhead was a steel I-beam with a chain looped over it, and a sturdy rope tied to the end.

Two goons stripped me and knocked me down. They tied the rope around both ankles with excruciating force and hoisted me up until my head hung about a foot off the floor. With fists and the truncheons, they began to beat my sides and stomach. After my core muscles failed, I started gasping for air. I couldn't get enough.

They brought over a bucket, and all pissed into it. They told me to do the same. A little blood flowed out with the urine, causing a quick conference among them off to the side. Perhaps *El Patron* had imposed limits. More likely, they had been warned to prolong my agony until death. This thought relieved me of the glimmer of any hope. They added water to the bucket and lowered my head into it. I had trouble holding my breath, and soon inhaled some of the foul liquid, producing convulsions in my body. They quickly pulled me out to cough, spit, and gasp for air. They shocked my testicles with a cattle prod and then put it in my mouth. My body jerked and convulsed, but I was unable to scream until they took it out. I was sobbing, with saliva running out of my mouth and out my nose. They shoved needles under my fingers and toes, and I screamed some more until blackness settled over me.

Minutes later, they threw a bucket of cold water at my face. The process began again.

The room had no windows, just a row of flood lights aimed at me. They were never turned off. Time had little meaning as I drifted in and out of consciousness.

Revenge

"Hello, Alvaro. I understand Sixkiller is your guest."

"Fuck you, Marcus."

"Listen you scum-sucking psycho, you steal from us, then kidnap and torture my best pilot, and you think you haven't crossed the line? This is what you're going to do..."

"I do what I please in Barranquilla."

"Not anymore. If you don't follow these instructions exactly, I'm going to kill you, tie your bullet-ridden body with a rope in front of your house to ensure everybody sees it floating in the river, and replace you with a new manager. So listen carefully."

"Why should I pay attention to any of your Miami crap."

"In case you think I'm bluffing, two-hundred of my best troops are getting their gear together as we speak. The following demands are non-negotiable. Get a pencil out because you're too stupid to remember everything:

1. Stop the torture now.
2. Call a reputable medical doctor to come to your office with his passport and treat Sixkiller.
3. A flight leaves for Miami in a little less than three hours. The doctor will escort Sixkiller onto the flight and stay with him until my men relieve him at the Miami airport.

Is there anything you don't understand?"

"If I do this, everything is fine between us? Business as usual?"

"Sure, Alvaro. We realize why you're upset. Don't worry. Just do what I said."

"Okay. Okay. You and Tyrone take things too seriously."

"Goodbye, Alvaro. I will personally be at the airport to greet Sixkiller. Don't fuck it up." Click.

Tyrone had planned past Alvaro. Two hundred soldiers, dressed in civilian clothes and heavily armed, were already boarding a charter plane. He had paid the bribes necessary to ensure no problems at the Barranquilla airport. Marcus and Tyrone agreed upon a professional manager to ride with the soldiers to keep product moving until a permanent replacement could be found. A few soldiers would stay in the plant to exterminate any militants loyal to Gonzalez. All of his security forces were marked for death. Alvaro failed to comprehend that he was a dead man walking.

Juan's account of the abduction, plus what he had overheard, clinched the implementation of the plan against the ever-cautious Tyrone. Juan also gave the soldiers a good description of the building, its entrances, deployment of security forces.

So, while the security forces were flying to Mexico, a second plane would be airborne in opposite direction flying to Miami.

I remember the bucket of cold water hitting my face. The torture would begin once again; I prayed for death. My body remained attached to the chain over the I-beam. The water ran down from my shoulders and chin, into my eyes, and dripped off my eyelids. Upside down had become normal. This time, however, they lowered the chain and cut the rope from my ankles. Unable to move, I lay motionless in my own waste. They pulled the needles from my fingers and toes.

"Stand up," ordered one. I moved a little, but could not get up. A brief conversation produced a garden hose. Terror replaced momentary relief, a new form of torture. The goons hosed me down heavily where I lay. A minute later, one pulled me to a slightly different area, and they hosed me again.

"You stink, gringo," laughed one. "A doctor will visit you, and he doesn't like gringo shit." All I focused on was the word *doctor*.

The two men got under my shoulders and half-carried me into an adjoining room with a sofa. I had lost sensation in my feet, and they couldn't support the bodyweight. I was dizzy and disoriented. They laid me down on the sofa, naked. I couldn't talk because my tongue was swollen from the electric cattle prod; my testicles felt on fire and were horribly inflamed; my ankles had second or third degree rope burns; and my entire body hurt like no other pain I've ever known.

In walked a doctor in a white smock. His entrance produced a startled response, my body shaking involuntarily.

"I am a real doctor," he said in good English. "I'm here to treat you."

"Why?" I tried to say.

"I will explain later. Did they hit you hard in the head with anything?"

"No. Need water."

"I'll have some brought in," he said to me, and then he said something to a person outside of the door.

"Follow my finger with your eyes. Good. Where are you?

What is the month and year?"

I answered his questions as well as I could with a tongue that seemed to fill my mouth.

"Are you allergic to any medicine?"

I shook my head.

"You don't appear to have a concussion. I'm going to give you morphine to ease the pain, but not as much as you probably need. We have a plane to catch to Miami in about one hour."

"To Miami?" I said in a distorted voice. I felt a prick in the shoulder and saw a syringe. He must have seen my eyes widen. It was all a cruel trick. Alvaro would never bring a doctor to treat me. He was entertained by the torture, and now it was time to poison me.

"It is morphine, and I'm taking you to Miami. Put this cold compress on your testicles and another for your lips while I try to find you some clothes."

"My boots..."

"You want your boots?"

I nodded my head, and he left.

The trip to the airport was hell with a driver so determined to be on time. I never realized the roads had so many potholes. I sat in back with the doctor. If I couldn't walk, one or both would get me to the departure gate. The doctor told me several times I had been "in a bad car wreck," and he needed the medical facilities in Miami. A wheelchair waited at the gate. After the stewardess seated us, the doctor gave me more morphine, and I felt sleepy. Morphine, named after the Greek god of dreams, Morpheus, was...

"It's time to wake up now," said a distant voice. "James! We are in Miami. We need to get off the plane now."

"Okay."

Keeping erect and focusing my vision required so much effort. The doctor was under one shoulder, but I felt my feet touch the ground. Maybe I'll walk again someday.

I heard Jamie squealing, "James, oh James."

I picked up my head and saw Jamie, Marcus, Ortiz, and another doctor. The two doctors walked off to the side and talked in animated voices. It was surreal. Marcus, who I wanted to put in prison, had just saved my life. He was the only one who could make Alvaro do this. I hated this job. I sat on a chair while the two doctors talked. Jamie wiggled and blew me kisses; and Marcus knelt next to me.

Marcus apologized, "I had no idea he would do something this crazy. We are taking care of the problem. He will never touch my pilots again." Tears rolled down my cheeks. This was so fucked up, I thought. He's a killer. A goddamn gangster. I needed to dehumanize him, but all I wanted to do was embrace him.

"A private ambulance is waiting outside to carry you to Mercy Hospital, the finest in the city. They can do a complete evaluation there and give you the best treatment. I think your sister wants in." Marcus motioned her to come. She rushed over, looked intently at me, took my hands, and kissed me on the forehead.

"Hey, Sixkiller, you're the best Indian pilot I've ever known. Of course, you're the only one I've ever known." I tried to smile at his feeble attempt at humor, but my mouth still didn't work well, and the morphine affected my thinking. With Jamie looking at me I said, "Karen?" Jamie shot me a stern look, and Marcus half-turned, then went back to talking in Spanish with Ortiz. After arriving at the hospital, I had a hard time answering the questions from doctors as Jamie held my hand. A technician drew blood; another sent me for a full-body CAT scan. While examining my entire body, doctors asked more questions about what hurt and where.

Later, Dr. Wilson entered my private room. His aura of calmness and authority made it clear he was actually in charge of what seemed like chaos around me.

"Apparently, your tormentors were instructed to avoid

egregious damage and obvious scaring. You are still urinating a little bit of blood from heavy blows to one of the kidneys, and you continue to be dehydrated. The kidney damage will clear up without treatment, but you will require antibiotics prophylactically for the blisters and devitalized tissue on top of the burned areas, including your ankles. Keep putting cold compresses on your testicles and lips until the swelling subsides. The nurses will give you ice chips to suck on for your tongue, but not much else. Two ribs are fractured, but not broken. They will feel much better in about two or three weeks. No signs of a concussion or spinal trauma exist. The only bad news is I have asked a surgeon to cut away the areas irreparably damaged by the rope burns on your ankles tomorrow. We will numb you up and give you an IV morphine drip. Because you are dehydrated, nurses will continue changing bags above you to help rebuild body fluids. Any questions?"

"How long?" I said.

"Probably four more days here, two weeks of rest at home, and you'll be fine."

Chapter 24

The Calls

Miami and Washington, November 1969

According to Jamie, Ray asked few questions as she recounted events. The oblique reference made by Sterling at the airport about Alvaro "never touching my pilots again" had escaped me, like much of that day. Ray and Jamie both concluded Alvaro was dead, and they now had a new production manager. Ray said he would approach the U.S. Attorney regarding the need for jury appeal from baggage carts full of dope in the courtroom. Also, Ray was concerned about the danger to my cover posed by things I might say to the hospital psychiatrist. Jamie mentioned Jake had looked directly at her after the flight and called her Karen. Despite the concerns, Ray decided to keep the cover with no changes, including the delivery of parts to a Miami company. The kidnapping and torture occurred because of mistaken identity during a feud between drug traffickers who used the same airfield.

Jamie told me she would call Karen and give her a sanitized version of recent events.

"Jamie, you gave me a bad look in the airport."

"You looked at me and said Karen pretty loudly, a name they don't know. Marcus noticed and turned partially toward you."

"I did?"

"Yes. I hope they believe that you were confused. The morphine was talking about some woman somewhere. However, the incident concerns me."

Dr. Wilson discharged me three days later. He stipulated that I return to visit the psychiatrist three times a week. Jamie drove us home and seemed subdued. I was in pain and didn't feel like talking.

We hadn't been in the house long when Jamie announced, "You still stink, Sixkiller."

"Screw you, Jamie."

"You wish! The nurses gave you sponge baths, but they couldn't get rid of the stench from your hair, and other bodily crevices. Rest if you need to, then I'll bathe you in the shower."

"I like the stink."

"Seriously, the psychiatrist at the hospital told me to remove any sensory inputs from you that might trigger recollections. The smell from your hair is intense. Also, I bought you a new pair of boots, almost identical to your old ones."

"Thanks, I guess."

"You're welcome, I guess."

"You're going to get in the shower with me?"

"What do you want! That I put on a bathing suit?"

"No. Just strip and let's do it."

"Be careful what you ask for, Sixkiller."

The wisecrack produced a slight smile, but no laughter followed. I wondered if I would ever laugh again. What a strange thought. I'm okay. I'm home and safe. Jamie's taking care of me. The nightmares were becoming worse, however, as I used less pain medication.

"Don't make the water too hot."

"Right, thanks."

I sat in the tub with my feet over the side, and outside of the curtain. I looked and felt ridiculous. Jamie had put a couple of towels over the bandaged ankles to ensure they stayed dry. To make sure the water was tepid, Jamie stood in front of the showerhead so water was hitting her back squarely. She reached around to make small adjustments. A little spray touched my arms; I began to get nervous.

"Here comes the shampoo."

The water hit the top of my head and ran down my face.

"Stop it!" I screamed. Although confused, Jamie closed the faucet. I sat and shook as she put her arms around me.

"I understand now," she said. "I'm going to get more towels for your forehead and a bucket. I'll wash you from behind so the water won't touch your face. Will you be all right with that?"

"Yes," I said, without confidence. As she scrubbed my hair from behind, her breasts danced gently in front of me. Abstractly, it was a beautiful sight for any man. Right now, however, it aroused me the same as two empty tin cans on strings. I really did need a shrink. Using bath water and the bucket, she washed the rest of me. The soap and shampoo smelled good. It felt pleasant to be clean.

"Hi, Karen. It's Jamie. Jake and I are sharing a house on his project. I'm using what's called a secure phone so just ignore any strange noises. Um, I need to tell you something which is Jake has been hurt, but he's been released from the hospital and will make a full recovery."

"Who is treating him? Who says he'll make a full recovery"? Where is he, Jamie?" The panic in Karen's voice sounded barely under control.

"He was admitted to one of the best hospitals in the country, and has been evaluated and treated by several excellent doctors. We spared no expense on his care."

"Jamie, how did this happen? Could it happen again?"

"Karen, please don't push me so hard on details. I do want to tell you everything, but I can't. And no, it won't happen again.

"If I give you more information about his physical condition, you must swear on the blood of your ancestors not to say anything to *anyone*. Karen, the FBI will fire me if this leaks and comes back to me, which it will. More importantly, it puts Jake in danger. Do you understand and agree."

"I swear to say nothing."

"Jake was kidnapped and tortured for two days. He was

rescued; it's complicated. His tongue, lips, and testicles are swollen with first-degree burns. The doctors told me to keep cold compresses on them all day. They beat him around the body, damaging one of his kidneys, but it seems to be clearing up. His ankles suffered bad rope burns because he was strung upside down. A surgeon repaired the damage to his ankles. Right now, he says most of the pain is from his ankles and burned testicles. I put burn ointment on them three times a day in addition to the cold compresses."

"My God, Jamie. How much pain is he in?"

"The pain is better, now. It was very bad for a few days. He is my friend, Karen, but you're the luckiest woman in the world because he loves you dearly. I get to be with him for a while, take care of him, and send him back to you at the end. So, I'll cry, but be happy when he comes home to you."

"Have you ever been lovers?" asked Karen.

"No, we are close friends, working together in a hostile environment. I have too much respect for him and your marriage to go down that one-way street. I love and admire him as a partner, and we depend upon each other every day. Perhaps I can explain this better the next time we talk.

"Karen, I understand the jealousy, and appreciate your trust in me. You seem like such a gracious person. I hope to meet you someday. Jake said to say hi to Wuffe."

Jamie had changed the sheets and slept beside me for several nights. When the demons came, she quickly found my hand and whispered something in my ear. Maybe I had turned a small corner.

Dr. Wilson referred me to a shrink for sessions three times a week. The psychiatrist also gave me valium and a tricyclic for depression and sleep. He made me relive everything: the terror, the smells, the pain, the dread, the despair, the loathing, the hopelessness, and more. He kept pulling it out of me. After a few weeks, I felt better. My body had healed, except for soreness in my ribs and ankles. For the first time since the rescue, I noticed Jamie as a woman again.

For reasons beyond my reach, however, I remained restless and irritable. Ray and Roy considered closing down the operation after the U.S. Attorney relented on his show featuring piles of drugs. Yet, he still wanted them if possible. They could nab Ortiz coming into Valkaria one night, but I didn't like the plan for some reason. I had been confronting my demons in the quiet safety of a shrink's office. Although this approach had been helpful, it wasn't my style. I needed more direct confrontation. I was waiting for Jamie to return home after work.

She had hardly put down her purse, then screwed up her face and said, "What's wrong?"

"Why does anything have to be wrong?" I asked defensively.

"With the exception of Karen, I know you better than anybody in the world. Something is eating you up."

"Obvious, huh? Sit down, and let's talk. I need your advice."

Jamie sat down on the sofa at an angle to me and folded her hands in her lap, her face expectant, but unreadable.

"I want to make a final flight to Barranquilla, to bring the show drugs for the trial. I'll ask Sterling and Ortiz to meet me in Valkaria with one or two No Names for security, like a low-key celebration saying, 'I'm back to work for you again.' We can get Marcus, a couple of his professional killers, the two drivers from D.C., and the load of drugs. Every cop and fed in Florida could be waiting for the end of the party."

"We can close down the operation with Ortiz flying," responded Jamie slowly, "and pick up Marcus at the same time. Tell me what this is really about?"

"You're so matter-of-fact, brutally blunt."

"You asked me for advice, and I think it's a terrible idea. Speaking for both Karen and me, I..."

"Since when did you become her spokesperson?"

"I appointed myself because I know what she would say. Your physical well-being and emotional health concern both of us. I will ask, again. What's this really about? There is nothing to prove. This case is effectively over."

I felt cornered. Despite loving and respecting Jamie, laying bare my feelings of vulnerability and anxiousness was beyond hard. I wanted to deal with the problems my way. Of course, I realized she already understood this. Why was she so determined to make me justify my plan to her?

"Remind me never to play poker with you. Making the trip, seeing the welcome-to-Barranquilla sign, and flying back with a planeload of drugs – all of this terrifies me. I need to be *me* again. All the shrinks and their pills aren't going to do that for me. I need to walk into the mouth of the cannon and return. Any cop who says he's never been afraid is a liar. This was far worse. I had my dignity and manhood stripped from me. 'Despair' doesn't come close to depicting what happened to me. I prayed for death."

Jamie had not moved, tears now flowed down her cheeks. I stopped.

She sat on me with her arms around my neck, and said, "Damn you, James. You're a stubborn son-of-a-bitch. You need to let go. There is nothing to prove."

She climbed off and seemed to study me. Finally, she said, "Ask your shrink what he thinks of the idea, but first ask him if I can come for the session."

I was taken aback by the proposal. On the one hand, it wasn't, "No, and hell no." On the other hand, what was I thinking? She wasn't my mother. Why would I need her approval? Perhaps I didn't trust my judgment any more, and Jamie was so well-grounded. It should have been simple. Jamie had been talking to Karen, after all.

"James, are you still here?" inquired Jamie.

For a second, I looked at her. "I'll ask him. I'm sure he'll say yes."

He did say yes and remained subdued during the session. Jamie emphasized her no-compelling-need argument. Despite the improvement, I still had nightmares and became startled by innocent noises or events. Given my fragility such a trip would be inherently dangerous. What if I freaked out at the airport or while flying alone. She should have been a lawyer. Allowing her to come was a mistake.

"I agree with everything your sister says," began the psychiatrist, "but at this point, you are well enough to balance the obvious and substantial risks of your proposal against additional months on my couch. If all goes well, you may achieve a rapid breakthrough from your self-doubts and depression. Mind you. I am not endorsing this venture because of the risks. Another possibility is survival of the experience in a day's work, followed by an abrupt return to the symptoms you seek to overcome. You are still quite raw, but also quite resilient. That has come through in our sessions."

Jamie seemed to pale at this qualified endorsement, a change he noticed.

"Your brother seeks life on the edge. Eventually, age may diminish this need. Forcing him to move prematurely to a comfort zone that seems normal for us – well, this could lock him into a sense he has been defeated. Defeat is an alien concept to him, and now a terrifying one after what he has endured. He says he wants to be himself again. He is the James before Barranquilla, impetuous, tough, self-confident, yet thoughtful for such a man. This must be his choice. It's too important for us to attempt to interfere."

We walked out without talking. Inside the car, Jamie began, "As you know, the FBI, in consultation with the Intelligence Division, has devoted significant resources to this case because of its multi-state and international dimensions. Out of courtesy and their link to the U.S. Attorney, the Intelligence Division retains the nominal lead. Therefore, I'll make all the arrangements with the Florida Department of Law Enforcement[11] and the BNDD to be present at the take down. You call Roy or Ray and, of course, Sterling. He'll be delighted you're back on the job."

Her voice was flat. She never looked at me.

"Jamie, I need to do this. Please don't make it harder with your anger. I don't handle anger from you or Karen very well."

"It sounds like I'm your Miami wife."

"Don't be sarcastic. We have a wonderful relationship that defies any label. I know you love me and fear for me, but I ask you to support me on this. I prefer not to leave knowing you're angry. I can handle you thinking I'm stupid or macho."

She pulled the car over, put her arms around me and kissed me on the lips. "Yes. It's stupid and macho, but I will support you. The shrink made a compelling argument at the end."

Was that a goodbye kiss? Don't overanalyze it, I thought. Besides, the combination of excitement and fear was beginning to build. And I liked it.

Chapter 25

Back to Work

Miami and Barranquilla, November 1969

Roy signed off on the plan, and I phoned Marcus. He did seem delighted at my return to work and called me his best pilot. The compliment bothered me, but I had already concluded lots of things were going to bother me, so I brushed it off. I was set to fly down with No Name Two, a.k.a. *Napalm Josey* because of his penchant to firebomb houses. We assumed Alvaro's men had killed Number Four. Nobody had seen him since my last trip. Marcus was arranging my trip to Barranquilla for the day after tomorrow. Thus, I had time on my hands, and time with Jamie, neither of which I wanted now.

Jamie returned home upbeat, or at least pretending to be upbeat. She had made the Florida and federal arrangements. Only the most senior agency officials were briefed on takedown details; one leak and Marcus would flee the country.

She flung her purse down in its usual chair, apparently bought for that purpose, and plopped down on the sofa. "I don't like admitting I'm wrong, but I think your plan is the best one for you. I'm still scared, James. You're so important to me. But, I also want the old James back. I'm not in the mood to talk more about this. Let's watch TV." We selected *Laugh-in* for a comfortable evening after all.

I didn't like any of Sterling's goons, particularly this psycho. But we nodded to each other in the boarding line. After nestling into my seat, I turned to a book as usual. I noticed, however, my ability to remember the previous page deteriorated. Near the end of the flight, I was simply gazing at some page. As we taxied past the welcome sign, my stomach did a flip-flop. Somehow, I needed to prepare for worse.

After exiting the jet way, three people stood together, one with the familiar Sixkiller sign. Number Two and I walked up to them.

"I wanted to welcome you personally," began one in nearly flawless English. "I am Pedro Sandoval, the interim production manager here in Barranquilla. Mr. Sterling has said only good things about you. Only a brave man would return, and so soon. This will be a smooth and businesslike transaction."

"Your English is perfect. It's my turn to be impressed."

He continued. "I graduated from the University of Texas with an MBA. I've never seen this airstrip or the planes, and would like to be familiar with all aspects of the operation. You and Marcus may be interested in knowing the room you spent two terrible days in no longer exists as such. We partitioned the space into normal offices. Those who worked in there before have been...well, terminated."

The loading was routine. Oddly, having Sandoval at the airfield, asking a mix of good and stupid questions helped me relax. For him, this was more information for his job. I did the usual preflight of the airplane, said goodbye to Sandoval and his two assistants, and departed Barranquilla for the last time. My knees had been a little weak on the ride out with three strangers, but now I felt fine. With clear weather, the normally forbidding expanse of open sea welcomed me.

I avoided Papa Doc in Haiti and the Mig jets in Cuba. Matthew Town lay straight ahead. At least one of the two line boys, with nothing else to do most of the time, listens on the radio for the standard incoming traffic calls by aircraft. If they hear the word *Comanche,* it's an easy hundred dollars. I chatted with Rupert for a few minutes and told him I found a position with better hours. I paid the tab, got my usual free soda, and said goodbye. The line boy helped me into my seat. He appeared crushed after I explained about my new job.

"The others sometimes forget," he said.

I fumbled for advice, especially since there would be no more tips. "Did you keep most of the money?"

"Yes."

"Save as much as possible, be frugal, and work hard. Good things often come to an end."

He gave me a sad smile and waved goodbye.

Chapter 26

The Takedown

Monday Evening

Jamie, as one of two Supervisory Special Agents, had the point on organizing the takedown. Special Agent in Charge Floyd Wainwright agreed evidence was sufficient on her undercover case to arrest the mobsters. Jamie used a miniature camera for months to copy records. The opinion of FBI's General Counsel was that photographic proof, followed by a search warrant, and her testimony, would withstand any judicial scrutiny. As of now, she was full time on the Barranquilla Case, its informal nickname.

Jamie agreed with my warning that cops of any stripe view a takedown as sexy police work. This places pressure on local commanders who advocate an enhanced function for their bureau. Politics dictated the Florida Department of Law Enforcement and BNDD play a role, but keeping the number of them to a minimum was going to be difficult. One dirty cop or agent would compromise the most critical part of the operation. So far, so good.

A serious problem in multiple agency operations is radio interoperability. Each agency has its own frequency bands, and the separate agencies often can't talk among themselves. Chaos and even friendly fire are always possible.

Previously, Jamie and I discussed Sterling's insistence on at least one No Name to conduct counter surveillance before the plane's arrival to make sure we are not ripped off again. I told Marcus what Alvaro had said before he tortured me, about paying the Mexicans to split the load with him. He seemed interested, but noted they now know this was a regular operation, and where we landed the planes. Besides, counter-surveillance was cheap insurance.

As prearranged, I slowed a little early to alert the law enforcement officers. A blacked-out plane is not easy to spot, and the engine sound trails behind by a few seconds. As promised, Marcus had driven up and brought Ortiz along to welcome me back. Both were sitting in the car near the only access road on the west side of the airport. With swamps to the south and Highway 1 to the east, they assumed any rip off attempt would come from the north or west. No Name One was concentrating his efforts in these areas.

"That's odd," said Ortiz. "Sixkiller slowed down early. Normally, he likes to smoke in hot and do some stunt flying to set up for landing."

"He may not be fully recovered and returned to work a little early," replied Sterling.

"Yeah, probably."

At the same time, Number One banged breathlessly on the window of the car, startling both men.

"This place is lousy with cops hiding in the brush."

"Get in," said Marcus. "We'll drive away slowly, as if we had other business to attend to."

Two state police officers behind the airport office observed them leaving.

"Call the Major," said one. "Tell him to ask Supervisory Special Agent Jamie Hudson what she wants us to do? Give chase or stay put."

Although Jamie watched them pulling onto the airport road, she could not communicate directly with the Major, only with other FBI agents, all of whom who had left their cars and gathered for the takedown. The frequency interoperability problem had paralyzed effective communications. She stepped out of her car, grabbed the nearest FDLE officer, and told him to tell the Major to pursue Sterling and Ortiz, now heading south on the highway.

Precious minutes had passed, and Sterling's car was making good progress south on Highway 1. Unaware of the problem, I was lining up for a landing on runway 9.

"Call him again!"

The radio screeched, "Hudson couldn't talk to us. You dropped the ball. Give chase now! All other units rendezvous at the prearranged point after he finishes his taxi and shuts off the landing light."

I touched down, slowed, and used runway 32 to taxi back to the old hangar. When I saw the waiting truck, I began the shutdown sequence ending with killing the landing light.

The takedown seemed to morph into chaos. The airport was lit up like a circus of red lights converging on our location. Tyrone's two men appeared terror-stricken and made no attempt to flee or take cover.

"Pilot, come out with your hands up," blared the loudspeaker. I complied, was cuffed, and taken immediately to Jamie's blacked-out cruiser.

"All others on the ground, face down with hands on the top of your head."

After she uncuffed me, I started to congratulate Jamie, but she appeared somber.

"Marcus escaped, probably with Ortiz and a No Name. He's a high flight risk. Two troopers are in pursuit, and I already called Miami to stake out his office and house. Also, they are preparing a circular for the airline counters. I'm going to coordinate with the state police to put out an All-Points Bulletin on their car. Do you know the tag number?"

I looked at the back of my Flight Log, and it was still legible. I also emphasized the heavily tinted windows.

"Can you suggest anything else to do now?" asked Jamie.

"No. Hopefully, the troopers will catch them. I don't believe he'll go to his home or office or flee now. He has at least two safe houses in Miami. My guess is he will just lay low for a while in one of them, and pay a charter jet to take him and Ortiz to George Town in Grand Cayman. The good news is the U.S. Attorney has his show drugs, and this load won't be hitting the streets."

"True," she said thoughtfully, "and Tyrone has been under surveillance and should be arrested by now."

"How are you feeling?" as she eyed me carefully.

"Great, Nurse Jamie."

She smiled, kissed me on the forehead, and left to make sure onsite coordination was maintained to avoid later problems with the evidentiary chain of custody. I had to stay in the car. Despite an argument, a decision above my pay grade was to maintain the undercover status for now.

Rage

"That double-crossing, aboriginal, piece of shit has to be a fed or cop," growled Sterling. "He had a perfect cover. Only the feds can pull something like that together. I should have let Alvaro finish the job, then killed and replaced Alvaro. Sixkiller speeded up the process a little. Head for safe house number one. Everything we need for now is inside. Speaking of speed, step on it. They probably saw us leave.

"It couldn't be the FBI or BNDD," rambled Sterling. "BNDD is too incompetent. Besides, their pricks are so small you can cover them with a wad of gum, no *cojones*. The FBI has the skills and balls, but they don't do something Sixkiller does constantly."

"What?" asked Ortiz obediently. Sterling never touched guns, but Ortiz saw him order a No Name to waste somebody for disagreeing with him while he was in a rage.

"J. Edgar Hoover does not allow his agents to curse. There is such fear of being caught, or ratted out, they don't curse."

"How do you know that?" ventured Ortiz.

"The Efrem Zimbalist guy said so on the FBI show. Hoover

watches it regularly. One day he called the show's director and told him to give Zimbalist a haircut. It was in the papers."

Ortiz thought Sterling had to be cooling off a little if he's talking about an actor's haircut.

"But that double-crossing, motherfucking Sixkiller, swaggers, stinks, and talks like a cop! It's typical FBI to sweet talk some city's brass into cross-deputizing a few of their best so they don't take the risk. I have a photo of a recent FBI graduating class. And it wasn't too hard to get. Now, how stupid is that if they're going undercover? They find some other poor bastard to do it for them.

"Jorge, do you recall when we greeted Sixkiller at the airport, and he was all messed up on morphine?"

"Yeah."

"He looked right at his sister and called her 'Karen.' Remember?"

"Yeah," said Ortiz. "I thought it was strange."

"Under those circumstances, whose name would you call out while looking at the face of another woman? His wife. Sixkiller's wife is Karen. How many cops are in D.C.?"

"Maybe three thousand," guessed Ortiz.

"How many full-blood Indians among those three thousand?"

They exchanged looks.

"Get an operator on the mobile phone. First, call the BNDD snitch on our payroll and find out who Sixkiller really is."

The corrupt agent answered on the second ring, and Ortiz came straight to the point.

"He says his real name is Jake Stone, a D.C. cop who works in the northwest part of the city, but he only learned that today because information was so tightly guarded."

"Hang up on him. I'll tell a No Name to kill him later for incompetence."

"Now, call Tyrone's office to find out if he has been arrested yet." Ortiz did as he was told. After a few minutes, someone picked up the phone.

"This is Sterling. Who's this?"

"It's JJ, Marcus, and the feds arrested Tyrone."

"Listen carefully, JJ. Maybe we can get Tyrone back. He uses a few clean-cut white boys to service the suburbs, right?"

"Yeah, five or six actually."

"Pick three of the most educated, sincere looks, sharp dressers, smooth; you got the picture. Tell them to drive—separately—into northwest and find uniformed cops who are shooting the breeze, eating, in short, not doing much. Each will tell the same story: I went to Northeastern State University in Tahlequah, Oklahoma with a Cherokee named Jake who works this area. I've met his wife, Karen, a couple of times and would like to say hello before I go back to work in Los Angeles.

"What I want is Jake and Karen's address. After the initial line, they may need to get creative. Of course, cops are not supposed to give anybody a home address. Maybe they can even say after a rejection. 'I understand. There is so little time before my flight. Perhaps I could slip a note under the door...'

"Tell them to use phone booths to call you to exchange progress and location every hour. We don't want cops to start talking among themselves about this address request. Rent three cars, all four-door types with a back seat fold down option from the trunk, if possible. Get duct tape, and go armed. Mrs. Sixkiller doesn't know it yet, but she is heading south.

"My office is staked out. Call my secretary who will give you directions to safe house number two. *Don't* mess her up. She is our ace in the hole and will tell Sixkiller how well we are treating her."

"Like an exchange," said an animated JJ.

"Yeah, like that. Let me handle the details. Now, roust those white boys and put them to work."

"With pleasure."

Monday night

"Oh shit," said Ortiz. "A cop just lit us up."

"Pull over, stop, and raise your hands where I can see them," ordered the trooper with the loudspeaker.

Meanwhile No Name One had slipped down almost to the floor between the front and rear seats to pull out an AK-47 with a 30-round magazine from a hidden compartment.

"When you get an opportunity, kill them," said Sterling quietly.

Sterling and Ortiz had their hands up. One trooper stood between his opened door and the driver's seat, calling the dispatcher about their vehicle stop. The other approached the car. No Name One opened the right rear door, catching both troopers by surprise. He nearly cut them in half with two, two-second bursts, spitting bullets at a rate of six-hundred rounds per minute. As they drove off, he casually put in a fresh magazine.

"Marcus," began Ortiz. "I don't have any special loyalty to Tyrone, and I'm one more person holding you back. What if we stop near Boca Raton, I'll steal a different car for you, and a plane to get me to Grand Cayman?"

Sterling turned to gaze at him, trying to decide what to make of the proposal. On the one hand, it sounded practical; on the other hand, his feelings were a little hurt because Ortiz wanted to escape all the new law-enforcement heat. Practicality won over, and they stopped in the Boca Raton airport parking lot. Ortiz hot-wired a good-looking Buick for his boss and casually strolled onto the tarmac looking for a plane to steal.

But Ortiz never arrived in George Town. In his haste to steal a plane without getting caught, he made the student-pilot mistake of not visually checking fuel levels. He didn't have enough.

Chapter 27

A Gambler's Chip

Miami, Tuesday morning

"Jamie, one safe house is in West Miami near the main airport, and the other is near Opa Locka, another airport. Coincidence? I put about 70 percent of Sterling's millions in banks on Grand Cayman. Why would he come back here? Why not drive north to an international airport in Georgia or Pensacola and leave while he can? By the way, we faxed those flyers only to international airports in south Florida."

"Good thinking. Let's fax them to all of the field offices in the United States and put the burden on them to get it out within their area. Washington would need to approve, but I'm sure they will. I'll call Floyd and ask him to request authorization."

Jamie added, "If Marcus and Ortiz do return to Miami, what do they want here? This is a high-risk environment for them. We're missing something."

Washington, D.C., Tuesday Morning

"Good morning, Officer Watson. I went to Northeastern State University in Tahlequah, Oklahoma with a Cherokee named Jake who works this area. I've met his wife, Karen, a couple of times and would like to say hello before I go back to work in Los Angeles. Is he nearby?"

"No, he's been transferred to headquarters."

"Perhaps I could slip a note under Karen's door saying I was here and at least tried to contact him."

"You can check the phonebook."

"Officer, forgive me, but all of you gentlemen use unlisted

numbers for good reason. Somebody at the station would know."

"Okay. Hold on." He was parked next to one of the ubiquitous blue call boxes. Officer Watson inserted his heavy, bronze key to open the box and took another bite of his sandwich while waiting for an answer.

"Yeah, Watson here. What's Stone's home address?" He scribbled the address onto a page he ripped from a small notebook used for preliminary information gathering.

"Here you go. Good luck."

"Thank you so much, Officer."

The drug runner, Frank, rounded the corner and found a pay phone to tell JJ.

"Pull the other two back. I have the address. What's next?"

As the others phoned in, JJ selected Frank and Morgan for the job. One of their cars had a fold-down rear seat.

"She's a housewife in Kenwood, a rich neighborhood off of River Road on the Maryland side," said JJ. "Back the car into the driveway like we are expected. Walk in, or pick the lock, handcuff her, and tape her mouth, *but don't hurt her* or get any ideas if she's a looker. Sterling will order a No Name to exterminate you for fooling around with the merchandise. Take some pillows from her bedroom, and fill these two boxes with heavy stuff and anything she needs from the house. She's going to be in the back with plenty of pillows, including against the boxes where the rear seat folds up. The idea is she has plenty of fresh air and cannot hurt herself. If necessary, you can fold up the rear seat, like at a rest stop or something. Questions?"

"She will need to pee, eat and drink," remarked Morgan.

"Good point. Write out a sign for all three and give her paper and a marker for other requests. Also, buy her water and food at rest stops, and drive to some rural dirt road away from people. She can eat, drink, and scream. Nobody should be near enough to hear anything. Take her to safe house number two in West Miami; here are the directions."

Kenwood, Maryland, Tuesday Afternoon

Karen went to investigate some odd noises at the back door next to the picture window. Maybe another bird had flown into the window, which has to be kept clean. Why would a bird want to fly into a house anyway? Why is the dog barking? She scanned the lawn behind the house.

"Down on your knees, Mrs. Stone," said the intruder with the pistol. He quickly cuffed her from behind. The other was bringing duct tape into the room when Wuffe rounded a corner and tore out a piece of flesh from one of his legs. Frank screamed, rolled face up, and shot at the dog's head. The bullet only grazed an ear, and the hundred-pound Sheppard clamped down hard on Frank's throat, ripping it from side to side.

As Wuffe turned toward Morgan, his upper lip rose and a guttural snarl escaped his mouth, his fangs still dripping Frank's blood. Morgan, who had always feared big dogs, was paralyzed by the horror of dying like Frank. He knew he was next. As the big dog leaped from Frank, he almost covered the distance to Karen and Morgan. Remembering the gun in his hand, the terrified Morgan emptied the 15-round clip on Wuffe.

Morgan and Karen were both stunned by the sudden violence. He asked Karen where the phone was. After considering an obscenity, she merely nodded to a corner of the room.

"JJ, it's Morgan. Frank is dead. Her monster dog killed him, and I shot the dog. Do I take her alone or do you want me to meet with a replacement en route?"

"Get the hell out of there," said JJ. "With gunshots and screams, cops will be all over you. Go. Drive her yourself. Remember the rules. Call me or Sterling later if necessary."

"We're going on a long trip, Mrs. Stone," said Morgan. "Do you need to take any medications with you? Anything for your personal needs?"

"No," as tears began to run down her cheeks.

Morgan's trembling hands put duct tape across her mouth. "I won't hurt you, but you are going to use the bathroom while I grab some pillows for your comfort. My name is Morgan. If you cooperate, the journey will be long and uneventful."

Morgan led Karen to the open trunk, tossed in various pillows, and pushed her in, closing the trunk lid behind her. He gave her the various signs, some paper, and a marker. Over the tops of the boxes, Karen and Morgan could see each other.

Karen asked herself, *Why is he trying to be considerate to me? I am obviously merchandise, and they had strict orders to take care of the goods. Wuffe gave his life for me. Perhaps, Jake and Jamie caught the gangsters they were looking for, and this will be a trade.* Thoughts raced through her brain. *Maybe it has nothing to do with Jake, and it's a kidnapping because of my money. I wish my knees would stop shaking.*

Washington, Tuesday afternoon

"Lieutenant Dominik, I need to speak with you, sir," said Officer Watson.

Dominik regarded the officer's formality as a bad omen.

"Go on."

"I haven't seen Jake Stone since his assignment to Internal Affairs. Normally, officers run into each other at the usual watering holes, or at headquarters, despite being transferred. It's like he's dropped off the end of the earth, and I wondered if he's undercover and not at Internal." He recounted the address request in the morning and admitted to giving it to the stranger.

Lieutenant Dominik's face flushed, and he pointed a finger at Watson.

"I'll deal with you later!" and strode rapidly into the captain's office without knocking.

With no preamble, Dominik called out, "We may have a big

problem. Apparently, Jake Stone's cover has been blown, and they may attempt to kidnap his wife as we speak." He summarized rapidly what Watson said.

Captain Larson dropped his pen and stared at the lieutenant. He pulled out a flat wooden board from his large mahogany desk with a list of important phone numbers, furiously dialed and waited.

"This is Captain Larson across the line in D.C. Put him on."

"Hello, Chief. I believe the wife of one of my undercover officers is in imminent danger of a kidnap this afternoon in the Kenwood area. Here is the address... Please expedite some units as well as officials, to smooth things over in case everything is fine. If she is all right, then please assign Mrs. Stone twenty-four-hour protection until I can resolve this matter. Thank you."

Fifteen minutes later, the captain's private line rang.

"I'm sorry, Tom," said the assistant chief. "They found a dead intruder mauled by a German shepherd. A second intruder apparently shot the dog and kidnapped Mrs. Stone. The only good news is the blood seems to be concentrated around the dog and the dead guy. We have his prints, and we will run them as quickly as possible. Witnesses report seeing a white van with D.C. tags beginning with the letter R. So, they're driving a rental car for now. We can help more if we knew where they are headed."

"Probably south, but I need to phone the FBI anyway."

"Tom, please let me know what else we can do. Our forensic people just arrived. We did find duct tape."

"Call us after your forensic evaluation with any new results. I expect the FBI will be knocking on the door shortly."

The next phone call was to Ray.

"Ray, this is Captain Larson. Do you know Jake Stone's cover is blown, and they kidnapped his wife about an hour ago?"

"Tom, I'm sorry, and I don't understand how this happened. The takedown last night went smoothly, with Stone led away in handcuffs. Sterling, Ortiz, and one of their professional killers escaped – a communications breakdown. Later, they gunned down two state troopers in pursuit about twenty miles south of the airport. I can imagine them guessing Sixkiller fingered them, but how they got from there to Jake Stone, much less Karen is hard to understand."

"Although the FBI has the lead on any kidnapping, please keep me informed about new information and progress," said Captain Larson. "Unfortunately, we know a serious lapse in judgment by one of my officers provided them the address of Mrs. Stone. How they got from Sixkiller to Stone remains a mystery. I'm going to call the Special Agent in Charge of the Miami field office to ask what he can tell me, and to make damn sure that the FBI tells Stone about his wife – not a gloating Marcus Sterling."

Miami, Tuesday afternoon

"Jamie, I can't find the safe-house addresses. More than likely, he mentioned the two generally. We need those addresses. Time is slipping away. Can you check on whether the judge signed the search warrant for Ex-Pat Reality? Sterling probably put them in the folder I made with information on his cash and offshore accounts. Also, ask your office to prepare an arrest warrant for his bitch secretary. She's up to her eyeballs in the criminal side of his business. She needs to go down anyway. We can squeeze her and promise her anything. I'm sure she'll break easily and give us the safe houses."

"Good plan," said Jamie. "Let me jot down the secretary's full name, and I'll get an arrest warrant for her while I check on searching the realty company. Probable cause to arrest her should move a lot faster than a review of what we want in the business, its location, and the relationship to the case.

"Also, you gave me an idea," continued Jamie. "A heavy

patrol presence would deter him from going to either of his safe houses. He'll run counter surveillance before he commits to parking and entering. If he's returning back to Miami, we want him to go there. He needs something, the folder perhaps, or he wouldn't take the risk. Once we have the addresses, let's ask the plainclothes FDLE officers to form a loose perimeter that's not intimidating around both houses. Later, you and I split up, one covering each house. When he shows up, we can make the arrest and legally search the place."

A loud knock on the door startled both of us. Instinctively, we drew our service weapons.

"It's SAC Wainwright. Open up, Jamie."

Jamie stared at me. We knew the news had to be especially bad. The Special Agent in Charge does not make house calls. Jamie opened the door and Wainwright nodded politely to her and said, "Officer Stone, please take a seat," gesturing to one behind me.

"This is extremely difficult for me because we do not know of any security breach. Nevertheless, members of the Barranquilla gang kidnapped your wife this morning and are driving south. No law-enforcement agency has received any communication from them. They are heading south because they abandoned the first car they used near the Virginia – North Carolina border. We're sure it's the correct car based on witness identification and other evidence. At this point, no evidence suggests your wife has been injured. I'm sorry, Jake. In partnership with the other agencies, we'll throw every resource we have at resolving this so that she is not harmed."

He stopped talking. My mouth moved, but made no sound as tears filled my eyes. I felt Jamie's hand rest on top of mine.

He was talking again. "Please, you both may know something that seems insignificant, but might help us."

Jamie spoke. "Sterling employs a mobile phone in his car. For this to happen so quickly, he probably used the phone to call one of Tyrone's lieutenants in Washington. I think those calls go through an operator. Since each call generates a separate item on the monthly invoice, we can demand a record of when and who from Ma Bell."

The SAC was taking notes.

Jamie continued, "One more thing I recall is the doctor who brought Jake from Barranquilla had given him plenty of morphine to help him make the trip. After we arrived, Jake gazed directly at me and called me Karen. Both of them noticed because they stopped speaking for a moment and half-turned. At that time, they probably paid no attention; the morphine was talking about some woman somewhere. Later, they most likely deduced the name belonged to his wife. But I still don't understand how they converted Sixkiller to Stone and found the address of Karen."

"We do know how they did it, and that officer will face Trial Board and probable dismissal from the D.C. Police."

Incredulous, I asked, "How could a patrolman know what we're doing here?"

The SAC replied, "He knew nothing about this operation and was duped by one of Tyrone's men into providing the information to an old friend of yours passing through town."

As I tried to absorb this, I remarked, "Sterling has millions in Grand Cayman. Why does he want Karen?"

The regular phone rang, and Jamie answered and listened for a moment.

"You know, Marcus, the FBI Special Agent in Charge of the Miami field office is here, and I'm sure he would like to chat with you."

Wainwright took the phone, "You killed two state troopers," said Wainwright. "Then, you ordered Tyrone's lap dogs to kidnap a policeman's wife. We're not off to a good start here unless you like our electric chair."

After a pause, Wainwright turned and said, "Jake, he says you can talk to Karen now."

I snatched the phone from him, "Karen, have they hurt you? ... *Polite?* Okay, that's good. Follow his instructions until we can rescue you. Where are you?"

Sterling's voice returned, but the sound quality from the conference call was poor. "Now, you know we can't let her tell you that, Jake. I'll call tomorrow afternoon with more specifics on the trade. Goodbye."

Jamie and Wainwright each had an ear on either side of me. *A trade*? For what?

"Sterling escaped the net; he got a lucky break Monday night because of the interoperability problem," said Jamie. "So, instead of running to his millions, he orders a No Name to kill the troopers and heads back to Miami. It must be a trade for both him and Tyrone, free passage to George Town."

"I'll tell you what else he wants," I added. "For security reasons, I convinced him to make all of his accounts in George Town numbered. He can't walk in and show his driver's license or passport. He needs those codes. The only places they could be are his office, the two safe houses, or a bank safe deposit box."

"Sir," began Jamie. "There are two things that would really help us out. One is a flyer to area banks regarding the safe deposit box. Second, we need the locations of those two safe houses, and a search warrant for each. If we can break Sterling's secretary, then she is the one person who can give us the information. She was fully cognizant of and participated in his criminal enterprises. We need to arrest her on an intimidating list of charges, state and federal, and promise her the moon for cooperation. The U.S. Attorney would never blink later at our false promises. If you happen to have a judge in your back pocket..."

Wainwright stiffened visibly at this comment.

Treading more carefully, Jamie continued, "...that is to say, on good terms with, agents could put together an interrogation team with the primary purpose of getting those addresses. A secondary purpose would be to fill in the gaps on Sterling's crimes, especially if another reason exists for him to take the gamble of returning here.

"Also, the search warrant for Sterling's office is on track. I was planning to call when you arrived. Do we know anything regarding the car or van they are currently using?"

"No, but I'm dedicating four additional agents to this case. I'll tell them to contact all rental companies along the likely route between North Carolina and here. In addition, I'll ask them to coordinate with police agencies for reported stolen cars from the same area and to the south. One more task for tonight: If they don't stop, it's twenty-four hours of hard driving to Miami. The warrants should be ready by morning, and I will walk them personally over to a friendly judge. Finally, I'll negotiate with or threaten the phone company to obtain information regarding Sterling's mobile phone."

As he got up to leave, both of us thanked him, and he gave us his direct line.

I sank down in the sofa. Everything seemed so unreal. Jamie sat down next to me and hugged me tight.

"You're going to hug Karen soon."

I hardly reacted to her encouragement. "She's only a pawn to him – dead the moment Sterling believes she's no longer useful.

"James, you talked to her, and she was fine. You know SAC Wainwright and the state police will take every necessary measure to ensure her safe return. She is a policeman's wife. This is not another routine kidnapping case."

"Thanks. Let's get some sleep. I can't deal with tomorrow right now." I went to my room, but sleep did not come. Sure, Karen was fine during my conversation with her. But what came next? Anything might happen.

Miami, Wednesday morning

Jamie and I were drinking coffee after an early breakfast when the secure phone rang.

"The secretary has been picked up? Great! Yes, we'd like to go with the team to the realty office. We can be outside in forty-five minutes. Thank you, sir."

Jamie turned to me. "He said they are already interrogating the secretary, threatening her with a list of real and bogus charges good for about one-hundred-and-fifty years. He expects her to fold quickly."

"Jamie, one No Name is dead, another is with Marcus, a third is probably in a safe house, but I haven't seen Number Three for a while. We need to make sure Wainwright understands how lethal these goons are. He got a taste of their methods when the troopers were shot about twenty times."

Jamie and I, plus four other agents, assembled on a side street near Ex-Pat Realty to go over entry and clearing plans. I glanced over at one of two agents carrying AR-15s with thirty-round, box magazines.

"The SAC warned us about the No Names," he said. I nodded in reply.

We burst into the front door as a team yelling "FBI," and ordered everybody onto the floor. I saw Number Three in the corner, partly shielded by the opening door. My weapon was out, but he already had his in hand. We traded shots, both missing. The agent behind me fired an eight- or nine-round burst, ending the career of one more professional killer. After confiscating a few weapons, the agents cuffed several persons working in the real estate office and set about filling paralegal boxes with potential evidence.

Personally, the question of who was a legitimate realtor and who was part of the criminal enterprise could be sorted out later. I understood, however, FBI agents are investigators trained to build solid cases for prosecution. My goal at this point was much narrower: We needed the two addresses.

Three agents began their work of cuffing and frisking employees. Jamie and I, along with the agent who brought tools, headed straight to Sterling's office. We pried open everything that was locked while another carried in empty boxes to help collect anything useful. We trashed Sterling's office to no avail. Neither the addresses nor the bank account numbers was here. I had put them in a special file for him, which was gone.

Sterling's private line rang. I looked at Jamie, and she pointed at me like the ringing phone could hear us if we talked.

"Yes," I said into the phone.

"Jake? It's Floyd Wainwright. How did the raid go?"

"One dead, No Name, but no other injuries. The addresses aren't here."

"No problem. The secretary broke, and we have them."

"*Yes!*" I shouted, pointing to Jamie with a thumb up.

"By the way, Sterling called me and wants free passage to George Town for him and his pal Tyrone, in exchange for Karen. I told him everything is negotiable. Give me a number to ring you later. He laughed, and said he would call back soon and expected a favorable answer.

"Ultimately, the approach we use is up to me. I'm open to ideas from you two as how to handle this."

"We had an idea. As a demonstration of good faith, we actually send Tyrone to George Town. At the same time, we request the Justice Department to send Interpol a 'red notice'[12] which authorizes his arrest later. Without the account codes, Tyrone will not attempt to run until Sterling arrives. Sterling, in turn, releases Karen, and we give him a ride to the nearest jail."

"We can try that as an opening gambit, but I don't think he will agree to release Karen, even if Tyrone calls him from George Town. The new offer buys us time, however, and I'll see how he reacts."

Chapter 28

Showdown

Miami, Wednesday afternoon

"Try this on for size, Jamie. I know Marcus better than anyone. He has a thin veneer of polish and culture, but he is very self-centered, and only one cut above the No Names he employs. He needs the brainpower and organizational skills of Tyrone to get back in the business again. This is not about loyalty; accordingly he will reject the proposal because of a lack of ironclad guarantees. I doubt he would tell us where Karen is, even if he and Tyrone were in a bar together in George Town knocking back a few. She is not part of his plan. Once he believes she's irrelevant to his escape, she is dead. I fear we are rapidly approaching that point.

"Moreover, I presume he's in the house near the Opa Locka airport with a No Name; and Karen is in the West Miami house with the other surviving No Name. The Fixed Base Operator of Opa Locka is a crook with a long history of doing favors for Sterling. He could put Sterling in a private jet, and he'd be over international waters in minutes.

"I propose we split up. You and two heavily-armed agents free Karen, and I'll leave with two agents to arrest Marcus, and make certain Karen is not there. The Florida Department of Law Enforcement should tighten the perimeter around both houses in case things go south."

Jamie gave me an enquiring look. Avoiding her gaze I continued, "Karen might be with him after all, and my plan is based on assumptions. If she is not in either safe house, I'm more likely than strangers to get Sterling to tell me where she is. At this point I would persuade him that cooperating and freeing Karen offer the best chance of avoiding the electric chair." Jamie nodded her head; the last item seemed to resonate with her.

SAC Wainwright called to say Sterling had rejected the proposal, saying it had no safeguards for him. Wainwright proposed he bring Karen with him to the airport and release her on the steps to the plane. Sterling asked how many FBI snipers he planned to deploy on the adjacent rooftop. He also advised Wainwright that time was running out.

I laid out the plan to Wainwright as I had with Jamie, and suggested we implement it tonight, given the implied threat by Sterling. I added that Sterling might be wondering whether we had located the houses through land records, or by some other means. If he feels cornered, I warned, Karen is dead, and he is on a plane at Opa Locka. A long silence passed.

"Normally, we would go in with such a large show of force that surrender is the only option. Why do you want just two agents at each house?" asked Wainwright.

"Each house, I believe, uses a No Name to protect the primary occupant. These killers will not surrender. From the shell casings found near the dead trooper we can expect a firefight with automatic weapons. Forgive my directness, with more cops or agents being shot at from the house, the more return fire it will receive. It's human nature to hold down the trigger during a gunfight. With all that lead flying, we still have no idea where Karen is within the house."

"I agree in principle to your main point. We could bring night-vision equipment if necessary with a smaller, simultaneous entrance to the front and back."

"That sounds good," I said. He was clearly mulling over the size of the teams.

"I insist on a team of three at each entrance, and each house has two entrances. Don't forget you are still a federal agent. Are you ready for this?"

"Is there a choice?"

"Yes. We can handle this."

"No. I know and get along well with Marcus. Despite his anger at my betrayal, I need to negotiate with him in private if Karen isn't at either house. He may disclose her location to me after he realizes how hopeless his situation has become. Can I say the death penalty is off the table if he releases Karen?"

"Sure," said the SAC. "It's not off the table, but what you tell him has no legal relevance."

"Can we hit West Miami a few minutes before Opa Locka?"

"Okay. We have the phone numbers. Call the Opa Locka house and me with a report after securing West Miami. I'll coordinate with the police. You and Jamie meet me in my office in one hour."

Miami, Wednesday night

SAC Wainwright had blown-up plans on the walls with the entrances circled. Jamie, ten additional agents, plus myself, were present for the planning. A judge had approved "no knock" arrest warrants, given the kidnapping and danger posed by the fugitives. The first priority was to arrest, disable, or kill any No Names, followed by other armed collaborators who may be present. If Karen was not at the second house, I was to question Marcus. Failure to find Karen would land Sterling in front of a special interrogation team. The SAC planned to grant Sterling's entreaties for a lawyer – after he disclosed her location. Suppression of evidence for kidnapping was not a major concern.

Wainwright had set midnight for West Miami and 12:15 a.m. for Opa Locka. Each team began its approach to the entrances about ten minutes before the raid, taking advantage of trees and darkness wherever possible.

At 12:15 a.m., I, and the other agents, were in place. I looked at my watch; we exchanged nods and kicked in the door. No Name One was dozing on a chair with an AK-47 lying on a table in front of him. As he went for the AK, an agent cut him down with a short burst from an AR-15. Sterling was reading and jumped out of his chair. We motioned for him to sit down with his hands up.

"Any others in the house," demanded the agent.

His head moved from side to side in slow comprehension of his circumstances.

"Frisk him," said the lead agent. "We'll search the rest of the dwelling."

Of course, Sterling didn't touch firearms. He had No Names to kill for him. I was waiting for the phone call. Finally it rang! I snatched the receiver so fast I knocked the base on the floor.

"Jamie, is she with you? How is she? That's wonderful! A little shaky? I understand. Put her on."

"Jake, I love you. I'm sore from the trip, but I'll be all right. Jamie is taking good care of me."

"I love you too, and don't go away. I need to take care of a couple of things, and I'll come down."

Two other agents were now standing behind me. I stood up slowly and turned to look at them.

"Marcus and I share a long history together, including a few things to discuss in private. Would you fellows go outside and check the perimeter for a few more minutes?" One headed for the door; the younger one hesitated, but followed him.

"James, James. I am delighted to see you again. My best pilot and most trusted advisor is a fed. You played your role perfectly, my compliments. James, what are you doing?"

"Getting a good sight picture on your head."

"Stop! I've surrendered. Besides, I saved your life. Alvaro would have tortured you to death."

I dropped my elbow, raising the gun toward the ceiling. Sterling looked relieved and smiled.

"I'm immensely grateful for the rescue, and I will always be indebted to you..." I said as I lowered the gun and shot him between the eyes. "But, you crossed the line when you kidnapped my wife." I was speaking to his lifeless body.

The agents rushed in after hearing the sound of a shot.

"He went for the AK on the table while we were talking."

Reunion

"Karen," said Jamie. "Let me help make you pretty before Jake arrives. Give me your clothes and get in the shower. I'll hand wash them in the sink and put them in the dryer."

The agents had left with No Name Two in custody. How fitting, Napalm Josey would die in Florida's electric chair.

Meanwhile, I found a trooper who could give me a red-light escort to West Miami. I told him my hot-rod Ford could keep up with him. Traffic was light at 1:00 a.m., but the trip seemed endless. My heart and mind were racing faster than the cars.

I opened the door, and Jamie was standing directly in front of me.

"Nice to see you, too," I said. "But where's Karen?"

"Not quite ready yet."

"Huh?"

"I'm in charge of preparations tonight. So, sit down here."

I got a kiss on the forehead, and she was gone. I heard what sounded like a clothes dryer. Then Jamie rounded a corner, ignored me, pulled out clothes and went back into a bathroom, then some giggling.

Karen came out, followed by Jamie, who was smiling and crying as Karen and I embraced. Then, I kissed her hard and long.

"I wasn't sure this day would come," I said, beholding her beauty and thinking I almost lost her. We held each other by our forearms just to touch and appreciate each other. Again, we hugged, but not so tightly. I detected a wince the first time. Jamie was standing near us with tears running down her face.

"Jamie, come here and put your arms around both of us," said Karen.

After a few moments, the three of us began to sway a little, side to side, forward and backward until we laughed.

Chapter 29

An Odd Triangle

Miami, December 1969

Jamie stood up and announced, "I need to go. You both stay here tonight. James, don't forget the paperwork tomorrow regarding Sterling and other matters. Come by after work, pick up your clothes, and say goodbye to me." She stood motionless, tears coming freely now. Jamie ran to me and hugged tightly. I hugged her back.

"Damn you, James! Why weren't you another asshole? I'm going to miss you so badly. You son of a bitch! You walked out of a prison and into my life, and now you're leaving me. Who will I talk to? They don't make men like you." Jamie turned to Karen immediately.

"Karen, I'm so sorry. I have no right to say these things in front of you."

"Everybody, please sit," said Karen.

"Jake tells me everything, including the initial sexual interest in him and the massage incident." Jamie sat, eyes wide, frozen in place as Karen continued. "But an important change in your relationship with Jake occurred when you apologized for the seduction attempt. To me the apology was a broader statement, saying, 'I now view you as my partner, friend, and even a confidant.' Jamie, I deeply appreciate the candor and willingness to confide in me after Jake was tortured, despite the profound career risk it entailed. Most importantly, you learned how to honor our marriage as well as respect and love Jake in a different way – something that has eluded you in prior relationships with male friends. Both of you share a much deeper friendship than you have realized. The demands of your work, combined with the realization it must end at some point, pulled you together and pushed you apart simultaneously. In many respects, it was an affair without sex. I suppose this should threaten me more than an episode of casual sex.

"With time on my hands, I thought about this situation quite a bit, especially after Jake's rescue from Colombia. An interesting article I discovered during my research is titled: *Urban and Undercover Police Work: Marriage Killers*. The short version is that policemen are afraid to confide in their wives about their fears and emotions. More than a handful are even incapable of accepting and owning their own feelings; they are a lost cause, usually to alcohol. For those who approach their wives, many are rebuffed because this is such an alien world to the wife or, perhaps, she cannot accept such raw feelings from her macho husband. Either way, a communication barrier is erected that becomes self-reinforcing, and the marriage ultimately fails. Jake's love for me is different from the love he has for you, Jamie. I like you; and you could teach me, as a woman, a few of the skills and realities necessary to help preserve our marriage in the future, if you are willing."

"Yes, Karen. But I don't know what I know."

"More than you can imagine. I come from privilege. The worlds you two inhabit on a daily basis are alien to me.

"Jamie, I also want to thank you from the bottom of my heart for the care you gave Jake after he was tortured. You tended his physical wounds; you slept beside him at night to calm him when the nightmares came; you bathed and cared for him; most of all you were a rock for him during such a critical time. Your support was vital in helping Jake overcome his violent treatment and not succumb to it. I may have been too emotional to do such a great job."

"You give me undue credit, Karen, but thank you for your kindness."

"Finally, my feelings are conflicted about an abrupt

separation of you two. Having lost friends who moved because of work, I often wish a few of them were close. Letters are not the same as dinner. What if the FBI transferred you to Washington? Your friendship continues, and you help me understand your world. All three of us win. Besides, Jake would be morose and a pain in my ass without you. After such a successful operation, the transfer might be justified as an award."

"I'd like that," answered a stunned Jamie.

"If the front door approach doesn't work, then talk to me. Getting things done in Washington often depends on connections."

She paused, clasped her hands, and looked up toward the ceiling. "Mother will kill me. First, I marry a cop, and later bring his Miami wife to Washington." The wisecrack brought restrained chuckles.

Jamie and I were both in shock after the conversation with Karen. I discovered new respect for Karen's intellect and shrewdness.

Jamie gave Karen a hug and, releasing her, said, "You are an amazing woman. I am not sure who will be the teacher, and who will be the student. Goodnight."

"Where's my forehead kiss?"

"Coming up. Such a pain in my ass!"

After Jamie left, I turned to Karen and said, "Let's sit and talk for a few minutes on the bench outside."

We walked out holding hands and sat down, Karen looking at me expectantly.

"Although I love Jamie's company, I can foresee problems if Jamie comes to Washington. You are my only wife, and this decision may create a rift between your mother and both of us. Three is an awkward and somewhat unstable relationship, with one person on the outside. In this situation, Jamie will feel excluded. She can't live with us; she will be one more agent assigned to the Washington field office or headquarters and living by herself. Despite the pain from losing a dear friend, I'm not sure this is a good plan."

"The beauty of love," began Karen, "lies in its ability to flourish on many levels at the same time. It is not a one-dimensional emotion. We love flowers, parents, spouses, children, pets, and friends all at the same time, but in different ways. Your affection for Jamie got off on the wrong foot. Both of you were undercover, living together, and emotionally needy. Mutual physical attraction was a natural first step, which would have caused significant damage to our marriage if you had not recognized and corrected the problem. In the beginning, drifting was easier than painting a brighter line for Jamie. Perhaps, with the challenging work problems demanding your time and attention, you did not want to quarrel with your housemate, someone you cared about and depend upon. Jamie deserves a lot of credit for her unsolicited acknowledgement about how toxic further seduction attempts would have been for all of us. The point is both of you worked it out and were rewarded with a deep and unusual friendship. In fact, it is an ongoing and mutual gift of love between you. Our marriage is a mutual gift of love of a different type.

"I don't take this step of supporting your friendship with Jamie reluctantly. You two are exploring new ground together. I am a bit envious of the experience, never having had the opportunity. But envy of an experience and jealousy are not the same. I'm proud of what you accomplished, and the time away from you has strengthened my love for you. By the way, I will take care of Mother. Jamie doesn't know it yet, but she is going to help me do that."

I looked deeply into her beautiful green eyes. "I'm so lucky to have you, and I'm a little lost for words."

"Well," she said, "you can begin by giving me a nice kiss, and think of something to say later."

The first kisses began tentatively, but rapidly grew longer and lustier. We raced each other back to a former safe house. Clothes began flying off as soon as the door was closed.

"Where's the bedroom?" I asked. We laughed and ran naked through the house until we found one. Karen was in my arms again. Yes, this was a different love.

Chapter 30

A Pact

Miami, December 1969

Jamie confronted me outside of the Miami's FBI Field Division offices. With a curt motion of her head, she directed me to a bench under one of the palm trees and away from normal foot traffic.

"You shot him down in cold blood! Didn't you? We are law-enforcement officers. Our standards and conduct are what separate us from the scum we pursue. And now you want me to cover for you. Right!"

"I have always liked the way you come directly to the point. You were not there. Nobody can contradict my version of events."

"That's because you requested the two agents behind you to check the perimeter again. They also suspect Sterling didn't go for the AK on the table. Both of us know that Sterling never touched guns, even less a gangster gun like an AK. James, you have put me in a thorny bind here."

"Sterling kidnapped and was about to kill my wife. I confess to nothing, and he got what he deserved. May he rot in hell."

"I don't want a confession, unless you enjoyed your time in Coleman."

"What do you want?"

"To vent at you before I sign official papers as the Supervisory Special Agent in charge of the Barranquilla case saying your use of deadly force was reasonable and necessary. Do you agree we cannot speak of this matter again?"

"I agree, Jamie."

She kissed me on the forehead and left wordlessly.

Chapter 31

Afterthoughts

Washington, D.C., December 1969

Karen pulled back the curtains of the master bedroom, and stood at the rear window overlooking the manicured lawn and garden. The leaden sky was producing a few harmless flakes of snow. She watched Jamie and Jake walking, talking, and occasionally gesturing. She was thinking: *I've grown quite fond of Jamie. When I heard her real name was Lucy, I asked to keep calling her Jamie, a name she now prefers. I don't yet understand their worlds, the management of fear, the unspoken assumptions and arrangements, the secrets. Something happened regarding this outlaw, Sterling, which involved Jake. They change subjects, however, if they suspect I am around. Perhaps some things are best left alone.*

Mother is outraged they sometimes hold hands "where others can see." Although I understand her view, no competition exists between Jamie and me. I do not want to take any steps hinting at competition. This friendship does not humiliate me, nor has it affected our marriage. In fact, Jamie possesses remarkable depth and is a good friend to do things with, especially when Jake and Mike visit their civil war battle-fields, or go flying together. The ultimate course of their relationship lies in uncharted waters and is between them. Jake, and even Jamie, remain comfortable in talking with me about bumps in the road.

Jamie's physical attraction to Jake is still a potential problem, and he cannot meet that need. She is a young woman, and needs a man who can understand her life. Their friendship will survive the transformation caused by Jamie's marriage someday, and the odd triangle will continue. I could never love another man the way Jamie loves Jake. I don't know how, and the ingredients are missing. I am not an urban or undercover cop. I just married one.

Chapter 32

Sparks

Washington, D.C., December 1969

Karen's parents threw a catered, annual Christmas party. Surrounded by their closest friends, the liquor flowed, and the chatter was loud. The gossip about Jamie and me had died down except for a few sanctimonious old women. Jamie had even charmed Mother, a feat I never thought possible. Like most of these parties, it was interesting at times, but mostly boring. I noticed frequent eye contact, however, between Jamie and Mike.

Sitting next to Karen, I whispered in her ear, "Do you see what I see?" She nodded her head.

When nothing else happened, I stepped up to Mike and said, "She likes you. Don't be a chump; go talk to her." He finished his drink, a little too fast, got another, and walked over to her. She lit up, what a smile! I suppressed a pang of jealousy while I hoped they would become an item someday.

High-Altitude Bonding

Mike and I had the same days off not long after the party. I asked him if he wanted to smash some bugs the next day over the snow-covered mountains of West Virginia. (*Smashing bugs* is pilot talk for having fun with no particular place to go, flying for the pleasure of flying.)

"Yes, but no drug runs," he said. "I can't handle the stress."

We departed Frederick, Maryland, in the same Cessna 182 that landed in Baltimore a lifetime ago. The winter day was beautiful with unlimited visibility. We flew low toward Harper's Ferry, West Virginia, a picturesque town sitting above the confluence of the Potomac and Shenandoah rivers. I turned southwest, roughly paralleling the Shenandoah River, and climbed to sixty-five-hundred feet for a better view, including one of Hawksbill Mountain at forty-one-hundred feet. Sunglasses allowed us to take in the stunning snow-covered landscape from the valley floor to mountain peaks.

"Mike, I noticed the way Jamie lit up when you walked over toward her. Did you ask her out?"

"Yes, for dinner. Both of us had a great time."

"Jamie and I became close friends in Miami. She is a first-class lady. Don't let this one slip through your fingers."

"Jake, it's strange how she was reassigned here after the operation. Stranger still is Karen and Jamie have become very tight. They are probably together now. You have told me some of the highlights—if that's the right word—of your undercover work. Can you tell me more about you, Jamie, and Karen? I want to keep seeing her, but I need to know where my best friend and his wife stand regarding Jamie."

Of course, this was the main reason for the invitation to go flying with Mike. Despite knowing the question was coming, I experienced a flash of discomfort at the level of intimacy required for a complicated and personal answer. I looked around. The beauty of the land and scenery fortified my resolve to be direct with Mike.

According to the Cherokee creation myth, a Great Buzzard was sent from the sky to prepare the wetlands for the people. As he got tired, my mother told me, his giant wings would touch the ground and carve out vast mountains and valleys, which remain to this day. The valleys, mountains, and land are eternal, she said; individual trials and triumphs are fleeting.

"Jake? Are you still here? Remember, I can't fly."

"Mike, I'm going to give you the unabridged version. I've never had to organize thoughts on these events for someone else. Telling a personal story is difficult, especially to a hard-edged, ass-kicking cop."

Mike smiled at the jibe. He had sensed my discomfort. "Stay in your comfort zone, Jake. I don't need all of it."

"The bottom line first. Karen and I both hope you and Jamie explore this new relationship and, we want to assure you there is no problem, nor will it change anything between us."

I gave Mike the unabridged version, which spilled over into lunch at the airport café in Elkins, West Virginia. As we departed Elkins on runway 32 for the trip home, Mike seemed quiet.

"Jake, you can make a crowbar complicated. This story raises my esteem of all involved. In your case, my esteem for you normally hovers at an all-time low, so a boost was sorely needed."

"Fuck you, Mike. This crowbar was complicated. Although we began with different agendas, we ended up getting it right. I remembered how much I missed your abuse."

"I'm relieved to hear that. I had started to worry," he said. "I've seen you and Jamie holding hands."

"I'd offer to do the same with you, but you're not an Arab and you're way too ugly."

Mike smiled and flipped me off.

"I still love Jamie in a platonic relationship," I said. "Having a female friend who is a confidant, who understands our world, who views things a little differently because she's a woman, and who likes my wife, is a rare gift."

"I can tell she loves you too. I didn't want to cause problems."

"Go for it Mike."

"I'd like that."

EPILOGUE

I was promoted to sergeant, received the gold medal for Valor, and a bonus of one-thousand-five-hundred dollars. Awarding the medal was an event. The Chief of Police read the citations and presented me with the medal. Ray and Roy were there, along with some other brass. Family and friends were also invited. As I sat down and while others received various awards, Karen gossiped to me how close Jamie and Mike were sitting.

The next day, the FBI called Inspector Ray Schmidt of the Intelligence Division with an unusual request. They noted the only people who know James Sixkiller is a fed are dead, except for Tyrone Jones, who is serving two life sentences. Accordingly, they would like to preserve his identity by spreading false information saying he escaped shortly after capture and is a federal fugitive. Part of the disinformation package includes reports of Sixkiller flying drugs across the Texas border and living in Cartagena, Colombia.

Roy called to ask if I would approve their request. He pointed out the obvious; this was a feeler for whether they could use me again sometime in the future. He also mentioned questioning and arrest by local police is possible but unlikely. An inconvenience the FBI could fix rapidly. I told him to let me consider the proposal.

I called Jamie and asked to meet with her. She knew nothing about it, but tears came to her eyes when I explained the request.

"Haven't you suffered enough?" she said. "A gold bar to pin on your chest and fifteen-hundred dollars. Have you slowed the drug trade? Most gold medals are awarded posthumously. Maybe you could get another one. What do you think Karen would say?"

"Straight to the point, I see."

"Karen won't say no, but her heart will scream it. Jake, how can you be so smart and so stupid at the same time? Both of us love you, and we know you need more time to heal fully. Another undercover assignment is too intense now. You still suffer from nightmares?"

"Karen told you?"

"Of course. She tells me almost everything about you, especially remaining fallout from the Barranquilla case. Tell them you need more time. Urban police work is enough excitement for now. Say you will consider a proposal in the distant future, and let them make you a fugitive because right now you don't care what they say or do."

"I always value your advice, Jamie. Thank you. You and Karen seem tight. Although I had initial doubts, I'm happy about the outcome."

I changed the subject. "How are things with you and Mike?"

"He's really sweet," she beamed.

We hugged, and she kissed me on the forehead. As she walked away, she looked back at me with a mischievous smile.

Notes

1. Washington Area Law Enforcement System was an early computerized system which maintained information on such things as outstanding arrest warrants and stolen cars. It was also used by the neighboring counties.
2. In a cage car the prisoner sits in a steel cage which surrounds the back seat.
3. A speedball is a mix of heroin and cocaine.
4. "10-99" is a common code for a one-person unit.
5. A vortac looks like a round cone about ten feet high. It gives any pilot who uses it his position along one of the 360 degrees of a compass. With sufficient altitude, the DME allows the pilot to fly a perfect arc around Cuba and then "home" on the Non-Directional Beacon located on the Matthew Town airport.
6. CDW: Carrying a Deadly weapon, usually a gun.
7. A hummer is a minor thing to be overlooked.
8. Among the most important codes are: 10-33 (policeman in trouble); 10-7 (out of service); 10-8 (in service); 10-20 (location of person or place); 10-4 (two-man unit); and 10-99 (one-man unit).
9. The Major Crimes Act of 1885 gave the federal government jurisdiction over specific heinous crimes committed in Indian country.
10. Pilot's Operating Handbook or POH.
11. In Florida the state police go by the name of Florida Department of Law Enforcement.
12. Interpol uses seven color-coded notices for different purposes. For example, Yellow is for missing persons; Black is for help with unidentified bodies; and Red is arrest and hold for extradition.

Roundfire Books put simply, publish great stories. Whether it's literary or popular, a gentle tale or a pulsating thriller, the connecting theme in all Roundfire fiction titles is that once you pick them up you won't want to put them down.